THE CONSERVATOR'S COLLECTION

DERELICT

LIMITED EDITION

JOHN DURGIN · JAY BOWER · JOHN LYNCH

Let the world know:
#IGotMyCLPBook!

Crystal Lake Publishing
www.CrystalLakePub.com

WELCOME
TO ANOTHER

CRYSTAL LAKE PUBLISHING
CREATION

PRAISE FOR THE CONSERVATOR'S COLLECTION DERELICT

"The three novellas within 'The Conservator's Collection: Derelict' are rock solid. But what would you expect from these three authors? Each story is visceral, unnerving and has a unique bite, though the feeling overall as a reader is elation—at being taken to three places in the hands of some of the strongest horror writers out there today!"

—Steve Stred,
2X Splatterpunk-Nominated author of *Mastodon,*
Churn the Soil, and *Incarnate.*

"Let the Conservator guide you through the darkest part of his archives, where men fear to tread. Be warned these pages contain vengeful revenants, urban legends come to life, and subterranean monsters. Durgin, Bower, and Lynch present a collection of ghastly tales that ring both classic and fresh, that haunt and harrow."

—Brennan LaFaro,
author of the Slattery Falls trilogy.

"This collection is set up like an awesome issue of Tales From the Crypt. Guided by the iconic Conservator, we are given a hearty serving of horror from Durgin, Bower, and Lynch. No shorts here: these are fully fleshed-out stories with plenty of meat. There's not a single weakness in sight in this absolutely solid collaboration. I can't wait to see what the Conservator finds for us next!"

—Megan Stockton,
author of *Bluejay, Quiet Pretty Things,*
and . . . *and Nobody Knows It But Me.*

"A triad of horror delights that, despite being created by three different imaginations, feel they could all be at home within the same literary nightmare. Durgin, Bower, and Lynch's killer collaboration is a must-read this fall!"

—Joshua Marsella,
author of *Hunger For Death.*

INTRODUCTION
PERFECT HORROR

TIM WAGGONER

MANY HORROR WRITERS and critics believe that the short story is the most effective form for the genre. I won't argue that a really good horror short packs a punch that you just can't get at any other length, but I believe the perfect form for horror is the novella.

Like most things in art, the definition of a novella is fuzzy. My favorite definition is: *A long story or a short novel.* Various writers' organizations classify its length more precisely, primarily for their awards, as a story between 7,500 words to 40,000 words.

So why is the novella so effective for horror fiction? It combines the best features of a short story and a novel, while avoiding the limitations of each form. Unlike a short story, in a novella there's more room to develop character—and horror is all about character. Horror is an emotion, and we can only experience it through a specific character's point of view. And the more developed the characters are, the more we can empathize with them and fear for their safety. One of the major problems with scary novels is that horror/suspense can only be sustained for readers for so long before they lose their effectiveness. Ride an extreme rollercoaster once and it's terrifying. Ride it fifty times in a row, and you get so used to it that it's boring. Novellas allow you to sustain horror and suspense to the end of the story without either aspect overstaying their welcome.

Because the novella form is relatively short, there's opportunity for experimentation, and readers will have more patience for experimentation at novella length than they might at novel length. And since a large part of horror comes from the unknown, it can be effective when your story is experimental because readers don't know what might come next. They literally can't anticipate what's going to happen—and isn't that what we ultimately want in our horror fiction? Many readers and critics love Mark Z. Danielewski's novel *House of Leaves*, but I bet its experimental approach would've kicked even more ass at novella length.

In order to write novellas, you need to use both short story techniques and novel techniques. There is no specific formula for which techniques you use when or how many to use. You'll need to experiment to find your way, and you may use a different "recipe" for different novellas. But for the writers among you out there—and for readers who want to appreciate the form more fully—here are some techniques for writing effective novellas.

First, some short story elements that novellas share:

•Compression.
•A short time frame: minutes, hours, maybe a day or two.
•Two or three main characters.
•Not many supporting characters.
•One basic setting.
•One point of view.
•One main story problem.

Next, novel elements that novellas share:

•Expansion.
•A short story is an event; a novel is a series of events that add up to a much larger journey.
•Stronger character development. Greater exploration of history/background.
•Deeper, widespread, increased conflict.
•Deeper exploration of theme.

Hitting the sweet spot between a short story and a novel can be tough, though. Here some techniques for keeping your novella from getting too long.

- Keep the story problem/concept at a smaller scale.
- Focus on one main character.
- Stay in that character's point of view the entire time.
- Try to limit the number of specific settings your story takes place in.
- Focus on one core story problem.
- Incorporate enough obstacles that the story is long, not so many that it's too long.
- Avoid incorporating too much exposition. You have more room to work with in a novella than in a short story, but not a lot of room.
- Avoid overly complex plot structures—lots of flashbacks, a number of subplots, etc.

But you also need to make sure you get the necessary length out of your novella. To help, here are some techniques for keeping your novella from being too short.

- Use the Triangle Technique. Instead of two elements of conflict, use three. Take the movie *Jaws*, for example. Sheriff vs the Shark as well as the Mayor who wants to keep the beach open during the 4th of July holiday weekend at all costs.
- Employ Murphy's Law—Have some things go wrong for your characters. Having something go truly wrong in a scene can send the story off into interesting and unexpected directions— and lengthen your story in the process.
- Keep your characters from cooperating and have them work at cross purposes. The more conflict there is between the characters, the longer you story will be.
- Create greater and varied obstacles to challenge your characters. (The final number of obstacles will determine your story's shape and length.)
- Reversal of fortune. Have a situation reverse for characters. For example, they were winning (or at least *thought* they were winning), but now they're losing.

So what does all this stuff about novellas have to do with *The Conservator's Collection: Derelict*? What you have in your hands is a collection of three novellas, all excellent examples of how to do long horror fiction well—*very* well. Read them, enjoy them, experience the thrills and chills they have to offer, but if you're also a writer, pay attention. You can learn a hell of lot from the stories of John Durgin, Jay Bower, and John Lynch in this volume. This is horror done right—*and* done at the perfect length.

Why are you still reading this introduction? Turn the page and get to the good stuff!

Unless, of course, you're too afraid . . .

THE CONSERVATOR

DIGGING THROUGH THE dusty tomes that I've collected over the years, I discovered manuscripts written in blood and wrapped in human flesh. Naturally, my curiosity was piqued, and I cracked the spines to see what was inside.

To my delight, I discovered stories I'd never read before. Rapturously caught by the words on those vellum pages, my life's purpose crystallized. Undead and cursed with everlasting life, I knew what I needed to do. A new direction materialized, and a smile cracked my lips.

Some call me a sinner. Some an abomination. I prefer to consider myself a conservator of horror. Just call me The Conservator.

When I first discovered my hidden stories, I wanted to keep them all to myself. I imagined I was the only one in the world who had access to these nightmares. But then I considered that others might enjoy them as much as I. After careful consideration, I decided it was time to unleash these stories into the wild.

Delving into the dusty, cobweb infested shelves, I soon discovered patterns within the stories. Themes emerged that called to me, and like a true connoisseur of the macabre, I answered.

What you hold in your hands are stories that dealt with abandonment or derelict situations. I found different themes in stories not included here, but those are for another time.

I open this collection with a story from John Durgin titled *Blank Space*. Children are not all sweet and innocent. Not when something far more sinister lurks in the darkness. I dare you to read it all in one sitting.

My next offering is *Eyebiter's Revenge* from Jay Bower. When a group of high school seniors decides to visit an abandoned school looking for a supernatural experience, they discover the school is not as vacant as they once thought.

My final offering is *Expiration of Sentence* from John Lynch. A man sentenced to rot in prison for a homicide that many would call justified, he soon learns there's more to the prison than he ever knew. But what lurks in the darkness is more frightening than the horrors behind the walls.

I hope you enjoy these wicked offerings. I have many more tomes to uncover and stories to share. Someone must conserve these stories, and I've got nothing but time.

VOLUME 1: BLANK SPACE

JOHN DURGIN

CHAPTER 1

THE WALLS ARE *painted in blood.*

That was the only thought going through Officer Natasha Briggs's mind as she walked through the group home, gun at the ready.

A family had called in what they believed to be a murder after a scheduled visit to meet a potential adoptee didn't go as planned. They'd driven almost two hours to meet little Becky Finch. When nobody answered the door after multiple knocks, the husband looked through the window and spotted what appeared to be a child's leg, covered in blood. Upon further observation, he realized the body was no longer attached to the leg. Just a jagged stump leaking out whatever fluids remained.

Briggs was the responding officer, with others on the way. After she looked through the window to see the same leg, she told the family to stay in their vehicle until other officers arrived and instructed them further.

The deeper into the home she got, the more she wished she'd waited outside with the distraught family. It was a scene straight out of a horror movie. Considering the home's haunted past, it was easy to get spooked. She shook the thoughts off and continued moving.

Loose body parts lay scattered across the floor like chewed-up dog toys. She forced herself to hold down the vomit at the sight of the first dead child, but by the fourth, she stumbled into the closest bathroom and threw up her breakfast into the toilet. Hopefully, they wouldn't give her too much shit for messing up evidence.

As she rounded a corner, heading past the dining room toward the kitchen, she spotted the first adult body in the house. A lady in her mid-forties sat slouched on the kitchen floor with her back propped against the counter beneath the sink. Her head hung

3

forward, facing the floor as blood dripped from her mouth like a leaky faucet.

Briggs prepared to radio in another casualty when the lady lifted her head and looked into her eyes. Briggs jolted backwards.

One of the woman's eyeballs was missing, revealing an empty socket with thick sludge seeping down her cheek.

Her teeth were shattered into tiny fragments that stuck out of her gums like sharp rocks poking through a sandy beach.

"Ma'am, can you hear me?" Briggs asked, wondering if the lady was truly alive, or if the body was just fighting off an inevitable death. Probably a bit of both.

"It's *her* . . . She did this to all of us . . . " the lady mumbled through swollen lips.

"Who? Who did this to you, ma'am?"

Briggs waited for an answer that never came. The lady's head dropped back down, and after a few seconds of raspy breathing, she went silent.

Briggs carefully stepped around the pool of blood and quietly walked to the next room. The body of what she assumed was the family pet—approximately the size of a small dog or a large cat, although which species it was remained indistinguishable through all the gore—lay torn apart at the bottom of the stairs heading to the second floor. The house looked as if a tornado of buzz saws had blasted through the downstairs, slicing up everything in its path. She had the feeling it'd be no different on the second floor.

She debated going upstairs, wondering if maybe she should wait for backup to arrive. But then she heard a soft cry from one of the bedrooms. She didn't think. Instead, she sped up the stairs, stepping over the unidentifiable animal on the way up. Briggs's nostrils burned as the aroma of copper invaded her airways. Crimson stains soaked the carpeted stairs all the way up, like someone had dragged one of the ravaged bodies through the entire house to mark their territory.

Her heart hammered in her chest, and for the first time in her career, she noticed her gun shaking as she aimed it in front of her. The soft cries of a child were coming from the second bedroom to her left, behind a closed door. She tiptoed down the hall, aware that someone could be in the room with the kid. Briggs stopped just outside the door and listened for any signs of a second person. Instead, just the sniffling cries of a scared child continued.

Slowly, she opened the door, trying to hold the gun as steady as possible. She pushed the door open enough to see in, but the room was shrouded in darkness, the curtains drawn shut. Scanning the room, she squinted from corner to corner, seeing two more dead children who couldn't have been more than twelve years old, torn to pieces.

The sun pushed a small sliver of light through a crack in the curtain, spotlighting the decapitated head of a preteen. The poor girl's dead eyes stared at the door, frozen in terror.

The whimpers started up again, coming from the closet.

Briggs entered, sweeping the room with her pistol aimed. There was nobody else in the bedroom that she could see. She approached the closet, taking concentrated breaths with each step. She'd seen many bodies over the years, but nothing came close to the massacre on display here.

The trail of blood from the hallway traveled across the floor, stopping at the closet. Someone either crawled into the closet bleeding out or dragged another body in with them.

Briggs swung the door open, prepared to fire.

A little girl sat huddled in the corner, the body of a small boy lying across her with his head resting in her lap. The girl looked up, her blond bangs soaked in blood, and she flinched at the sight of the gun. The boy, however, didn't move.

"Hey, honey. Are you hurt?" Briggs asked.

The girl continued to sob, then averted eye contact and looked at the face of the deceased boy in her lap.

"Is . . . Is everybody dead?" she asked in a timid voice.

Briggs thought back to all the bodies she'd passed on the way. There were six casualties. Seven, counting the kid in this girl's lap. But right now, that was the last thing this girl needed to hear.

"Let's get you somewhere safe and cleaned up, okay? What's your name?"

The little girl lifted her face, blood smeared across her cheeks. "Katie Ripley."

CHAPTER 2

Three Months Later

MONICA PAGE WAS six years old the first time her mom and dad decided they wanted to be foster parents. At first, she was excited. The thought of having a temporary brother or sister for a while and then getting her parents all to herself again seemed like the perfect situation. She could play with the kids, even share her stuff. As long as she knew there was an expiration date on their stay. But as the last few years passed, that excitement turned to resentment.

She'd often get attached to the children who came to live with them, only to have the kids ripped right out from under their roof to go back to their abusive parents who'd apparently cleaned up their act. Or she'd despise her interim brothers and sisters and count down the days before they were out of the house forever. Monica was now nine years old and ready to be alone with her parents for good. For a few months, she thought her wish had come true. She hadn't heard as much as a peep from her parents about taking in another kid. Until the last few days.

After they caught her eavesdropping on their conversation before bed the previous night, she now found herself sitting at the kitchen table just wanting to enjoy her bowl of Lucky Charms in peace, but instead, she sat in awkward silence as she watched her parents trying to figure out how to break the news to her. She only got Lucky Charms when they were trying to suck up to her. She should have seen this coming.

"Hey, hon? We have something we need to talk about with you," her mom said, then eyed her husband, waiting for him to remember his part.

"It's been a bit since we fostered a kid. We know you said you didn't want us to do it anymore, and we try to respect your opinion.

But we have to do it this one last time, okay? We should've told you the minute we decided on it."

Monica wanted to storm away from the table but constrained herself to stay seated. Besides, she hadn't been saving all the marshmallows for last just to get up and leave them behind to drown in the milk.

"Why? You told me we were done! That it would just be us now," she said, keeping her eyes on the floating rainbows in her bowl.

"Sweetie . . . we had to. This poor girl needs someone that can help her get her life back on track. She's been through so much these last few months," her mom said.

"That's what you always say about them. How is this kid any different? It's just going to keep happening," Monica responded, realizing she was pouting but not caring in the slightest.

Monica stopped eating her breakfast, wondering why her parents weren't continuing with their sales pitch. Her mom and dad looked at one another like they were debating on whether they should say something or hold off.

"She deserves to know the truth, Faith," Monica's dad said.

"*Dan* . . . " her mom hesitated, then sighed before turning back to Monica. "Honey, do you remember the story a few months back about the group home just out of town?"

"Yeah. My friends at school said everyone in the house died. Why?"

Again, another look of concern between her parents. This time, her dad spoke.

"Well, *almost* everyone died. There was one little girl who they found alive. Her name's Katie. After spending some time with people that could help her and talk with her about everything she went through, she's ready to live with a family. They reached out to us because we've helped so many kids from that home over the last few years. They sounded desperate to get this girl some stability. What they call a 'crisis child.' Do you see why it was so hard to say no?"

"I guess . . . How long does she have to live with us?"

"That really depends. But we promise, *this* is the last time. As someone who grew up moving from home to home, you know how important this is to me, Monica. Right?" her mom asked.

"Yeah. I guess it'll be fun to have another sister around for a while. Dad isn't very good at playing with my dolls," Monica said, surrendering a smile.

"Hey! I do the best voices. You said so yourself," he said, then got up from the table and kissed Monica on the top of the head. "The social worker is bringing her over today to see the house and meet you. If all goes well, she'll be moving in tonight. Mom and I have a lot to prepare. Gotta get one of the spare bedrooms set up. Wanna help?"

"Okay. I'll pick some toys of mine that she can borrow."

"Thanks for understanding, sweetie. It means a lot to us," her mom said. They all headed upstairs to prepare for Katie's arrival.

CHAPTER 3

MONICA WATCHED FROM the window as her parents greeted the man getting out of his car. He had spiky red hair, and a perfectly lined beard to match. Her dad always said anyone who had time to groom a beard that nicely clearly didn't have kids. Red beard opened the car's backdoor and a little girl with blond hair exited, staring at the ground. It was nothing new to see them shy at first, but this one seemed strange. Something was different about her, but Monica could hardly blame the girl after what she went through.

Monica couldn't hear what the grownups were saying, but the man kneeled and talked with Katie for a moment. Monica's parents stood side by side, her dad wrapping his arm around her mom's shoulder. They were giving those over-the-top smiles that grownups tend to give when trying extra hard to cheer up a kid. If Katie was anything like her, she'd read right through it. As they continued talking, Katie finally lifted her head, looking at her soon-to-be foster parents. She forced a smile, then peered up to Monica's window, locking eyes with her.

Her gaze sent chills down Monica's spine.

One of the rumors her friends discussed about the "group home massacre" was that the surviving kid had killed them all. Monica had thought the idea of a little girl killing a house full of people to be silly. Until she looked into those blue eyes. She hadn't even met the girl yet and already couldn't wait for the moment someone came to pick her up and take her to her permanent home.

When she realized Katie was still staring at her, and that now all the adults were as well, she faked a return smile and waved. Taking a deep breath, she headed downstairs to introduce herself.

***

After the man with red hair—Barry, he had introduced himself as—left the house, Monica's parents led the two girls into the living room. As they did on every occasion that they took a child into their care, once Katie was comfortable enough, they told Monica to give her a tour of the house while they carried her bags in from the porch. The two girls walked upstairs in silence, both waiting for the other to break the ice. Monica tried to forget about the creepy stare she got from the window, knowing her parents would expect more from her. They raised her to not judge others, especially kids who came from rough backgrounds.

Monica opened the door to the spare bedroom they'd prepared for Katie and walked in.

"Here's your room. I thought you'd like this one because it has pink walls. The bed's comfy, too," she said, turning to Katie.

Katie took in the bedroom, her eyes gravitating to the closet, which remained shut. Monica recalled the story of how they found Katie in the closet, hiding from the killer.

"I'm sorry about what happened . . . My parents told me not to talk about it with you."

Katie pried her eyes from the closet and brought her focus back to Monica.

"It's okay."

"Do you like playing with dolls?" Monica asked.

"Yeah. I lost all mine in the home."

"I have a lot. I'll share them with you too. My parents have helped a bunch of kids. I think you'll like them. Even though they can be annoying."

A slight smile cracked beneath the sadness that seemed permanently etched on Katie's face.

Maybe she won't be so bad after all, Monica thought.

CHAPTER 4

FAITH UNDERSTOOD SHE had to be patient whenever they brought a foster child home. Not just for the new kid who was experiencing their foreign surroundings for the first time, but for her daughter. Faith felt selfish, knowing Monica didn't want any of this, yet was made to go along with it through the prime years of her childhood. There was always some guilt burrowed deep inside Faith for putting her daughter through it. Being a mother to the most amazing daughter in the world was the best thing that ever happened to her. Yet, there was something about taking a child in who had experienced trauma and trying to help them get their life on track that was rewarding far beyond anything she'd ever felt in her life.

Growing up, moving from group home to group home herself, Faith knew how tough it was for kids. She knew how flawed the system was. How kids often went back to their abusive parents until the next time they got taken away again. Or how they were living with a family that was only in it for the money, taking the payments given to them each month only to treat the child like a stray dog begging for scraps. She vowed to give whoever they looked after an experience that would help mold them into better people. To help take that pain and use it to become a stronger person. It was never easy to see the kids leave after becoming attached, but she could sleep at night knowing that every single child who slept under their roof left in a much better place than when they arrived.

So far, Monica appeared to be getting along well with Katie. She couldn't help but smile at the realization they were raising a near-perfect human. Sure, Monica had her moments like any kid. But she handled fostering with a selflessness that not many children could. Faith was so proud of her.

She watched quietly as her family finished their dinner—the first step in trying to win Katie over. It was tradition to cook the favorite meal on a kid's first night in the house. Katie had selected Kraft Mac & Cheese, and Monica wasn't complaining. Nor was Dan, who, while pushing his mid-forties, no longer carrying the flat stomach of his youth, never hesitated to devour kids' food like it was a medium-rare steak at a five-star restaurant.

Faith committed to keeping a close eye on Katie, monitoring for any signs of trauma that could possibly be keeping its hold on the poor girl. For everything the kid went through, she at least appeared to have herself under control on the surface.

Dan was telling the kids some of his horrible dad jokes while they ate, hoping to break the ice and help Katie feel more comfortable. It was nice to see her smile so early on. Some of the kids were tough to crack, but they always found a way. It appeared that Katie would end up being one of the *easier* ones, surprisingly. Faith left the kitchen and walked over to join them.

"Why'd the bicycle fall over?" Dan asked, a smile already spreading beneath his scruffy maw.

Monica rolled her eyes—a habit she shouldn't be picking up for at least another few years—and then bit on her dad's punchline.

"Why, Dad?"

"Because . . . it was two-tired! Get it?"

Monica cringed, burying her face in her palms and shook her head, but Faith saw a smile beneath her hands. Katie covered her mouth and giggled.

"Please don't laugh at his bad jokes. He'll only keep going if you do," Monica teased.

For the most part, Katie hadn't said much since arriving, but that was normal. It was just good to see her laughing and smiling.

"Okay. Who wants some dessert and a movie?" Faith asked.

"Me!" the girls and Dan all shouted.

***

Dan kicked his feet up on the couch and grabbed the remote. They'd decided on watching *Frozen*, a movie they'd watched more times than he could count. But seeing the excitement of Katie, who'd only seen the movie once, plus the girls agreeing so easily, made it worth it. Faith dimmed the overhead lights to get rid of the glare on the television and sat next to him.

"Okay, girls. I know the ice cream's freezing, but the cold never bothered me anyway," Dan said.

The girls both groaned in unison, then laughed at their mirroring reaction. Dan turned on the TV, going to the app he was forced to pay for, even though he had no desire to give the corporate companies a dime. *Gotta make the kids happy, right?* He thought.

The screen went dark momentarily as the movie went to the opening credits. For a brief second, the dim light created a reflection on the flatscreen.

Dan saw a large silhouette standing behind the couch, behind *them.*

He stopped himself from jumping out of his pants, not wanting to spook the girls, then turned to look behind him.

There was nothing there.

After waiting a second, he shook his head and turned back to the screen again, but the movie had already started, brightening up the surface too much to see the glare.

"Better eat that ice cream before it melts," Faith said.

Dan snapped back to reality, looking down at his bowl to see the start of a chocolate puddle forming at the bottom of the bowl.

"Yeah, just thought I saw something, is all. I need to get my eyes checked." He shook his head again and ate a large spoonful of half-melted ice cream. He couldn't help feeling like someone was watching them through the entire movie.

***

After the movie was over, the girls went upstairs to brush their teeth and get ready for bed. The night couldn't have gone any better. Monica and Katie appeared to have an instant connection, even though it was clear Katie wasn't ready to fully let her guard down just yet. But Monica was used to that after multiple foster kids. Faith heard the girls giggling in the bathroom while they brushed. They exited and Faith climbed the stairs to tuck them in while Dan cleaned up downstairs.

"Okay, let's get you kiddos to bed. Hon, why don't you go on in your room and read a book until Dad or I come say goodnight? I'll get Katie situated and be right in, okay?"

"Okay," she agreed, and Faith kissed her on the head before leading Katie to her room.

Katie hesitated in the doorway, scanning the room.

"It's okay, hon. Nothing to be scared of here," Faith said, but quickly realized it would take more than calming words to comfort the girl. "How about I stay in here and rub your back until you fall asleep? Would that help?"

Katie nodded, her eyes glistening.

"I know it's hard to adjust. But I promise we'll take care of you, Katie. And if you ever want to talk about anything with us, please don't be afraid."

Katie didn't say anything. Instead, she entered the room and climbed into bed, pulling the neon-pink comforter up to her chin. Faith sat at the foot of the bed, smiling down at her.

"Would it help if I sang to you? Monica thinks she's too old for it these days, but I didn't take years of vocal classes for nothing. I don't think I'm exactly the target audience for *American Idol* anymore," she said with a grin.

"You took singing lessons? That's so cool."

"Yep. One of the things I learned after growing up in foster homes was that I needed a way to take my mind off the bad things I went through as a child. If we can go through what we went through, why be afraid to chase the dreams you always wanted, right?"

"I love singing . . . Thank you for being so nice, Mrs. Page."

"Oh, darling . . . you're so welcome."

Faith proceeded to sing calming music, watching Katie's eyelids flutter before eventually giving in to sleep. Even once the little girl was no longer awake, Faith couldn't help but notice the uneasiness behind her closed eyelids, her eyes flitting back and forth. She wondered if Katie had even enjoyed a good night's sleep since the massacre. All she could do was continue to be the support system Katie needed, and she planned to do just that.

CHAPTER 5

MONICA CLOSED HER book and set it on her nightstand. As much as she wanted to read and force herself to stay awake until her mother came in and said goodnight, she found herself beginning to doze off, reading the same sentences over and over as her head bobbed down every few seconds. She rolled over and faced the window, staring out into the night. The bedside lamp remained on, but she had no intention of turning it off until her mother came in. Instead, she watched as the tree branches swayed in the night sky. They used to scare her when she was younger, but over the years, Monica had come to enjoy their fluid motions, as if they were trying to aid her to sleep.

She thought about how the day went, meeting Katie for the first time and how easily they were getting along. It wasn't always so simple becoming friends with the foster kids, but Katie seemed nice, even though she was super shy. Monica recalled how every time they entered a room, Katie looked around skittishly, as if she needed to make sure nobody else was there before going in. Then while they were brushing their teeth, Monica couldn't help but burst out laughing when Katie stared in the mirror—toothpaste sloshing around in her mouth—and whipped around to lock eyes on the tub as if something was going to jump out from behind the curtain and scare them. At first, Katie's attention remained glued to the shower curtain, but once she realized Monica thought it was a joke, she conceded a laugh.

I wonder what scared her so badly? Monica thought.

Still, all things considered, they had a lot of fun together. Katie even laughed at her jokes, which not many kids at school did. Hopefully, after a few days of living with them, she would become more relaxed and learn to enjoy herself again.

Monica closed her eyes, deciding it would be okay to doze off for a few minutes before her mom came in. It had been a long day, and with the summer heat wrapping around their bodies like a suffocating cocoon, her energy had been completely sapped. She nuzzled into her pillow, the air conditioner blasting cool air into her face to help her relax.

She drifted off to sleep, only waking slightly when she felt her mattress dip as one of her parents sat on the edge of the bed to rub her back. The gentle strokes comforted her. And then, the soft humming of melodies crawled into her head, something her mom hadn't done in quite some time. Considering it had been so long, it made sense the song wasn't one she recalled hearing her mother sing before.

Then her mom stopped rubbing her back, continuing to hum. As the song ended, the tickling of a soft whisper came. Her mom began to rub Monica's exposed arm, her pointy nails sending gooseflesh across the skin. The whispering sped up, as if her mother was chanting something under her breath. The nails slid from her shoulder down to her elbow, pressing harder, the comfort turning to pain.

"Mom, that *hurts.*"

Monica shot her eyes open and realized her room was now dark. But the hallway light was still on, shining in her bedroom and reflecting off the window.

She looked at the window, no longer seeing the branches slowly dancing in the dark, but instead the reflection of someone standing over her bed, far too tall and skinny to be her mom.

Monica's throat tightened, ready to scream.

Without moving her head, she looked down at the hand rubbing along her arm. The fingers were covered in filth, the nails longer than the fingers themselves, and caked in blood. Unnatural veins traveled beneath the weathered skin.

She screamed, then whipped around in her bed.

Her room was empty.

***

Faith jumped out of bed and ran to her daughter's room. She turned the light on and Monica screamed again as she came into view, as if the sight of Faith in the open doorway terrified her.

"Monica! It's okay, hon. It was just a nightmare," Faith said.

"Mom! It wasn't a nightmare. Someone was in here with me. They were singing to me like you always used to. They started rubbing my back and . . . " Monica couldn't say anymore as the tears choked out her words.

Faith turned to see Dan following down the hall, rubbing the last bit of sleep from his eyes.

"What is it?" he asked.

They both entered the room and sat on the edge of Monica's bed.

"I know it can seem real, but it's not. There's nobody here besides us, Monica," Faith said. She attempted to rub her daughter's arm, but Monica flinched, acting as if she was about to be struck instead of calmed.

"Kiddo. It's okay. Take some deep breaths," Dan said.

"Someone sat on my bed! And turned off my light. I know I wasn't sleeping," Monica cried.

"That was me that turned off your light after I came in to check on you, hon. I know things can feel real when you first wake up, but it'll fade away, and you'll realize it was just a really bad nightmare. Do you want me to stay in here until you fall asleep?" Faith asked. She really had no desire to do that after finally getting Katie to sleep, but it was clear her daughter was still worked up.

Monica hesitated before responding, again glancing toward the door, then the closet. Dan followed her eyes and got up off the bed.

"Here, let's do the old-fashioned monster inspection, shall we?"

He walked to the closet and opened the door, revealing a dark space littered with piles of clothes that should have been on the hangers but were instead tossed aside after Monica tried them on and decided on another outfit.

"See? Nothing in here could be scarier than this mess you left," he said with a smirk. "Shall I check under your bed?"

Monica smiled, and Faith knew she was coming around.

"You might find another clothes monster hiding under there. Better not," Monica said.

"Uh oh, I heard they bite," Dan said.

He grabbed her favorite stuffed animal and sat it next to her.

"We can leave your door open if that's better. You want the light from the hall? I told Katie I'd leave it on to make her more comfortable," Faith said.

"Okay."

Dan kissed her on the head and smiled.

"Thanks for being so helpful today, Mon. You made Katie's first day great," he said.

"You really did. We're so proud of you. I say tomorrow we spend the day in the pool. What do you say? We can play some music, have some snacks, and just hang out all day," Faith said.

"Sounds good. Goodnight."

"Goodnight, Money Monica," Dan said, then kissed her on the head again and walked out.

Faith rolled her eyes at his horrible nickname for their daughter and kissed her cheek.

"Love you, hon."

"Love you too, Mom."

Faith turned off the light and left the room. All she wanted was to fall back into bed and pass out. She walked down the hall, past the room Katie now occupied, but didn't think to glance over at the door. If she had, she would have noticed the door slightly ajar. A set of eyes peering out from the darkness, watching her as she passed.

CHAPTER 6

AFTER BREAKFAST, Monica sat at her desk, drawing a picture of butterflies and flowers to give Katie to hang in her room. She worked hard on it for a good part of the morning, excited to give it to her new friend. When she felt the drawing was the best it could be, she got up from her seat and left her room, approaching Katie's closed door. She stopped outside the door and listened, making sure she didn't hear Katie doing anything in private that would embarrass her. As she went to open the door, her hand froze a few inches from the knob, a soft melody muffled from inside the room.

She immediately recognized it as the song she'd heard in her dream last night. Whatever entered her room had hummed it while scraping their ghastly hand along her skin. Monica didn't know what to do, but suddenly she had no desire to open the door. A chill traveled down her spine, and she prepared to walk away when the song stopped. Before she realized why, footsteps approached the door and she had nowhere to go.

The door swung open, and Katie stared into the hallway, surprised to see Monica already standing there.

"Oh, hey. Whatcha doing in there?" Monica asked.

Katie stared at the ground before bringing her focus back to Monica.

"I was just getting ready for the day. What about you?"

Monica glanced over Katie's shoulder into the room, spotting a small notebook on the edge of the bed. When Katie realized she was staring at it, her face reddened with embarrassment.

"Sorry, I didn't mean to be nosy," Monica replied.

"It's okay. My doctor told me to write and draw every day in my book to help me get better. She told me the more I do, the better it would make me feel."

"Does it?"

"What?" Katie asked.

"Make you feel better. Whatever you write in there?"

"Oh. Yeah. Sometimes at least. I don't like my private thoughts out for anyone to see."

Monica picked up that the topic was an uncomfortable one for Katie, so she changed the subject.

"I was coming to your room because I made you something," she said, holding out the drawing.

Katie stared at the drawing, her eyes beginning to water.

No! She hates it, Monica thought. "What's wrong?"

"Thank you. Nothing's wrong. It reminds me of a girl in the group home who used to draw flowers all the time."

Monica felt sick. She'd drawn the picture to help Katie feel better, but instead, it reminded her of one of her dead foster sisters.

"I'm really sorry. I was trying to do something nice."

"I love it. She was my best friend in the house. Her name was Becky. Thank you so much," she said, then hugged Monica tight.

Monica wasn't sure what to feel. She was relieved Katie liked the drawing. But that song kept coming back to her. Why would Katie be singing the song that until her nightmare Monica had never heard before? She pulled back from the hug.

"That song you were singing . . . What was it?"

Katie raised an eyebrow in confusion.

"Song?"

"I heard you humming something when I was gonna knock on your door."

"Oh . . . That's a lullaby my mom used to sing to me before . . . before she died. It's a German song my grandmother used to sing to her."

Monica swallowed down a gulp of fear. Maybe she just thought it was the same song. It made no sense that she'd hear it, even in a dream.

"What's it called?" Monica asked.

"Der Mond . . . something. It means the moon has risen. She used to hum it to help me go to sleep."

Again, Monica wanted to scream. She was too embarrassed to say anything to Katie. Too embarrassed to mention it to either of her parents, for that matter. Instead, she decided to try to push it aside and think about swimming.

"Let's go swim. You're going to love the pool!" she said in forced excitement.

***

Monica squinted through the bright midday sunlight, standing on the edge of the diving board. Her mom lay relaxed in her lounge chair with one of her cringe romance novels—the kind where a shirtless man stood in an unnatural position to show off his muscles on the cover. Her dad cooked on the grill, flipping burgers as the flames attempted to take hold of the grease-lathered meat. She couldn't help but smile, thinking back to all the cookouts they had where her parents' friends would pick on his grilling skills, always on the verge of an apparent grill fire.

Her mom looked up from her book and smiled.

"Hon, remember to show Katie where the soft spot in the liner is, k?"

"Okay."

Katie sat at the edge of the deep end, her legs dangling over the side into the water.

"Just be careful. There are a few soft spots beneath the liner, but the pool man said they were fine as long as we didn't jump right on them. It could pop a hole in the liner because the sand is sinking underneath it," Monica said.

"Thanks for telling me. But I don't swim very good anyway, so I'll probably just stay here . . . Sorry."

Monica tried to hide her disappointment, but she knew Katie saw it in her eyes.

"You can't swim?"

"It's not that . . . I just don't like the feeling of being trapped in a spot. My doctor said that'll go away someday . . . *hopefully*."

"Well, you can use my float if you want. That way, you don't have to go all the way in the water," Monica said.

"Thanks, maybe I will."

Monica's dad shouted from the grill. The flames now engulfed the food as he swore under his breath and tried to get it under control. He noticed the girls watching him and held up the metal spatula like it was some sort of majestic weapon.

"This grill will not defeat me!" He laughed. "Hey Monica, let's see one of those famous cannonballs you do."

She smiled, then bounced on the diving board, trying to get as much power behind her jump as possible. She counted to three and launched herself, soaring through the air until her body splashed the perfectly heated water and plunged below. Monica sank, her feet hitting the pool floor. She prepared to push herself off and swim back to the surface. Only she couldn't separate from the bottom.

Something was holding onto her foot.

Her eyes shot open, desperately seeking whatever was unwilling to release her from its grasp. Water invaded her pupils, clouding anything more than a few inches from her face. But she was certain she saw movement below her. The problem was there was nothing below her except the white liner of the pool. Her foot stuck to the floor as if someone had doused her skin with superglue. And then she noticed a shift below.

Beneath the liner.

The water played tricks with her eyes, but she was certain something rippled beneath the floor. She glanced at her ankle as panic quickly set in. The liner stretched beneath her, raising a few feet from the floor, and wrapped around her ankle like a python. It slowly transformed into the shape of a hand from the soft spot in the liner, stretching the material like putty as it tightened around her.

Monica screamed. Bubbles forced their way from her lungs, floating to the surface above. Her eyes bulged, frantically scanning the surrounding area for anything to help her. She wasn't close enough to the wall to reach out and grab it. *Why weren't her parents jumping in to save her?*

With her free leg, she kicked at the strange hand as it continued squeezing tightly around her ankle. Stars began to float around her vision. She opened her mouth out of instinct, attempting to take a deep breath, but instead filling her lungs with water, suffocating her even more. And then something else pressed against the floor from below. The outline of a face. A nose sharp enough that it looked as if it could tear the liner with even one more ounce of pressure. The mouth opened wide, continuing to expand until a set of finely sharpened teeth pushed against the material.

Monica knew she was close to drowning, but that didn't stop her from screaming again, the sounds muffled by twenty-two thousand gallons of water. She began to fade. The water above her swirled around, and she looked up, fighting to stay conscious. She faintly made out her mom swimming toward her. She reached for her mother's hand, then realized she was now floating toward her. Whatever had gripped her leg had let go. Her hand linked with her mother's. As Faith began to pull her toward the surface, Monica searched below, hoping to see the monster who had done this to her. Instead, her vision faded, her heartbeat slowed. Everything faded to black.

CHAPTER 7

FAITH PUSHED HER daughter's limp body to the surface, where Dan awaited to lift her out of the water. *Please, no, not my daughter*, Faith thought. Everything had happened so fast. She'd been reading her book, Dan, cooking on the grill. When Monica jumped into the water, the flames on the grill began to spread across every burner, forcing their way up a few feet and causing Dan to step back and trip over the patio step. Faith had run to Dan to help him up, and together they tried to get the grill fire down. For a brief second, she could have sworn she saw a face forming in the flames as they expanded, reaching for something else to consume.

That's when Katie screamed, yelling something about Monica not coming up and being trapped in the deep end. Dan shouted for Faith to go help their daughter while he kept working to get the fire under control. By the time she dove into the pool, Monica was already floating toward the surface, still alert enough to look up at her, but Faith saw her eyes start to fade.

Dan now kneeled over Monica, prepared to give CPR. Faith stood behind him, praying that it wasn't too late to save her. For a moment, they forgot all about Katie, who now sat hugging her knees, rocking back and forth while she stared into the deep end. Dan pressed his hands below Monica's sternum, ready to push. Then Monica curled into a ball and rolled to her side, coughing up water. She continued to cough, taking forced breaths to fill her lungs.

"Hon, oh god. It's okay. It's okay," Faith said.

"Monica. Keep taking breaths, sweetie," Dan said while rubbing her back.

Monica screamed at his touch, not in pain, but fear. She was terrified.

"It's okay," he repeated.

They all remained silent while Monica attempted to regain her breath. When she finally had herself under control, she looked at the pool.

"Did you see it? Something grabbed me at the bottom!"

Dan and Faith looked at each other with concerned stares that were impossible to hide.

"Hon, there's nothing down there," Faith said.

"Mom! It was something under the liner, I swear. A hand came up and grabbed my ankle. It wouldn't let go."

Faith instinctively looked at her daughter's ankle and gasped. Three bruises, roughly the width of fingers, lined the skin.

"I . . . How?" she asked.

"I'll go down to see if something could have caught on her foot," Dan said.

"No! Don't go down there, Dad. What if it tries to get you, too?"

"Sweetie, I can see down there from here. It's possible there's something hanging on the liner that I can't make out from up here, but look . . . There's nobody down there," he said, gesturing to the deep end.

Monica glared at Katie.

"It's her fault! Ever since she got here, weird things have been happening to me."

Faith gave Katie an apologetic glance.

"That's not fair to say, hon. You can't blame her for having a nightmare and . . . whatever happened in the pool. She wasn't even in the water," Faith said.

"I don't care! There's a reason she wouldn't go in the water. I know it was her."

Katie remained silent, staring at the pool. Faith felt awful for her. She walked over and crouched next to Katie.

"She's just upset right now. I'm sorry."

"It's okay. After what happened at the home, bad things keep following me around." Katie wiped her tears away.

"Don't say that, hon. Monica didn't mean it, okay?"

Faith helped Katie to her feet while Dan supported his daughter. Dan remained focused on the deep end, but Faith knew she needed to change the subject, to lighten the mood. But those bruises worried her. *What could have done that?*

"Well, Barry's going to stop by for lunch to see how things are going so far. How about we all go inside and relax while your dad and I set the table?" Faith suggested.

Monica wouldn't look Katie in the eye. Faith needed to speak with her in private before she did any more damage to this poor girl's confidence.

They all walked into the house, forgetting about the pool for the time being. Dan grabbed the tray of overcooked burgers and hot dogs on the way in, prompting Faith to look at the grill. She couldn't shake the image of those flames, wrapping around one another like fiery serpents from Hell reaching for the sky, the face that she *knew* she saw staring back at her from the flames with a sinister grin.

CHAPTER 8

NO SOONER THAN the table was set, the doorbell rang, and Faith saw the blurred figure of Barry waiting on the porch through the stained-glass window on the front door. She wiped her hands on her apron and sped to the door, not wanting to make a bad impression after only one day of having Katie. She opened the door and smiled.

"Barry! Come in, come in. We're so glad you could make it for lunch. Usually, the caseworkers look for any excuse they can not to come check on the kids, but you clearly care about your job."

She hoped she wasn't laying it on too thick. But it was the truth. In their years of fostering kids, the sad reality was that most caseworkers moved on to the next kid without much thought of the ones left behind to foster parents. At least not until an official adoption was close. Faith had always found it strange how someone could get into that line of work only to treat the children like case numbers instead of human beings. The fact was that caseworkers were expected to check in on the kids at least once a month. They were expected to keep in regular contact with the foster parents, developing a plan with the family that outlines the path to permanency goals. They were supposed to be part of a much larger support system to help make sure the children got what they needed. Yet, far too many times, Faith had been let down by the system. Both as a foster child herself, and as a foster parent.

"That I do. These kids have been through so much I feel I owe it to them to make sure they get proper treatment. Especially one such as Katie, after what she went through and all," Barry said.

He followed Faith into the house and approached the dinner table, where Katie and Monica sat while Dan placed the food in the center dishes.

"Hey, Barry! Good seeing you again," Dan said.

The men shook hands, and again Faith felt they were trying too hard. She wasn't sure why; they had been through this with many kids. Maybe it was because of the struggles Katie had dealt with leading up to coming here. Or, more likely, the fact that their daughter almost just drowned and blamed Katie for it.

Barry sat at the table, pulled up a chair next to Katie, and smiled.

"Hey, Katie. How have the first few days been?"

"Good . . . Mr. and Mrs. Page are really nice." She smiled, then looked toward Monica and stopped. Apparently, Barry picked up on it because he also looked at Monica.

"Well, that's wonderful to hear. The first few days can be an adjustment with a new family, especially when they have kids. How are things between the girls?" Barry shifted his attention to Faith and Dan.

The parents exchanged glances. Faith decided she'd better speak up before Dan said anything, as he had the tendency to ramble when he was nervous—a tic she normally found cute, but right now, that was the last thing they needed.

"For the most part, it's gone really well. A few incidents out of the norm, but Katie has been a darling."

"Incidents? What do you mean?" Barry asked.

A knot tightened in Faith's stomach. She knew it was ridiculous. Nothing that happened was in any way an indication of how they parented. Monica had a bad dream the night before and a freak accident in the pool. So why did Faith feel as if they were being judged?

"Monica woke in the middle of the night screaming last night. She said someone was rubbing her back and humming a song, but then they started to hurt her. It was just a bad dream. And then she got stuck in the pool today after jumping in . . . " Faith trailed off, eyes locked on the pen that Barry wrote with.

"Got stuck in the pool? Like underwater?" He furrowed his brow.

"We think something on the liner snagged her ankle when she jumped off the diving board," Dan said defensively.

Watch the tone, hon, Faith thought.

"Well, that surely doesn't sound safe. Did you figure out what it was?" Barry asked.

"I'm going to go down after lunch and see if I can find anything.

It's strange though . . . from the surface, we couldn't see anything out of the ordinary," Dan replied.

"While this sounds terrifying for your poor daughter, I'm wondering what Katie has to do with it?"

Faith wished the kids were in another room so they could talk freely. She didn't want to upset Katie any more than Monica already had.

"Monica seems to think the two incidents were Katie's fault. That bad things started happening to her when Katie arrived," Faith said.

"I see," Barry said. Something in his eyes didn't sit right with Faith. It was as if the mention of strange occurrences spooked him.

"Care for a burger or dog?" Dan asked.

"Yes, please, I'm starving. And this food looks great," Barry said while rubbing his hands together in anticipation.

They all filled their plates, making small talk while they ate. Faith was thankful they were no longer focusing on the kids' relationship, feeling it wasn't appropriate to do that in front of the girls. Katie acted as if she didn't care, but Faith knew better. There was no way the poor girl wasn't feeling guilty for something she had no control over. If she was already getting blamed for stuff, what would happen when she went back to school?

When all the mean kids would be waiting for the first chance to throw the massacre in her face, calling her a monster. While they never did find out who was responsible for the murders in the group home, they deemed Katie innocent. For one, she was such a small child, there was no way in hell she could have torn bodies apart with her bare hands. Secondly, Katie had been bounced around from home to home over the last few years leading up to the group home massacre, yet the most trouble she'd been in was for pushing a boy who picked on her regarding her dead mother.

After lunch, the girls went to their rooms, allowing Barry to give his full attention to Faith and Dan.

"I just want to say . . . you guys have an incredible reputation with foster kids. I didn't want to say anything in front of Katie, but it's not you that I'm focusing on as much as it is *her*. Normally, these appointments are to come up with a plan of action, but today I just wanted to touch base and see how things were going for her. Even in the little time I've spent with her, there's always this sense of eeriness floating around. It's not fair to her. But I can tell by your reactions that you both feel the same way."

"It's not us you have to worry about. Monica doesn't usually act like this with anyone we bring in. And at first, she was getting along great with Katie. But as hard as she's trying, she's never tried to make one of them feel unwanted or different. Just in the span of one day and night, it's like she thinks Katie's a monster. It can't help that all the kids at school talk about the massacre and spread those nasty rumors," Faith said.

Barry continued to look uncomfortable, swallowing a large gulp of air.

"I had a few strange moments with her in the days leading up to bringing her here. Nothing too strange, but I was in my office, filling out paperwork while I talked with Katie. I noticed she kept looking over my shoulder as I made small talk. The only thing behind me was the wall, cluttered with folders and books on the shelf. I turned to see what she was looking at, but nothing appeared out of the ordinary. Then I went back to filling out the paperwork, asking her questions that needed to be asked. Something tickled the back of my neck, and I shot back around—again, nothing. When I turned back to Katie, she looked terrified. I asked what was wrong, and she just shut down. I can tell you that I've been scared before, but nothing has ever sent chills down my spine like that. And that wasn't even the worst of it. As I continued filling out the paperwork, feeling like something was breathing in my ear, a hard pinch squeezed the center of my neck. I've never sworn in front of the kids, but I'd be lying if I didn't tell you I hollered 'FUCK' and jumped out of my chair."

Faith and Dan listened in awe.

"The reason I'm telling you this is that I just want you to keep an eye out. It sounds like your daughter has experienced similar occurrences. Have either of you?"

"Not at all. Business as usual for me, at least. You, Faith?" Dan asked.

She considered the face floating in the flames. Was that enough to admit to? Monica had a nightmare. All kids have nightmares at some point. The pool incident was confusing, but they didn't see anything in the water.

"No, nothing to me specifically."

"Okay. Just be careful. I'm sorry that I'm putting this on you guys now after you already took Katie, but until you mentioned the story with your daughter, I just thought I was losing my mind. Katie's a wonderful girl. She deserves to start fresh. Have a blank space, if you will. If you run into any more of these occurrences, please reach out to me," Barry said.

"Will do," replied Dan.

They walked Barry to the door and said their goodbyes. Faith wanted to tell her husband about the flames. About how something wasn't sitting right and maybe Barry and Monica were correct. But it felt ridiculous. Katie's past was messing with her. She shook off the unsettling feeling and started to clear the table while Dan went out to look at the pool.

CHAPTER 9

FAITH LAY IN BED, reading the same sentence in her book over and over as her mind wandered back to the conversation they had with Barry at lunch. The rest of the day had gone by without any issues, but after hearing Barry's story, she was struggling to view Katie in the same light she had earlier. It made her sick to her stomach that she was letting awful thoughts about this little girl infiltrate her normally levelheaded mind. It wasn't just Barry's story. Monica had never acted this way toward one of the foster kids. While the first day went well enough, ever since the pool scene, Monica didn't want to be in the same room with Katie.

She looked over at Dan, who scrolled through social media apps on his phone with heavy eyes.

"Hon? Do you think we have anything to worry about with Katie?"

He set the phone on his chest and considered her question.

"Nah . . . It's easy to get spooked when you know her backstory. I think everyone's putting this stigma on the poor girl that she's cursed or something. What has she done that would lead us to think she's anything but some lost soul looking for care?"

"I know. It's just they never put those murders on anyone, and she was the only one left. I'm not saying she was capable of killing all those kids. Hell, I wouldn't have taken her into our home if I thought there was even a chance of that. But I never expected this strange feeling anytime we're around her. I feel awful about thinking like this, Dan."

He smiled, rubbing her leg.

"Babe . . . there's nothing to feel awful about. We're still trying to help her get her life back together. We're still the ones going out of our way to be even a small part of giving a kid some hope. Isn't that why we started this in the first place? To do something you always wished was done for you? Think about that for a minute. You spent your entire childhood bouncing from home to home and never felt you had anyone to look out for you."

Faith closed her eyes and sighed.

"I know, I know. And thank you for saying that." She leaned in and kissed him on the cheek. "But what are we going to do about Monica? It's going to be a rough few months if we can't get those two on the same page."

"I'll talk with her tomorrow. Take her to lunch and the mall or something. Maybe you can get some bonding time in with Katie and try to get some more out of her. Have some faith, Faith." Dan smirked.

Faith rolled her eyes but couldn't help smiling at his terrible jokes.

"Okay. I love you."

"Love you too. Goodnight," Dan said.

Faith set her book on the dresser, then turned the bedside lamp off, sending the bedroom into darkness.

***

Monica curled up in her bed, staring toward the hallway. She'd requested that her mom leave the door open and the hallway light on. After the nightmare the previous night, she had no desire to sleep, even with her body telling her to close her eyes. Monica squeezed her stuffed bear tight, sitting up every few minutes to keep herself awake. The more time passed, the more she was beginning to think the strange lady rubbing her shoulder the night before was, in fact, a nightmare. But she'd never felt pain from a dream, and when she awoke, screaming to her parents, her shoulder was throbbing where the phantom hand squeezed.

She sat up, feeling her eyes forcing their way shut. *Don't sleep. Stay awake.*

Every shape in her cluttered room looked as if it was waiting for her to let her guard down before crawling from the shadows to finish what they had started last night. Her heart jumped in her chest as she focused on the far corner of her room, where the light from the hallway struggled to reach.

A tall, warped figure hugged the wall.

While she couldn't see any eyes, she sensed it watching. Waiting. Something scraped along the window, and Monica threw her hand over her mouth to stifle a gasp. *It's just branches*, she thought. She needed to remind her dad to trim them, because this wasn't the first time they had scared her.

Her attention shifted back to the corner. The large shadow remained in place, as still as before. Part of her wanted to scream for her parents, but she was afraid if she shouted, it would come for her. Monica also realized that she could be overreacting, that her imagination was playing tricks on her. Without taking her eyes off the shadow monster, she reached over to her nightstand, feeling blindly for her lamp. She almost knocked it off the dresser, catching it at the last second. Her hand found the switch and turned the light on . . . and stared back at the culprit of the shadow—her towel she'd used at the pool earlier, hanging off her closet door.

Monica shook her head in disgust at herself. She was letting Katie's past mess with her. What had Katie actually done to her? Nothing. Yet Monica found any reason to blame her for whatever was happening. *But what about the pool*? Nobody believed her. Even her dad, who went to check on the liner after lunch, said there wasn't anything that could have caught on her foot. Bruises don't form from things in your imagination. *Something* grabbed her. And she knew it was a hand, pushing from beneath the liner like it was living under the pool, waiting for the chance to grab someone and pull them below.

As she went to turn the light off, Monica decided to get out of bed and check the hallway, making sure there was nothing lurking around the corner. She tossed the blankets down to the foot of the mattress and slid her feet over the side, then considered something could be *beneath* the bed. That was all it took for her to jump out of bed and separate herself from the dark unknown. When she felt there was enough distance between her and the bed, she turned to look below the dangling sheets. The scariest thing staring back at her was the mound of dirty clothes she promised her mother to take care of earlier.

Entering the hallway, she found herself alone, but that somehow didn't make her feel any better. Knowing it was clear, she decided it was best to get back to her bed, where she could at least cover herself with her blankets and remain still. But then she heard a voice down the hall. At first, she assumed it was her parents talking in bed, but their room was deeper in the house, so there was no way their voices would carry this far. The voice was coming from Katie's room.

Monica took a deep breath and snuck down the hallway, her heart drumming in her ears. The voice got louder but remained softened behind the closed door. It was definitely Katie, and it sounded like she was talking to herself. Monica made sure the door was completely shut, noticing there was no light coming from beneath the door. Katie was talking to herself in the dark. *Maybe she's talking in her sleep?*

Monica put her ear to the door and listened.

"No . . . I need to get rid of her . . . I can't leave yet."

It was a struggle to make out the words, but Monica knew what she heard. Her legs turned to jelly, and she was suddenly struck with a bout of lightheadedness. She leaned against the wall, trying to hold herself up. Trying to listen some more. Whether Katie was talking in her sleep or not, it sent a chill down Monica's spine.

"Monica could've died today. I could have stopped it, but I didn't."

Tears slid down Monica's cheeks. She didn't know what to do. Her parents wouldn't believe her. There was nothing to prove that Katie had anything to do with the pool incident. And her parents would be really upset if she woke them in the middle of the night. Should she confront Katie? Go in and demand she confess everything to her parents? She wasn't sure she had it in her to open the door. With a trembling hand, Monica reached out for the door, ready to open it . . . but stopped when the talking resumed. Something was wrong.

The voice was different. Monica realized it wasn't Katie's voice anymore. Someone else was in the room with her.

"They will be ours, girl. They belong with the children."

The voice was deep, hitting an extremely low octave that sent gooseflesh across Monica's arms. She had heard enough. She turned and sped down the hall, back to her bedroom, and jumped into bed, pulling the comforter over her head. Suddenly, she didn't think she would need to force herself to stay awake the rest of the night. Her hands shook, her heart rammed against her ribcage. She lifted the blanket just high enough to create a small viewport to the hall. That was how she planned to lay the rest of the night.

CHAPTER 10

DAN STOPPED AT the red light and took the opportunity to glance over at his daughter in the back seat. Monica had been mostly silent since she woke up this morning. The bags under her eyes could be mistaken for black eyes if someone looked quick enough. After everything that happened to her the day before, it was easy to see why she struggled to sleep. He wished she'd felt safe enough to come to them in the night instead of going to bed in fear.

"Let's talk, love dove. What's on your mind? You look like you didn't get a minute of sleep last night."

Monica stared out her window for another minute before finally turning her attention to him. She was on the verge of tears.

"Daddy, I . . . I'm scared of Katie. She seemed nice at first, but she's the reason this stuff is happening to me. I know it."

Dan knew he needed to be careful how he answered her. The last thing he wanted was to lose the trust he'd established over years of effort. He also knew he needed to make her realize how ridiculous it all was. The light turned green, and Dan brought his focus back to the road.

"Honey. What makes you say that? Because of her past? That's not very fair to her. I know it's odd timing for sure and that you never have nightmares, and then the first night she's here, you wake up terrified. But even if there was any truth to her being involved with those kids dying—which there *isn't*, or we would have never taken her into our home—that would have nothing to do with you having a bad dream. You see what I'm saying?"

"I knew you wouldn't believe me. I know it sounds stupid. But Daddy, the song I heard in my dream was the *same* one Katie was singing in her room after I had the nightmare. She said her mom used to sing it to her. I never even heard the song before."

That was an odd coincidence. He'd give her that. There had to be an explanation behind it, though. Maybe Monica had hummed it in her sleep before waking up. There was a chance Katie overheard it.

"I don't want you to think we don't believe you, Mon. It's just so strange. One thing we agree on, though, is that Katie's a nice girl. And that she has been through hell and back the last few months. We're trying to make a difference in her life and help her get her feet back on the ground. If we make her feel like some freak, how do you think that will make her feel?"

Monica closed her eyes and dropped her head back against the seat.

"What about the pool, though? I know you didn't find anything down there, but *something* grabbed me. I didn't make that up. You can see it right on my leg, Daddy."

Dan considered it for a moment. It really didn't make sense to him.

"I know, hon. I don't think you made it up. But again, even though whatever happened to you was strange, Katie wasn't even in the pool. How could she have done anything to you?"

"Yeah . . . I know. I keep feeling like something is following her around, though. Something we can't see. Last night, I heard her talking in her room and thought she was talking to herself. But then I heard another voice talking back to her. I ran back to my bed after that. I know it makes no sense."

"What was she saying? You sure she wasn't watching something on TV?"

He saw the defeat in Monica's eyes and hoped it was because she realized he was right and not that he didn't believe her.

"Yeah, I guess it could have been. I thought I heard something about us, but I don't know. Maybe I'm wrong. I promise I'll try harder."

"Well, I'll make a deal with you. You pick out a few dresses today for yourself. My way of thanking you for being so understanding of all this and knowing how important it is to your mother." Dan smiled.

"Thanks, Dad! Maybe we can get a matching one for Katie, too, to make her feel included?"

It warmed Dan's heart to hear her trying so hard to change her mindset. It couldn't be easy sharing your parents with kids that weren't your real family.

"I think that's a great idea. Good thinking, hon. She'll love it."

***

Faith threw the load of wet laundry into the dryer and started the machine. She wiped away the sweat on her forehead and left the laundry room, deciding she should have a talk with Katie soon. She wasn't sure why, but she found herself trying to keep busy and put it off. After what Barry had told them and what Monica had experienced, Faith was embarrassed to admit she was a bit spooked by it all.

The importance of why they were doing this in the first place came back to her. Faith dedicated her time to fostering kids after what she went through growing up. Moving from home to home herself. She experienced firsthand the damage of having foster parents who only fostered kids for the extra cash it brought them. People who would take the extra hundreds of dollars each month for their own selfish reasons and have the foster kids living off scraps for a fraction of the money they received for the care.

That was only the beginning of it, though. She wished that was the worst of what some kids went through. Verbal, physical, and sometimes sexual abuse. The thought made her sick to her stomach. Faith could fill a bingo card on experiencing each and every one of those nightmares. She vowed to help kids growing up in similar situations as what she grew up with, to make them feel safe and wanted. When the chance to take Katie was proposed to them, Faith begged Dan to agree. She was worried that because Katie qualified as a "crisis care" child—which happened to pay the highest daily rate to someone caring for the kid—it would lead to someone agreeing to foster her for all the wrong reasons. Throw in the history of what Katie went through, and there were bound to be some sickos throwing their name in the hat.

Right now, Katie was sitting in the living room watching the movie *Frozen* again. Faith noticed the smile on her face and decided to hold off just a few minutes longer before confronting her. Instead, she folded some of the clean laundry and brought it into the spare bedroom, which Katie had been sleeping in. She sat the pile of clothes on the bed and grabbed one item at a time, placing it neatly in the proper drawer. Once the last item of clothing was taken care of, Faith grabbed the comforter to tidy up the bed. As she pulled the blanket up, a notebook stuffed between the comforter and sheet fell to the floor.

She picked it up and went to toss it back on the bed, but

curiosity got the better of her. Faith turned to the doorway to make sure Katie wasn't there, then looked at the book. *What are you doing? Invading a little girl's privacy. You should be ashamed of yourself*, she thought. Yet, she couldn't help it. She opened the first page, displaying a drawing of a rainbow and a unicorn, similar to the ones Monica drew. She turned to the next page and was surprised to see writing much nicer than a nine-year-old typically had. Faith decided reading the words was too much of an invasion of privacy and shifted her focus to the right-hand page, seeing another drawing. This second drawing was a far cry from the unicorn. It was an older lady in an old-fashioned dress. Her eyes were colored a dark red. The hands had abnormally long, sharp nails connected to each finger, as if the lady was wearing elongated knives.

"What the hell?" Faith whispered.

The image sent gooseflesh across her skin, and she brought her eyes back to the words on the left-hand page so she could stop looking at the image. Before she could stop herself, she was reading the words, and they made her sick to her stomach.

I need to get rid of them. They are evil. They want to hurt kids. I can't let the Page family know about what I can do. But I think it might be too late for them.

Faith couldn't read anymore, but her eyes remained glued to those few sentences. She read them over and over, trying to figure out what Katie was talking about. Who was evil? She couldn't be referring to Faith and her family, could she? All they had done was go out of their way to help Katie. And too late for what? Dread sank its teeth into her veins as she contemplated all the possible answers. Once again, the story Barry told them came back to her.

"Faith? Why are you looking at my journal?"

Faith gasped and whirled around, coming face to face with Katie.

"Hon . . . I'm so sorry. It fell while I was making your bed and I saw . . . saw what you wrote. I think we need to talk."

CHAPTER 11

DAN PULLED INTO the driveway, surprised to see Faith's car still home. Either the girls hadn't gone out as long as expected, or they never left. As soon as he parked the car, Monica jumped out, grabbed the shopping bags and took off toward the house, excited to share the new clothes with Katie. Dan checked his cellphone to make sure he hadn't missed any calls. No missed calls or text messages.

He got out of the car confused, not sure why he was chalked full of nervous energy. What was the big deal about his wife changing her mind and not leaving? After talking to his daughter about the importance of not judging Katie, he appeared to be doing just that. Still, he walked a bit faster than usual to the front door. When he opened it, he was relieved to see Faith and Katie sitting at the table. That relief quickly drained when he noticed the expression on not only his wife's face, but Monica's.

"What's wrong?"

"Come have a seat, hon. Katie has some things to tell us." Faith held a small notebook in her hands. Dan realized that was where Monica was staring. Not at her mother, but at the notebook in her mother's hands.

Dan hesitantly sat at the table and took a deep breath.

"Okay. I'm all ears. What's going on?"

***

Katie knew she wasn't supposed to talk about her secrets. Her mother's dying wish was for her to never tell anyone about her past. Or her ability. She told Katie that if anyone found out, they would keep Katie locked up and run tests on her. They would treat her differently than other kids and never let her live a normal life. But it felt important to tell the Page family. Their lives were on the line.

BLANK SPACE

When Faith said they needed to talk, Katie refused to comply at first. She sat in silence at the table as tears slid down her face. Faith was so nice about it, though. She made sure Katie felt comfortable, telling her she wasn't in trouble and that she only wanted to help. More than anything, Katie believed Faith.

And so did her dead grandmother, who stood in the corner undetected by everyone except Katie.

"Hon, you don't have to talk if it gets too uncomfortable. Just remember, we are here to help you. And please understand that what's in this notebook is very concerning to me. But we will do whatever we need to do for you, okay?" Faith said.

Katie wiped a tear away and nodded. She looked at her grandmother, who gave a nod and a smile from the corner as her image rippled like the surface of a calm lake.

"I have something my mom called 'sensed presence.' It lets me see ghosts and things that other people don't know are there. But it's more than that, and she didn't tell me until I got a little older. I *can* see ghosts. But I can bring them to our world too. Sometimes I do it by accident because I can't always control when that part of my brain works." Katie paused, waiting for one of them to call her crazy or worse. Instead, they gave her concerned looks, but in a nice way. So, she continued, "When I was in the group home, something really, really bad got out into our world. It wanted the kids. She said she wanted to kill them and take their souls and make them suffer. When I was hiding in the closet, I could hear it ripping them apart. I could hear the screams while it played with them. If Officer Briggs hadn't saved me, it would have got me, too.

"I know that sounds make-believe, and I wish it was, but that thing got out and killed everyone in the house. It was the first time any of the ghosts had hurt someone."

Faith and Dan looked at each other, concerned, but Katie pretended not to see it. Monica sat in her chair, staring at Katie like she was the monster herself.

"Oh, hon. You poor thing. Why didn't you tell the police any of this? Even if it's hard to believe, at least it would have been *something* for them to go on instead of thinking you had something to do with the murders for months," Faith said.

"I *did* have something to do with it. I let it out. And it's still out there somewhere. I don't want her to hurt you guys like she did all the kids. She wants to come here." Katie couldn't hold the tears in

41

anymore and began crying uncontrollably. She looked at her grandmother again, who smiled and mouthed, "It's okay." Faith noticed Katie looking in the corner and turned to see what she was staring at.

"What are you looking at, hon? There's nothing there—" Faith paused mid-sentence as the realization hit her. "Is there a ghost here with us now?"

Katie nodded.

"Is it going to hurt us?" Faith asked.

"No . . . it's my grandmother. I called to her last night when I thought you were in danger. She's the one that told me to tell you guys my secret because she trusts you."

Katie wasn't sure what the Page family believed, but unloading the weight off her shoulders was a huge relief. Even if it did lead to her getting taken away, it'd be worth it if it saved them. She couldn't tell if Faith was just going along with it or actually believed. Dan looked confused by it all.

"Okay. So, this stuff I found in your book . . . Is that a picture of your grandmother?" Faith asked.

Katie shook her head and almost laughed. "No, no. My grammy doesn't look scary like that. That's the lady who killed all the kids. But she can change what she looks like or sounds like. She tried to tell me she was going to kill you all last night."

"Jesus Christ!" Dan yelled. "Monica, why don't you go wait in the living room, so you don't have to hear this stuff?"

It was the first time Katie recalled hearing him raise his voice since she'd been in their home. She understood why, but it was still upsetting.

"Hon, let's stay calm, k?" Faith said to Dan, then turned to her daughter. "Monica, I think your dad is right, though. Some of this is stuff you shouldn't hear."

"I think she should stay," Katie interrupted. "If it wants her, she shouldn't be left alone. That's what happened in the pool; it tried to take her."

Monica's eyes opened wide, the realization of something trying to kill her setting in. "I'm scared, Mom and Dad."

"It's okay. We won't let anything happen to you. You know that," Dan said.

"I thought you said it *wanted* to come here. But you make it sound like it's already here. And if it talked to you last night, why didn't it hurt *you*? Are we in danger right now, Katie?" Faith asked.

"I don't know why it didn't hurt me. I think maybe because I'm the one that brought her here, so if I'm gone, so is she. I don't know if you are in danger yet. It can show itself sometimes, but it loses power fast when it's far away from its home."

"What can we do to protect everyone?" Faith asked.

Katie again looked at her grandmother. At first, she didn't realize what gesture the ghost was giving her. Then it hit her.

"You pray."

CHAPTER 12

FAITH **DIDN T KNOW** what to say. What to believe. Everything Katie told them sounded preposterous, yet it somehow still made sense. After talking with Dan, it was clear he didn't believe any of it. Instead, he thought Katie was crazy and a danger to them all. Whether it was ghosts or a crazy child hell-bent on murdering their family, they decided they needed to take Monica somewhere safe. After Katie was done with her story, the decision was made to drive Monica to her grandparents for the night and keep her away from the house. They rarely asked Dan's parents for childcare help. Faith didn't agree with how much they disrespected the boundaries set with Monica from an early age. Dan's parents also took any chance they could to remind Faith they didn't approve of bringing so many foster kids into their care and robbing their only granddaughter of the important parent/daughter time they believed a child needs.

Katie agreed that getting Monica away from the house could help save her since the ghost's only connection to the world once released from their purgatory was Katie herself. They were at their strongest when they were close to where they crossed over, but without Katie in close proximity, they were even weaker. Dan quickly packed an overnight bag and got Monica in the car. Now that they were gone, Faith wanted to talk to Katie some more.

Faith walked back to the kitchen to find Katie still sitting at the table, staring off toward the wall at nothing. Or at least nothing that *Faith* could see. Even though she told them it was her grandmother in the room, Faith couldn't help getting the creeps as she watched the little girl smiling at the empty space. Whether Katie told the truth or not, the idea of a child seeing and interacting with something that wasn't there was almost worse than if there was, in fact, a ghost moving around their kitchen.

44

Katie asked them not to say anything to anyone else, but Dan insisted that they get in touch with Barry to let him know what was going on. Because Dan didn't think any of it was real, his biggest concern was making sure Katie got the proper help she needed—something he didn't think they were equipped for anymore. Faith didn't feel right telling anyone after Katie begged them, but Dan would have none of it. He planned to call Barry after he dropped Monica off with his parents. He was set on coming up with a resolution before his daughter came home. The sudden change in his approach with Katie was jarring, but Faith couldn't blame him. He had their daughter's safety in mind, first and foremost.

Faith sat next to Katie and smiled.

"Hey, hon. Thank you so much for telling us all that. That took a lot of courage to put that trust in us."

"My grammy really likes you. She says you're good souls. That she knows you want to help me."

The phantom compliment was unsettling, but at least it wasn't some threatening presence similar to what Katie had been dealing with.

"That's true. You know, I grew up in foster homes like you. My parents died in a car accident when I was a kid, and we had no close family besides my uncle, who was a mean man. He didn't want me, so I moved from home to home for most of my childhood. So, I know how tough it can be for a little girl to grow up that way."

"How come your uncle didn't want you?" Katie asked.

Faith considered the question. She hadn't really thought about it in years. She recalled how awful she felt when her uncle Henry told her he didn't have time in his life to parent a child. He even went as far as saying his sister should've been smarter than going to a party with her deadbeat husband. Saying had Dan not consumed any drinks, maybe they wouldn't have crashed and left her an orphan. She liked to think that it was just his way of grieving the loss of his sister and that having her daughter around every day would be a terrible reminder of her loss. But Uncle Henry was much meaner than that.

"I think sometimes, people just aren't meant to have kids, you know? I don't want to hold that against him. He didn't ask for my mom to die and leave me in his care. We never had a relationship before my parents' death, so why would he change that after the fact? But that's why I grew up telling myself I'd never do that to a child. That I'd help any kid in need that I could and provide them stability."

"You're so nice. I'm sorry this is all happening because of me." Katie closed her eyes, fighting off more tears.

"Hon. This *isn't* your fault. Whatever is happening isn't something you asked for. We have helped kids that have anger issues, defiance issues, and even disorders. None of them asked for the cards they were dealt. It's our job as adults to help guide kids through tough times. This is no different. So please, don't blame yourself for any of this."

"Thank you. For everything. I hope it's not too late."

That last sentence tied Faith's stomach into knots. None of what Katie told them seemed remotely realistic. But everything was starting to give her no choice but to believe. She was struck with an idea, something that could possibly lead her to get an answer on how real this all was.

"Katie. I want to believe everything you are telling me. I hope you understand that it's not easy to comprehend. Then again, nothing outside of our normal day-to-day lives is. Is there a way you can prove to me that your gram is here? Have her do something that would show me?"

Katie's eyes lit up, excited by the idea.

"Yes! Maybe I can have her move something."

The idea freaked Faith out, but if this turned out to be true, it meant far bigger issues ahead for their family. It meant that it wasn't just Katie's grandmother in their house.

"That sounds good. If she can hear me, ask her for a sign . . . I'm sorry, I don't know how this works . . . if I'm supposed to talk to her directly . . . or it only works with you."

"Both! You can't hear her, but she can hear you. She said to hold on a second."

Faith's mouth dried with anticipation. Her heart rapped against her chest as she eagerly watched the empty corner of the room for something, unsure what to expect.

The lights flickered for a second, then went completely out.

There was still enough daylight to keep the room lit, but the feeling of being draped in darkness still overcame Faith. Before she could respond, a cupboard door slammed shut, jolting her from her seat.

"Okay, I believe you! She didn't have to scare me like that."

Katie laughed. "She said you need to restock on canned goods. Whatever that means."

Faith smiled, but then realized it was all true. Katie's *entire* story. There was some other ghost, far more sinister, roaming their house.

"Katie, what can we do to get rid of this other ghost, or whatever you call it?"

Katie thought it over before responding.

"My gram says we have to go back to the group home. I need to send it back where it came from." Katie looked uncertain.

"Do you know how to do that?" Faith asked.

"I . . . I think the spirit needs to be reminded of their past. They need to be weakened, or vul—I'm sorry. I can't remember the word my gram said."

"Vulnerable. And how do we do that? We don't even know who or what this thing is . . . Do we?" Faith asked.

"Well, they usually come from wherever they died. My mom said most of them stay close to the place they remember most. So, this monster might have been someone at the foster home before they died."

Faith jumped to her feet and grabbed her iPad from the counter. The group home where Katie lived had a history. Faith recalled hearing about it when they had taken their first kid from the home after they moved to town. She didn't remember exactly what happened, but she needed to find out.

"What are you doing?" Katie asked.

"I'm searching the history of the home. Before the murders, long before you were ever there, something awful happened. Maybe we can find the source of where this thing came from."

The lights popped back on, startling Faith. Until it happened, she'd been so focused on finding info that she forgot they had gone off. Katie stood over her shoulder, watching as she typed away in the Google search bar. Faith wasn't sure what to search for. She typed in "haunted group homes in New Hampshire." Surprisingly, the search results brought up a ton of links. The most recent links were about the massacre Katie was involved with, so Faith quickly scrolled past them, hoping Katie didn't see.

"Apparently, ghosts have nothing better to do than haunt helpless kids," Faith muttered to herself.

She scrolled with her finger on the touch screen until Katie grabbed her hand.

"Stop! That's it! The house looks different, but the lawn and street look the same. I used to do cartwheels right there!" She pointed to the side lawn on the left side of the house.

The picture displayed an old orphanage from the 1920s. The windows on the home were shattered, with antique cop cars parked on the side of the road. Suddenly, the stories she heard when they first moved to the town came back to Faith. She read on, unable to stop herself.

KEENE ORPHANAGE SHUT DOWN AFTER MURDERS SHAKE THE COMMUNITY

Keene, Monday, May 25, 1921—Officers responded to a call on Sunday, May 24th. In a shocking turn of events, the quiet and peaceful neighborhood of Cliffton Heights was rocked by a string of brutal murders that left the community in shock and mourning. The incident came to light late Sunday night when concerned neighbors alerted the authorities about a disturbance at the local orphanage on Bluebird Lane.

Authorities arrived at the scene to find multiple lifeless bodies, mostly of children who lived in the home. The grisly discovery sent shockwaves through the close-knit community. Residents in the surrounding area reported hearing muffled screams and raised voices during the late hours of the night, but few suspected the horrifying truth that awaited them. The police cordoned off the area and began their meticulous investigation, leaving the community in a state of unease and fear.

While detectives combed through the crime scene, they initially revealed little about the motive or potential suspects while they continued their investigation.

BLANK SPACE

As evidence was gathered and witnesses were interviewed, more news came to light.

The matron of the home, Helen Crowe, was not one of the bodies initially found in the home. Locals described her as someone that appeared nice, but insisted she was very stern with the children. Whenever children were in her presence, it was clear they feared the matron.

Upon further investigation, the authorities found Helen hiding in the basement, covered in blood. They described her eyes as feral, with dirt and flesh caked in her nails and scratches lining her face, which they believed were from the children attempting to escape as she murdered them one by one. She refused to go into their custody, jumping on an officer and attempting to rip his throat out before she was shot dead on the scene.

The orphanage will be closed until further notice, and authorities are urging anyone who may have information related to the incident to come forward and assist. The community has rallied together, holding a candlelight vigil in the children's memory, hoping to show their support and solidarity during this harrowing time.

As the community grapples with the grisly murders, local authorities are assuring residents that they will do everything in their power to ensure the safety and security of the area. The memory of the slain children will go on to haunt the town of Keene as we all try to seek answers to what led Helen Crowe to commit such an evil act.

Faith felt sick to her stomach. Even though the murders were a hundred years ago, reading the details made her feel as if she had lived through the horrible events herself. She clicked on related articles, seeing child obituaries, forcing herself to scroll past until a picture of Helen Crowe came up, the image grainy and ancient. Helen stood in a stiff position, her hair in a tight bun. The start of a smile spread across her face, but her eyes told another story. The article talked about Helen's horrible upbringing, how her parents were abusive and would often torture her as a young girl. It was horrible. Faith looked at the picture of Helen again. Even through the scratchy filter, it was obvious where Faith had seen this lady before.

It was the lady from Katie's drawing.

CHAPTER 13

DAN ENDED THE call with Barry, immediately feeling better. Monica was with his parents, safe and sound. Barry was on his way to meet them at the house to come up with a plan for Katie. As much as Dan wanted to help Katie and support what his wife felt so strongly about, he wasn't about to put his own daughter's safety on the line to do that. He'd tried to look past the strange occurrences, past the unsettling stories that Barry and his daughter had told. But the notebook changed everything. Whether it was real or not, didn't matter. It was a lose-lose scenario. Either Katie was crazy and really did have something to do with the murders, or there were fucking vengeful ghosts lurking around the house trying to kill his daughter.

Faith wasn't happy Dan did the one thing Katie asked them *not* to do. Tell someone about her ability. But he was okay with that. He'd deal with her wrath later, after he knew his daughter was going to be okay.

After hearing the story, Barry seemed very eager to get to their house before anything happened. It was as if he believed they were up against time, which bothered Dan even more. Barry told him to worry about his family and get home, and he'd call the authorities to fill them in on Katie's situation. Even though he believed he did what was right, Dan couldn't help but feel some guilt. Regardless of what the truth was, Katie didn't ask for any of this. She didn't ask for her mom to die. Or for the far-from-perfect childcare system that foster kids had to deal with. And she especially didn't ask for the mental or physical condition that she lived with every day.

Dan thought back to watching a movie with everyone, and how he thought he'd seen someone standing in the reflection. It was something he truly had shrugged off after the initial few minutes of it happening. Now, he couldn't deny that the sense of danger overwhelming their home.

He pulled onto their road and sped up. The closer he got to the house, the more urgent the situation felt. Streetlights popped on as the evening sky invaded the neighborhood. When the house came into view, a sense of relief washed over him, as if he anticipated coming home to discover a pile of rubble in place of the house. Everything appeared normal on the surface. That was good. He parked the car in the driveway and killed the engine.

Before he even got to the porch, the front door swung open and Faith stood in the doorway, crying with her arm around Katie.

"What's wrong?" He marched toward them.

"Hon, it's all true. All of it. And we know who's behind the awful things happening to Monica," Faith said.

As they walked into the house, Dan's blood boiled at the thought of someone hurting his daughter. "Who? Who'd do something like this?" He asked the question, expecting a real, live human to be the culprit. When Faith answered, he became even more perplexed.

"Her name's Helen Crowe. In the early 1900s, she ran the orphanage where Katie's group home was located. Apparently, she went crazy and slaughtered a bunch of orphans and was killed by the cops when she refused to comply. The house shut down and remained boarded up and deserted for almost a hundred years before a couple bought it and remodeled it, then reopened it as a group home."

"How do you know this has anything to do with what's going on here?" Dan asked.

"Because I asked Katie to prove the ghosts were real. Her grandmother did and scared the hell out of me in the process. I'm telling you, Dan. We have to believe her."

"It's true, Mr. Page. The monster is going to come for all of you as long as I'm around. It will follow me wherever I go," Katie said quietly.

Dan turned to her for the first time since before he left to drop off Monica. He instantly felt awful for how he'd been treating her. One look into her terrified eyes felt like a slap to the face. How could he be so cold toward her? That's not what they set out to do when helping kids. And yet here he was, with the worst situation they had come across yet with a child, and he was ready to turn his back on her.

BLANK SPACE

Even hearing it from his wife, it was a struggle to believe any of this was possible. He always considered himself open-minded, willing to believe things that people who think in black and white wouldn't. As a child, he often wondered where people went after they died. He didn't grow up religious, so the thought of Heaven and Hell never felt like the only possible answer. He often wondered what existed elsewhere, if there was life beyond what they could see. So, now that he was faced with actual proof that there *was* something beyond life, why the hell was he finding himself wanting to doubt it so much?

"We won't let anything happen to you, Katie. I'm sorry I was so mean about it all before. It's just—"

A car door shut in the driveway, and Katie ran to the window, seeing Barry walking toward the house.

"Why is he here? Did you tell him?" She sounded panicked.

CHAPTER 14

AFTER BEING CAUGHT up in all the commotion, Dan had forgotten all about calling Barry to come to the house. Once again, he was hit with a feeling of letting Katie down. Any trust they'd built with her was likely now lost for good.

"I'm sorry, Katie. I called him when I was upset, not sure what to do. It's okay, though. He wants to help us. Do you trust him?" Dan asked.

She shook her head slowly, biting her lip.

"He cares as much as we do, sweetie. He told us how much he wanted to help you after everything that happened. It's okay," Faith said.

Still, Katie hesitated. A knock at the door led to tears falling from her letdown eyes. It was at that moment that Dan realized he'd made a huge mistake.

Faith opened the door and let Barry in. He thanked her and approached the table where they all sat. He was acting strange, but Dan hoped it was because Barry realized the horrifying story, he previously told them proved to be more than just his imagination playing tricks on him. Barry wasn't taking his eyes off Katie as he sat across the table from her.

"Hi, Katie. Dan tells me you told them quite the story. Can you tell me everything so I can try to help?"

She narrowed her eyes and scrunched her nose. "No . . . I shouldn't have said anything."

Barry glared at her, and Dan could've sworn he looked angry. *Why would he be mad at the poor girl?*

"Listen. If you want to make sure you get the help you need, I need to know *everything*. How do you do it?"

"Do what?" Katie asked.

"You know what I'm talking about, Katie. How do you bring them into our world? It's a miracle," Barry said.

What the hell? What is with this guy? Dan thought.

"Hey. That's not our biggest concern right now. We need to make sure she's safe before anything else is done. She's not up for answering your questions right now," Dan said, starting to get a bit agitated.

Barry's knee bounced up and down rapidly, a telltale sign of someone anticipating something. His whole personality had flipped completely since their lunch.

"I know that, Dan. The point is, if we know how she can bring them in, it can help us get them *out*. I knew I felt something in my office when you were there, Katie. Was there a ghost present then too?"

Katie ignored the question.

"So, how'd you do it?"

"For fuck's sake, Barry. Leave the poor girl alone, will ya?" Dan asked. He regretted cursing in front of the child, but his anger got the best of him.

Before Barry could respond, the lights flickered out again, only this time it sent the house into darkness as evening settled in. There was enough natural light to still see everyone, but with far less clarity.

"Can you tell your gram to turn the lights back on, please?" Faith asked.

"It's not her," Katie whispered.

As she said it, Dan spotted movement skittering past the opening of the kitchen into another area of the house. He stood from his chair, watching the open space.

"This is incredible," Barry whispered to himself. Dan couldn't tell if he was scared or excited.

"We need to get out of the house. Now. Is this the mean spirit you drew, Katie?" Faith asked.

"Yes . . . But she shouldn't be this strong here." The little girl's voice trembled as she talked.

Dan put his arm around Faith, preparing to pull her toward the front door. Katie screamed from behind them. Dan's first thought was that whatever this ghost was, it had come for Katie. But when he turned around, it was *Barry* who held Katie. His hand was firmly gripped around her wrist, and even in the dark room, Dan could tell it hurt.

"What are you doing? We need to go, Barry," Dan snapped.

"We aren't going anywhere until I know how this works. You don't understand. The whole reason I went through all the shit I did, was so I could find Katie. So, *we* could find her. I couldn't be sure until I saw it with my own eyes, which I'd say this freak show is enough proof. My boss will be a very happy person tonight. Now, Katie. I'll ask again. How do you do it? There's no use in fighting it anymore. You're coming with me tonight no matter what happens here."

"What is it exactly that you do? You went through all the steps to get this job, spent years working it, just to find Katie? How did you even know about her?" Faith asked.

"Of course, I didn't work there for years. My company fudged the paperwork to make people think that. After the massacre at the old orphanage home, they sent me out to this shitty town to keep an eye on the girl, to see if she might be the one we were looking for. I don't exactly have the time to get into who I work for or what we do, Faith. Just know that people like this need to be watched. They need to be controlled. Think about what we could do with her ability. About the possibilities. Picture creating a vaccine that allowed us to tap into this world and to communicate with the dead. All the cold cases that could be solved by communicating with murder victims. All the treasures we could find by talking with dead explorers," Barry said, his eyes lighting up.

"She can't help this, Barry. She's not some fucking guinea pig. Let her go," Dan said.

"Sorry, pal, I won't be doing that. If you want to go, be my guests—"

Behind Barry, something came forward from the darkness. Before he could finish his sentence, the figure swooped in, wrapping its hands around his head. Its disgusting nails were more of an extension of the fingers than actual fingernails, long and sharp with a needle-like tip. Barry screamed as the hands tightened around his skull like a vise, the tips of the nails piercing into the sides of his head.

"It's her!" Katie yelled as she ran to Dan and Faith.

The figure stepped forward, still holding Barry, forcing his body to move with her. Dan had never heard a pain as distinguishable as what forced its way from Barry's chest. He was unable to talk, the iron grip of the ghost's hands not only squeezing his head but forcing his mouth shut, only allowing agonizing groans to escape. Barry reached out toward them; his eyes wide as they peered between the thing's bony fingers.

As the figure stepped in front of the kitchen window, Dan finally saw the features of the woman's face.

The whites of her eyes were tinted yellow, like two rotten eggs. But that wasn't the worst part. Her irises were completely red, as if the eyes had gone bloodshot and all the blood pooled in the center. Her skin was a grayish white, sagging in areas that used to hold the bones firmly in place.

She snarled, then squeezed tighter. Barry kicked frantically, swatting at her deformed hands, to no avail. The veins in her neck bulged, then began to swim around beneath the skin with a life of their own. She squeezed tighter. Dan wanted to help, but Faith and Katie clung to his side as they all watched in horror. His mind told him they needed to leave. Get out of the house while she was distracted and get far, far away. But he couldn't take his eyes off her. Helen's dress was ripped and torn, its normally white color covered in a mix of dirt and blood. Her hair was pulled up in a tight bun, stretching the skin of her forehead so taut that it was nearly translucent, with dark blue veins that branched beneath the skin, none of which matched the sagging skin beneath her eyes.

Helen opened her mouth, exposing a set of decaying teeth. At first, Dan thought she was going to bite into Barry, but instead, she inhaled deeply, then screamed toward them in an ear-piercing octave.

"Heewp meeee," Barry managed to get out just as Helen Crowe forcefully twisted his head, the bones popping in his neck oddly reminding Dan of when he cracked his knuckles and drove Faith nuts.

Helen continued to twist Barry's head until it turned completely around to face them again, then she yanked. Skin stretched, ripping apart at the center of where Barry's Adam's apple used to reside, revealing the inside of his throat. The skin continued to rip, a sound similar to denim tearing apart, until his head came completely free. His limp body dropped to the floor beneath the ghost, landing in a puddle of his own bodily fluids. The legs twitched a few times, then went still. Helen removed one hand from Barry's head, her nails drenched in crimson, then pointed toward Katie.

"It's time to get your punishment, little girl."

Dan snapped out of his trance at the sound of her voice.

"We need to go. Now! Get to the car," he yelled.

They took off in a sprint toward the kitchen door, heading into the living room. The door slammed shut in Dan's face. Dust particles floated from the cracked door frame as he fought with the doorknob, but it wouldn't budge. Something whizzed by Dan and smacked off the door, falling to the floor. He looked down at his feet to see Barry's shocked eyes staring up at him. He instinctively kicked the decapitated head to the side, feeling sick to his stomach as he heard it roll across the floor.

"Open it, Dan!" Faith shouted.

"I'm fucking trying. It won't move!"

Katie screamed again, "She's getting closer!"

Dan turned and couldn't help but think the ghost was toying with them. Helen stepped over Barry's lifeless body, getting closer with each step. A raspy echo rattled against the inside of her chest, sounding like a diseased cat purring.

Dan kicked the door, aiming for the doorknob. A vibration reverberated through his leg, but he shook it off and kicked again. The wood continued to splinter apart, but not fast enough if they planned to escape.

"Dan!" Faith warned.

He turned just in time to see Helen Crowe grab Faith by the throat and lift her off the floor. He momentarily forgot about the door, scanning the area for anything that could help him. What the hell could help fight against some supernatural entity who'd crossed over into the real world? Faith kicked at Helen, far too similar to what Barry had just done before having his head torn off. Dan couldn't let it get to that point.

Katie looked to the far side of the room. "Grandma, help!"

Dan still couldn't see Katie's grandmother, but Katie clearly could as her eyes traveled in the direction that he assumed the second ghost approached from. Helen shrieked, her red eyes bulging. She threw Faith across the kitchen table, then turned to see what was interrupting her.

Faith's head smacked off the corner of the table on her way to the floor. Dan ran to her side and helped her up, noticing blood trickling from her temple. She blinked, her eyes temporarily in a daze.

"Are you okay?" he asked.

"I think so . . . We need to go."

Dan grabbed Katie by the arm and pulled her toward the door, but she couldn't stop watching her grandmother fighting off Helen. To Dan, it looked like Helen was swatting away at a swarm of invisible wasps.

"GO!" an unknown voice bellowed.

"Grandma, no!" Katie screamed.

While Katie continued to resist, she did so with less intensity. Dan pulled her toward the door, taking one last glance back toward Helen. She pried apart an open space in front of her as Katie continued to scream for her grandmother. Dan could only imagine what Helen was tearing at. He pictured her clawed hands pulling the jaw apart. Could ghosts hurt each other? Was that a thing?

With one final kick, the door flew open. Their escape was now within their grasp. Helen continued to shriek in the background as they opened the front door. They made it to the front porch; his beat-up Honda Accord was the most glorious sight Dan had ever set eyes on. Faith helped Katie into the back seat, then hopped into the passenger seat. Dan backed the car out of the driveway, then punched the gas. The tires squealed as they distanced themselves from their home, leaving the nightmare behind.

CHAPTER 15

FAITH DIDN'T TAKE her eyes off the passenger side mirror until Dan pulled into the parking lot of a gas station on the other end of town. She wasn't sure what she expected to see; it wasn't as if an evil ghost would float behind them, tailgating their car until they pulled over.

"Katie. You need to really listen to me, okay? We know you can't control these things, at least not fully. But you said you called your grandmother somehow, and she came. You must know a way to get rid of them as well," Dan said.

"I don't know. My mom told me I have to think the same way I do to open the door they come through, only the opposite. I've tried it and I never made it work."

"And you said the way to do it is by going back to where they came from?" Faith asked.

"Yes. But if we go back there, she'll be even stronger. I've never seen them this strong away from their home. She's different from the rest."

"Please tell me that Monica's safe out of town," Dan said.

There was a long pause, far too long for Faith's liking. Then Katie hesitantly nodded.

"She should be. But I really don't know. I'm sorry I'm not more help." Katie began to cry, aggressively wiping away the tears like it was acid leaking down her face.

"It's okay, hon. You're a nine-year-old kid. It's not fair to you for us to expect that you know all the answers. We're just trying to figure it out together. If you think there's any chance of our daughter being in danger, we need to know," Faith said.

She didn't like that she was interrogating a child who'd been through so much. Katie had already seen the dead bodies of multiple children, lived her life without parents, and then watched as a man who she thought was trying to protect her turned his back on her and attempted to take her like some lab rat before having his head pulled off.

"Right now, she wants us. If we can stop her, everyone will be safe," Katie said. She sounded far too intelligent for a child her age.

"Okay. So, we need to come up with a plan. We can't just show up at the orphanage and ask her to go back home. Do you know of anything that can hurt them? Fire? Gun? A damn vacuum to suck her up?" Dan asked.

Katie cracked a smile, and the moment made Faith love Dan even more. He could always make kids laugh, even in the worst of times. The smile ended when some sudden realization hit Katie and her eyes opened wide.

"My mom said something about making them face what they did wrong. But I don't know what that means. Maybe being in the old home will do that."

"How did your mom know all this?" Dan asked.

"I'm not the only one in my family with this ability. My mom had it, and so did my grandmother. It's why I'm able to communicate so easily with my gram and why nobody else can see her. She could show herself if she wanted to, but because we are connected with our power, she can make herself only seen by me. Before my mom died, when she was sick, she taught me everything she could. She wanted to make sure I knew how it worked since there would be nobody else to teach me."

"So why don't you communicate with your mom? Why just your gram?" Dan asked, immediately regretting his question when he saw Katie's reaction.

"I . . . I don't know. I've tried to bring my mom back before, but it never works. The last time I tried was in the group home and the mean lady came instead. I'm afraid to try again. And every time I bring one over to our world, I'm afraid people like Barry are going to find me and take me away. I wish I never had this inside me."

"Hey, it's okay. I'm sorry to keep asking all these questions, kiddo," Dan said, then stopped to think for a minute. "If you had to do it one more time, bring back some ghosts, if it could help us, would you?"

Katie sighed. "Yeah. I just don't know if I can make it work. If she's coming after us, I won't be able to concentrate. Those are the times where I mess up the most."

"Are we really doing this? Going to the old orphanage?" Faith asked.

Dan looked out his window at the night sky. The house was just out of town, about a ten-minute drive. The LED lights shined down from the canopy fixtures above the gas pumps, forcing Dan to squint. As he took a moment to gather his thoughts, Faith wondered what was going through his head.

"What is it? That's your 'I have an idea' face."

"Yeah, but we will need to come up with a distraction, so Katie has the time she needs. Let's send her back to Hell."

***

Katie sat in the back seat, feeling the nerves kick in the closer they got to the house. She never thought in a million years that she'd step foot back in the place where it all happened. Her life had been a living nightmare ever since. Images of all the dead children snapped back through her mind like a demented screensaver. Even with the passing trees on each side camouflaged in darkness, she recognized key landmarks that warned her they were getting closer. Her heart pounded. Her hands refused to stop shaking with each passing mile.

They rode in silence, forcing her to live in her thoughts for the time being. Her mother had not wanted her to tell anyone about her secrets. This was the first time she did, and it almost got her killed. Katie never trusted Barry. From the moment he flashed his unsettling smile, something felt off about him. But she assumed she'd just been paranoid after being raised to think everyone was out to get her.

And now she had to put her full trust in the Page family. Dan asked if she could bring ghosts back if needed, something that, just moments before, she had no desire to ever do again. Yet, she agreed to do it if it would help. What she didn't tell Dan and Faith was that when that door opens—when she calls to the spirits—anything could come out with them. Her mom told her that if she had time to train the powers, she could control that. But Katie was never lucky enough to get that help. She'd spent a good part of her life trying to figure it out on her own.

Up ahead, the outline of the orphanage came into view. Katie's chest tightened as if the presence of the home was pressing down on her. Dan slowed the car and parked it on the street, the same spot those antique police cars had parked in the old photo. Yellow police tape still surrounded the home, although it had ripped in some places, causing the loose ends to flap in the evening breeze. The large windows were boarded up, giving the creepy home an even more uninviting vibe.

Dan killed the engine, and they all sat quietly for a moment before he spoke.

"Whatever happens in here, please know that none of this is your fault, Katie. I know we keep saying that, but it's so important that you don't live with any burden on your shoulders that you can't control."

Katie nodded, but found herself too choked up to speak.

"So . . . what's the plan?" Faith asked.

"Follow me," Dan said.

Dan got out of the car and opened the trunk, grabbing the flashlight, and looked for anything else that could defend them. The closest thing he found to a weapon was a hammer he'd left in the back from when he helped his dad build a shed a few summers back. He shut the trunk and looked up at the home sitting on top of a small hill. The moon had risen above the roof, hanging over the orphanage. This brought another bout of tears from Katie. It reminded her of the lullaby her mom used to sing. "Der Mond ist aufgegangen." *The moon has risen.* She absorbed the happy memory, hoping it wouldn't be the last one she ever had.

CHAPTER 16

IN A PERFECT WORLD, they wouldn't have been doing this after dark. Nightfall only added to the terror that awaited them within. Who the hell were they kidding? In a perfect world, they wouldn't be doing this, *period*. Faith watched her husband attempting to pry back a sheet of plywood blocking one of the windows. She held the flashlight up so he could see what he was doing.

The house was in a sad state, even with only a few months passing since the massacre. Punk kids had apparently thought it was cool to deface the home, spray painting phrases like "Orphan House Massacre" and "Where's the Orphan House Killer?" To them, it was a game. A new story to add to the long list of town lore. But to Faith, the horrors of the orphanage were real. To *her*, it was a group of kids being helplessly murdered by a sadistic matron. It didn't matter that it was a hundred years ago. And now the same thing had happened to a new generation, by the same evil monster, Helen Crowe.

"I almost . . . got it," Dan said as the wood snapped in his hands and created a small opening.

He grabbed the hammer and struck the center of the plywood. The hole expanded as the condensed particles from the board fell to the ground. He struck it again with the claw of the hammer, knocking off a larger piece. The hole was now big enough to climb through.

"Okay, ready?" he asked, his words coming out between exerted breaths.

Katie nodded, but Faith stopped before approaching the opening.

"Why has she left us alone since our house? This feels too easy."

"I don't know. I think she's weak right now. After what she did

64

to Barry . . . and my gram, I think that took away a lot of her strength. Especially because she was away from here when she did it. But I don't know if that's right or not. It's just a guess," Katie said.

Dan shrugged. "Makes sense. Still, we have to be extra alert. Let's stick together in here."

"Before we go in, what's your plan? We can't go in here blind, Dan," Faith said.

"Katie. You mentioned that one of the ways to get rid of them is to bring their past back to them, right? We know what she did, not just to you and your friends, but to the orphanage all those years ago. Think about how many people she's killed. What are the odds that there are a whole hell of a lot of ghosts who'd love to get their hands on her for what she did? When I saw what she did to your grandmother—which I'm sorry you had to see—I realized they could hurt one another. Do you think you could call more than one if needed? Like a whole damn army of them?"

Faith didn't like any of it. It was too much to ask of a little girl. Too much pressure to put on her. She shook her head. "No. We can't ask her—"

"I can do it," Katie interrupted.

"Hon . . . are you sure?" Faith asked.

"Yes. I can do it. When you showed me what happened here before will help me picture it. I just need enough time to do it."

"Okay, so it's settled. I'll go first," Dan said.

He climbed through the opening, and it was as if the house swallowed him whole. Faith sensed a bout of panic overtaking her at the thought of her husband being gone forever. She fought through it and climbed in after him. She grabbed Katie's hand and helped her climb through. The house was dark due to the power being shut off. With all the windows boarded up, it completely eliminated any hint of light from the outside world.

Faith handed Dan the flashlight. He aimed it left to right, displaying the layout in front of them. The home looked like a scene out of an apocalypse movie after a group had ransacked it for any remaining goods. They were standing in what appeared to be the living room, although it was hard to tell with everything strewn about. A trail of dried blood traveled across the floor and around the corner into another room. Faith had always heard that a crime scene gets left as is outside of eliminating any health hazards. It was clear that someone had done a half-ass job of scrubbing away the blood, but the stains remained. Still, seeing it with her own eyes shook her to her core. She turned to Katie, realizing how traumatizing it must be for her to see this scene again after what she went through.

"You okay, hon?"

Katie bit down on her lower lip and nodded. *Such a strong girl,* Faith thought.

"Let's look around. She's bound to show her ugly face at some point, right?" Dan asked himself. He began to follow the trail of blood when Faith's cell phone rang in her pocket. They all jumped.

"Shit! That scared the hell out of me," Dan said.

Faith pulled her phone out and looked to see who it was. The screen illuminated the area around her face, displaying the confusion in her eyes as she read the name.

"It's your mom. Why would . . . " Her heart jumped in her throat. *Monica.* She quickly answered the call. "Hello? Is that you Monica?"

She put the call on speaker so Dan could hear as well. It was sobs coming from the other end, *Monica's* sobs.

"Mom . . . Help me. She got Grammy and Grandpa."

Dan rushed over to Faith. "Monica! Where are you? We'll come get you right now."

Before their plan had even started, it was falling apart. This was their worst-case scenario. Something they went out of their way to prevent.

"She took me to the orphanage. I'm here . . . " Monica whispered.

"Hon, are you with her now?" Faith asked.

"No, I'm hiding upstairs. Come get me . . . *Please!*"

Faith's eyes began to blur as the tears came. Their poor daughter, who never wanted this life in the first place, was in danger all because of them taking in a kid they knew could be a risk. They walked toward the stairs, the flashlight beam their only source of light.

"Stay on the line, baby. We are coming to you," Faith whispered.

"Okay."

A noise from the next room stopped them in their tracks. What sounded like bare feet slapping across the floor in the darkness, just out of sight. For a second, Faith forgot she had her daughter on the line, her whole focus locked on the open doorway heading into the next room. A figure walked by the opening, forcing Faith to suppress a scream.

"What is it, Mommy? Did she find you?"

Monica's voice. It sounded distorted. And Monica hadn't called her Mommy for at least a few years. Faith glanced at her phone screen as if that would somehow give answers.

"Hon, you're breaking up. Don't hang up," she whispered.

"I won't hang up, Mommy. The only thing hanging will be you . . . hanging by your neck on the stairwell." The voice got deeper, sounding more like a middle-aged man than a young girl.

Faith dropped the phone, suddenly feeling like she was holding a poisonous snake about to sink its fangs into her. Dan bent over to pick it up, briefly aiming the flashlight toward the floor to locate the phone that had turned face down. As he did, the space behind him returned to darkness. That's when Faith saw a tall figure standing in the far corner, watching them. Everything was camouflaged by the night except a set of red eyes. *Helen.*

"Dan!" Faith yelled.

He looked up, spotting the figure.

"Daddy? What's wrong?" Monica said on the phone. "Daddy? Come *FIND ME!*" The voice changed, turning from their lovely daughter to something not human. The voice began to laugh, a deep, unsettling level that a little girl had no right to reach. The phone call ended abruptly, but the laughter did not. It continued, now coming from the figure in the shadows. With Dan staring at Helen, Faith grabbed the phone from his hand and went to recent calls, prepared to call her daughter back. But there *were* no recent calls to Dan's parents. Somehow, Helen had found a way to play mind games with them.

"Monica never called. It was a trick, Dan," Faith whispered.

"Did you think you could come to my house and outsmart me? I had unfinished business here. And now you stand in the way of that," Helen growled.

She stepped forward into the room, still mostly hidden from the lack of light, but some of those horrifying features became visible again. She approached, one rigid step at a time, all while burrowing into them with her crimson eyes. They were trapped, standing at the base of the stairs, with Helen blocking any other way out of the room.

"We need to go upstairs to buy Katie some time. Let's go!" Dan said, pulling on Faith to snap her from her trance.

She couldn't take her eyes off Helen. Earlier, she'd been in shock the first time they saw her. Now it was fully hitting her that this was all real. That this savage killer had been dormant in the abandoned orphanage for nearly a hundred years and was back doing it all over again.

They climbed the stairs, running down the hallway with the beam of light swinging wildly in Dan's hand.

"In there, it was my room," Katie whispered, pointing to a room on their left.

Dan didn't question it, entering the dark space. Faith quietly closed the door behind them and locked it, whatever good that would do. Dan scanned the room, the light picking up the remnants of the massacre. Katie froze in place, taking it all in for the first time since she was rescued.

"Hon. Try to focus. I know it's hard, but we don't have much time. Can you do this?" Faith asked.

Katie wiped away a tear and nodded.

Unsettling noises continued to break the silence throughout the house. Every creak of a floorboard, every scratch against the wall. It was impossible to tell where Helen was or what she was doing. Katie walked to her old bed, now covered in dried blood spatter. She threw the comforter to the floor and sat on the bed. Faith looked at Dan, who shrugged, unsure of what Katie was doing.

"I need it quiet, so I can concentrate. I'm going to try to bring them back now."

CHAPTER 17

KATIE CLOSED HER EYES. The hardest part was getting the imaginary doorway open. She needed to drown out all the other sounds, which was nearly impossible with Helen walking through the house. At any moment, she could burst through the door.

Stop it. Concentrate, she told herself.

She imagined the photos from Faith's iPad of the old orphanage and the kids they saw obituaries for, and those of her group home brothers and sisters, including her best friend, Becky Finch. She reminded herself of what they went through and why they would want to come to this world to help defeat Helen. *Spirits, we need your help. We need your strength so that you can go in peace. She's back, and she's doing it again. Helen Crowe killed my friends. Please, spirits. Help us.*

"Please. Come, spirits."

She opened her eyes, listening for any sign of the children.

Laughter. She heard laughter somewhere within the house. Footsteps running through the halls. *It's working!* Katie again closed her eyes, envisioning the opening that her mind had created, forcing it wider. Whenever she completed this step, she had no idea where the actual portal was located, but her mind pictured a giant hole opening for them to come through from wherever they resided. She needed to close that opening before something else came with the children.

THUMP!

Something slammed against the wall from the hallway. Again.

The distraction pulled Katie from her focus. The noise continued, traveling down the wall approaching the door.

"It's her," Dan whispered.

Footsteps that sounded like someone walking with

cinderblocks on the bottom of their feet moved down the hall and stopped just outside the room.

Dan held his hand up, telling them to remain silent. He set the flashlight on the bed, aiming the light away from the door. Katie hoped it wasn't already too late. The odds Helen knew they were in here already were pretty high, but if they could do anything to buy extra time, they needed to. She closed her eyes again, but her attention remained on Helen, unable to shake the feeling of her standing outside the door.

Focus!

Everything returned to silence. The kids running and laughing abruptly ended.

And then something slammed off the door. Katie screamed. Dan and Faith stood by her side, ready to protect her, but uncertain how to do it.

The next strike against the door splintered it down the middle. Helen's extended nails appeared through the small opening. They hooked into the wood, gripping the inside of the door, and tore upward. The door split as Helen ripped through with brute strength.

Dan pulled the hammer from his belt loop, prepared to strike. Helen's red eyes appeared in the opening, staring at them. Her decaying lip lifted in an angry snarl as she gave one final rip, splitting the door completely. Dan charged at her with the hammer raised, but with minimal lighting, he didn't see the corner of the bed frame. His knee drove into the sharp corner of the metal frame. His leg buckled. He caught himself from falling, but he'd lost most of the force he intended for the strike.

Katie wanted to help, but knew this was her chance to close the realm. She forced herself to focus.

***

Pain pulsed through Dan's kneecap. There was a chance he'd chipped the bone, but he couldn't worry about that right now. He ran at Helen, lifting the hammer as he went. He heard Faith, who, while standing a few feet away, might as well have been miles in the background, shouting for him to stop. He heard children laughing deeper in the house. But his main focus was on Helen. The monster who'd killed countless kids. Who tried to kill his own daughter.

Helen stood in place, watching him charge. He wondered why

she wasn't reacting. When he felt close enough, he swung the hammer, striking her left hand that still gripped the door. The claws of the hammer punctured into the meaty part of her palm, the grayish skin splitting apart. No blood escaped the wound, but the hammer was stuck.

She didn't even flinch.

Instead, Helen shot her right hand through the opening, grabbing Dan by the throat. She squeezed. A jolt of pain burst through his neck as her nails pierced into his skin, forcing their way into the muscles and tendons. He knew she could crush his throat with ease if she wanted to, but she enjoyed making people suffer. The only hope going through his mind was that she would drag this out long enough for Katie to do what needed to be done. *Why aren't the kids helping yet?* They were running through the fucking house like it was playtime.

"Helen Crowe! We know who you are and what you've done. We know you murdered the children of this house—twice," Faith said.

Helen kept her hand locked on Dan's throat, but took her attention off him to glare at Faith. The red of her eyes narrowed, and her mouth opened wide, again revealing the discolored teeth that belonged to a corpse. She screamed, deep from within her chest, the breath of rot suffocating Dan's already strained airways. Faith was distracting her. He needed to get the hammer back, to strike again in hopes it would at least break him free. He reached for it, but it was too far from his grasp.

"Your parents abused you as a child. They created your twisted ways of disciplining kids. But that's no excuse. You're pure evil. You need to go back to Hell, where you belong. You died on May 24th, 1921. A cop shot and killed you. You aren't real!" Faith yelled.

Dan felt the grip tighten around his neck; breathing was getting more difficult by the second. But Helen was not paying attention to him. With all the force he could muster, Dan pushed his body weight toward the door, the sharp nails sliding deeper into his neck as he did. He grabbed the hammer, still sticking out of her hand, and jerked it free. Helen's eyes went wide, and she snapped her attention back to Dan, squeezing tighter, if that was even possible. Before she could act, Dan swung the hammer again, this time connecting with her face. The metal claws met the cheekbone with a wet smack.

Her grip loosened, and Dan fell to the floor. Blood started to pump from the wounds in his neck, which he instinctively reached for to stop the bleeding. He crawled backwards into the room to get away from Helen, who was staggering back into the hall with the hammer still lodged just above her top teeth. Dan assumed it didn't really hurt her, but it caught her off guard. Still, he'd avoided death for the moment.

"Dan!" Faith ran to his side, seeing the blood leaking down his neck onto his shirt. His collar was already stained red and only getting worse.

He began to feel lightheaded, the loss of blood draining any energy he had left after fighting for his life.

Katie screamed. Dan looked to the door to see Helen now in the room, slowly walking toward them. She reached up and tore the hammer free, the metal hooks bringing a chunk of dead flesh with it, exposing her rotted gums and teeth on the side of her face. It created a permanent smile on the left side of her mouth. She threw the hammer to the floor and marched forward.

Dan tried to slide backwards on the floor, but he was struggling to push his own weight. Faith stood in front of him, and he wanted to yell for her to get away, to save herself and Katie and leave him. But his voice was cemented in his throat.

The beam of light blasted from the flashlight toward the door as Katie lifted it. Behind Helen, Dan saw a group of small figures approaching the door from the hallway. Kids of different ages and sizes. Some of them wore old-fashioned clothes that were tattered and worn, while others had on modern-looking outfits. There had to be at least ten of them, their eyes all completely white and glossed over.

The children whispered as they entered, the words not clear, but just the tingling sound of their soft voices all talking in unison made the hair on the back of Dan's neck stand up. Helen violently shook her head like a dog trying to rid itself of ear mites. Their whispering chorus clearly bothered her. Faith still stood her ground in front of Dan. The light shined through her toward the hall, almost as if the beam was highlighting her as the star of the show.

Helen raised her hand to strike, but two of the children jumped on her back, their mouths stretching open wide—far wider than they had any right to. Dan thought he'd seen the worst things he could ever see tonight until both of the kids clamped down on her neck with razor-sharp teeth. Helen squealed, turning to face the kids still marching in.

"GET OUT!" she yelled.

The children didn't listen. They continued to surround her until there was no room left to move. Two more kids crouched low, grabbing hold of her ankles, and like their fellow orphans, they gnawed into her skin, this time ripping at the Achilles tendon. A boy with his brown hair falling out of his head in multiple spots and caved-in bruises spread across his scalp like craters on the moon, came forward. But instead of looking at Helen, he turned to Katie, his white eyes locking onto her.

"Thank you."

And then he clung to Helen's chest, clawing at her face with a ferociousness Dan had never seen. Helen fell to her knees, trying to pry the kids off her. The rest of the orphans piled on, swarming like a colony of ants, discovering a free meal left on the side of the road. They bit, clawed, hit. The sound was sickening, and the sight was even worse, yet Dan couldn't take his eyes off it.

Faith turned and kneeled next to Dan, checking the wounds on his neck. He'd lost a lot of blood, and his skin was turning a pasty white. She held his hand tight.

Helen continued to get torn to pieces, screaming in agony as the kids got their revenge. The pile of orphans completely blocked out her body, but the sounds were brutal.

"Katie, can you send them back now? Is that possible?" Faith asked.

Katie, who'd been silent, watching everything unfold, looked as if she'd just come out of a bad dream. She nodded without saying a word, too transfixed by the horror in front of them.

***

The truth was, Katie had no idea if she could close the door to the other world. The idea of it sounded a lot easier than actually doing it. She brought herself back to her mother, teaching her everything. But she was *so* young. Most kids struggled to remember what they ate for dinner the previous night, and yet she was expected to remember all the rules to control her ability.

She closed her eyes, left only to the sounds of Helen's dead flesh being pulled from the bone. She tried to block it out, to concentrate on the door closing and sending them all back to where they belonged. For the first time in her life, it was so clear what needed to be done. She heard the sounds of the kids disappearing one by one, their spirits going to their final resting place. When the room went silent, she opened her eyes.

The only thing remaining in front of her was unidentifiable. Helen's hair remained in a tight bun, but the face below it was gone. In its place was a featureless canvas covered in black sludge. Her decayed teeth were cracked and falling out. As hideous as the image was, Katie couldn't help but smile. She'd done it. Sent them all back and got rid of the monster who had killed all her friends. And best of all, she'd saved the Page family.

She ran to them, hugging Faith tight. Dan looked very sick, and she knew they would need to take him to a doctor. Hopefully, the injuries could be treated, and he would be okay. As she squeezed Faith tight, burying her face in her foster mom's stomach, she let out tears of joy. It was the first time she felt like a real family since her mom died.

Faith tensed up, and the first thought Katie had was that Helen wasn't gone for good, that maybe she was getting to her feet to come for them. She pulled back from the hug and turned to see what Faith was scared of. Helen's body still lay motionless on the floor. The flashlight aimed toward the far wall, where another tall figure stood, silently watching them. Katie couldn't believe what she was seeing.

"Mom?"

The word coming out of her mouth felt foreign.

"Hi, sweetie. I've missed you."

Katie ran to her, wrapping her arms around her mother. How did this happen? Everything hit her at once, and she began to cry so hard she was shaking in her mom's grip.

"Mommy. I've tried to call you so many times. It never worked. And the last time I tried . . . *she* came. All those people died because of me."

"No, *no*. Don't blame yourself for that. We didn't ask for this ability. But you figured it out, baby. You called me. I heard you, and I came as fast as I could. And you saved all these wonderful people that have looked out for you."

"Please don't leave me again. I need you."

Her mom pulled away and knelt to be at eye level.

"I know it feels that way. And believe me, I miss you too. But we both know I can't stay, honey. But I promise I will *always* be looking after you. People like this give me hope that there's still good in the world." She looked at Faith and Dan. "Thank you. Thank you for protecting my daughter and keeping her safe."

Faith was now crying as hard as Katie, but she smiled through the tears. "Of course. She's a wonderful young woman. We will make sure she's safe from those people. Her secret is safe with us."

Dan winced, attempting to sit up. "She saved my life. You raised quite the little girl."

"Thank you."

Katie hugged her mom again, knowing this could be the last time she ever did. Her mother kissed her on the top of the head, just like she always did when Katie was little. She whispered, "I love you," and walked to Helen Crowe's deformed carcass. She wrapped her arms around the limp body and lifted it up; the mangled head drooped back, staring up at the ceiling.

"Katie . . . You know what you have to do now," her mom said.

A final tear slid down Katie's cheek, but she knew her mom was right. She had to close the door. "Death's door," as her gram used to call it.

"I love you, Mommy."

"I love you too, baby."

Katie closed her eyes, fighting back more tears as she let her mind work. As sad as she was to see her mother go after working so hard to try to see her the last few years, it was also the closure she needed. For the first time doing this, she smiled.

When she opened her eyes, her mother was gone. Helen Crowe was gone.

CHAPTER 18

AFTER HER DAD was rushed to the hospital, Monica's grandparents drove her to see her parents. She'd been so worried the entire time she was with her nana and pop-pop, but she understood why they did it. Her grandparents sat in silence in the waiting room, and she took the opportunity to tell them she was going in to be with her parents. She entered her dad's room and, seeing him hooked up to a bunch of machines with bandages around his neck, really hit home with her. While she wasn't sure what they went through, she imagined he'd fought for his life.

She ran to his side and hugged him, noticing his pained grunt as she rested her head on his chest.

"Hi, Money. You treat your grandparents okay?" he asked.

"Yeah. They gave me an extra scoop of ice cream after dinner. I told them you would be mad, but they did it anyway," she giggled.

"Yeah, yeah. We'll let it slip this time."

"Is it over? Are we safe now?" Monica asked.

"Yes, hon. Katie saved us all," Faith said.

Monica saw Katie sitting in the corner, wiping her eyes. She looked like she'd been crying all night. Monica couldn't picture what she went through to get rid of the evil spirit. She wasn't so sure she'd ever know, nor did she want to. All that mattered was her family was safe. They all sat together for a while until a nurse came in and said a police officer was there to see them. Monica knew her family didn't do anything wrong, but the fact that so much had happened to them over the last few days still made her nervous.

A lady police officer walked into the room and smiled. She looked nice. Katie's eyes lit up at the sight of her and she jumped up to give the cop a hug.

"Hey, little lady. How've you been?"

BLANK SPACE

"Natasha!"

"You two know each other?" Dan asked.

"She's the one that saved me from the group home!" Katie said.

"Officer Briggs. Nice to meet you. I'm just here to ask some questions, but I couldn't pass up coming to see this rock star here," she looked back to Katie. "It's only been a few months. How have you grown so fast?"

"I'm almost ten, you know."

They all laughed. Natasha asked Dan and Faith questions about what happened. There would be a lot more questioning over the coming days, but for that night, they could be a family. Including Katie. After everything they'd been through together in just a few days, Monica didn't want her to go anywhere. She wanted Katie to stay with them. She wanted her to start over with a blank space.

VOLUME 2: EYEBITER'S REVENGE

JAY BOWER

CHAPTER 1

PETE AND HIS four closest friends stood on the concrete steps leading into the old abandoned elementary school, its exterior made of faded brown bricks. A sodium glow from the nearby streetlight cast them in soft shadows. Despite the late summer heat, they were all dressed in long sleeve black shirts with black pants, except Avery, who insisted that her hot pink hairband would not detract from their attempt to remain hidden.

Pete swallowed hard and stared at the entrance to the school. The metal door with glass windows was boarded up with weathered plywood and secured by three locks. It screamed "don't come in," but that was exactly what he had planned.

"You guys ready?" Pete asked.

Their senior year started in two weeks. Pete had taken all summer to build up the courage to break into the school. His friends Avery and Tom were anxious to reveal the ghosts roaming the halls, but Doug and Ray couldn't care less, mostly going along because they had nothing better to do.

"Can we just get on with it?" Ray said. He was the tallest of the group and the oldest, barely missing the cutoff to be in the grade ahead of them when they were in grade school, a fact he reminded them of often. His scraggly beard, that extended an inch from his face, was hidden in shadows and gave him a darker, sinister look.

"You don't have to be a jerk about it," Avery said. "We just got here. Are your panties too tight?"

Tom and Doug chuckled. Avery may have looked like the epitome of the American Girl with her blonde hair and green eyes, but she didn't take shit from anyone. It was one reason Pete became friends with her soon after she arrived in Brownsville with her mother. He laughed to himself at her response to Ray.

"I'm bored," Ray replied. "We're wasting our time. There's no such thing as spirits and ghosts and shit. There's probably some fucking psycho in there ready to gut us."

Avery smiled and stepped closer to Ray. Pete caught a hint of her sweet perfume. Even when breaking into an abandoned school, Avery had to make sure she was presentable.

"Afraid someone might touch you in your funny place?" she asked.

"If you're offering, I'm down with it," he replied.

She huffed and turned away, shifting the strap of the backpack on her shoulder.

All five of them carried a similar pack stuffed with essentials: black candles, lighters, a flashlight, and clothesline.

It was his intent to conjure the spirits within the school and communicate with them. The rumor around town was that the children who died in the shooting were still trapped within the walls of the school. Some claimed the adults were there too, which meant his father might still be there.

None of the five of them brought any fancy cameras to record the session, just the phones in their pockets, not that they were planning to record anything. They weren't trying to make money from the experience, just communicate with those souls trapped inside. And for Pete, it was his last chance to reach out to his father. If the school wasn't scheduled for demo in a few weeks, he doubted he'd have the nerve to break into the place. Haunted houses and ghosts scared the hell out of him.

"Damn, I gotta piss already," Doug said, pushing his glasses back up his nose.

"Fine, we'll get inside so you can break out your dick in the most haunted place in town," Pete replied, eliciting a murmur of laughter from all but Doug.

"Hurry the fuck up," Doug replied.

"Tom," Pete said.

Tom edged closer and pulled a black pry bar from his backpack. He handed it to Pete.

"Thanks, man."

Pete forced it under the bottom padlock and, with two quick yanks, pulled the lock off the weathered board.

"Easy as that," Pete replied. He swallowed hard. There was still time to turn back. He pushed that idea out of his mind. *Dad*, he thought. *This might be the last chance.*

Doug shifted from one foot to the other. Avery stood with her hands on her hips. Ray and Tom occasionally glanced behind them to make sure no one was watching. It wasn't likely as the school was set back from the main road. Two entrances cut through the trees that surrounded it, out of sight unless you wanted to go back there. Weeds and an unruly underbrush had encroached on the place giving it a more sinister, desolate look. To Pete, it was as if the town had discarded the memory of the tragedy, which meant discarding his father.

With a strained effort, Pete pried open the second lock, letting it fall to the cement steps. When he tried the last one, the lock held firm. The screws holding the latch in place resisted his attempt to snap them. After a couple of tugs, Tom stepped up and grabbed the pry bar with him.

"Ready?" Tom asked. A bead of sweat raced down his cheek.

"Dude, hurry the fuck up," Doug said. "I can feel my bladder ready to burst."

"Why don't you go pee in the grass?" Avery asked. "It's not like there's anyone here."

Doug looked out toward the overgrown weeds that extended from the school to the entrance and cocked his head as though considering it. Pete looked back at the door.

"I'm ready," Pete said to Tom. The two of them pulled, white knuckling it. A moment later, they ripped the screws from the wood with a loud cracking sound. The pry bar flew from their hands and nearly hit Avery in the head.

"What the . . . " she said, jumping out the way and bumping into Ray. The pry bar clattered on the sidewalk behind them.

"Sorry about that," Tom said. "Pete, let go of it."

"Screw you," Pete said with a smile.

Ray retrieved the bar and handed it to Avery. "You can hit both of them. I won't tell." She looked at it, then shook her head.

"Nah, not yet. But if they do something like that again, I might." She stuffed the pry bar into her backpack and zipped it shut.

"Open the fucking door," Doug said. He clutched his pants as though pinching a garden hose.

"Ladies and gentlemen. And Ray," Pete said. "I present to you Artemus Ward Elementary School. The most haunted place in Jackson County." With that, he swallowed hard and pulled the creaky door open, stepping inside. The others quickly followed.

CHAPTER 2

ONCE THEY WERE all inside the school, they stood in a tiled hallway covered in dust and debris. Cobwebs clung to the ceiling. Doug pushed past them with his flashlight in hand. The light bounced from one side of the hall to the other, illuminating posters and bulletin boards with hand cut letters and crudely drawn pictures that had curled in the heat over the years. Dust kicked up from the floor, a trail left behind him like footprints on the moon. Halfway down the hall, the beam from his flashlight pointed to his right, and he slipped into the darkness.

"This place is freaky as hell," Ray said. "Stinks, too."

Pete nodded, thinking the same thing. It looked as though the school could've been in use had it not been for the thick layers of dust covering everything. The place had been closed for over fifteen years, and it didn't seem like anyone bothered to clear out the contents. It kinda made sense. Crime scenes were often left untouched.

"How many died here?" Avery asked.

"Twenty-three," Tom replied.

"Including my dad," Pete whispered. Except for Avery, because she only moved to Brownsville four years ago, they all knew someone who died in the shooting. Friends, cousins, people from church. It was devastating.

Pete was there when it happened, but was too young to remember anything. He was in pre-k at the far end of the school. The memories of the tragedy eluded him, blocked by grief and his body's natural response to the shooting. However, he'd seen news stories about the Artemus Ward Shooting to have a sense of the tragedy. Everyone in town knew about it. When a kid shoots up a school in a town of just 8,000 people, it strikes home to everyone.

Pete shined the beam of his flashlight on the walls. A poster admonishing students to "Just Say No" was partially torn. He turned toward the opposite wall and gasped. The others followed the beam.

"Damn," Avery said.

There were three holes in the sea foam green cinder blocks. Bullet holes.

"He just walked in the front door, right?" Ray asked.

Pete nodded slowly. "Yeah, man, there was no security or anything." They stared at the evidence of the violent day in silence, the weight of the moment settling in.

After a minute or so, Avery broke the silence. "Where the fuck is Doug? How long does it take to pee?"

Her words broke the tension, and they left the entrance and headed down the hall toward where Doug left them.

Four light beams bounced within the hall like a wild Hollywood premier. Flashes of broken floor tiles and more bullet holes skipped across Pete's vision. Torn papers and toppled furniture lay strew across the hall beyond the bathroom door where Doug entered.

"Doug, come on, man. Let's get going," Tom said. There was no reply from the bathroom. A light inside indicated he was there, but he didn't say anything.

"Are you playing with yourself?" Avery asked.

"Why, would you like that?" Ray replied.

"Eww, gross. Especially not with you."

Pete and Tom laughed, Ray's face turning bright red.

"Maybe he's taking a shit?" Tom asked. "I need absolute silence for that. The little gopher likes to hide when it's noisy."

"Gopher?" Ray asked.

"Yeah, you know when it pops out and—"

"Dude, we don't need to know," Pete said. "Maybe he's having problems in there. I'll go check."

Pete entered the bathroom and turned to his left, where it opened up to three tall urinals with three stalls next to them. Two sinks lined the opposite wall, rust streaks extending from the faucets to the drains. In the furthest stall is where Doug's flashlight beamed brightly.

"Doug, are you ok man? Do you, like, need toilet paper or something? I might have some tissue in my backpack." Doug didn't reply. Pete stepped closer, following the footprints left in the dust. He crossed the gray-tiled floor and headed straight for the stall.

"Doug, what's going on in there? You aren't jacking off, are you?" He was hoping to elicit laughter, or at least a comment. It was eerily silent, not even the sound of piss hitting the water or grunts from a strained effort.

When Pete reached the stall door, he felt the hairs on his neck bristle. A cold chill ran across his skin. With the blood rushing in his ears, he pushed open the door.

Doug wasn't there. His backpack lay across the toilet seat and his flashlight was propped against the metal handle behind it. "What the fuck?" he muttered.

"Hey, guys, he's not here!" Pete yelled out. Soon, the others scrambled into the bathroom and stood behind him.

"Look," he said, moving to the side to show the odd tableau.

"Where the hell is he?" Avery asked. "There's only one way in here and none of us saw him leave."

"We would've seen his footprints in the dust, too," Ray said. "Did anyone see a set of prints coming *out* of the bathroom?" They all shook their heads.

"Something's wrong," Pete said.

"It's the most haunted place in Jackson County, right?" Ray asked. "Maybe a ghost got him." He snickered. Of all of them, Ray was the one most skeptical about the existence of anything paranormal. Pete was pretty sure that the only reason he agreed to come along was the prospect of getting into Avery's pants.

"Eyebiter got him," Tom said.

"We haven't even summoned her," Pete replied.

"Doesn't matter. She's here and we're disturbing her peace. I don't like this at all," Tom said.

"She's not real. It's all made up bullshit," Ray said.

"What about Doug? We gotta find him," Avery said.

"I agree," Pete said. He stared at the flashlight, following the beam to the ceiling, hoping for some sort of clue as to where he disappeared to. Nothing looked out of place. It was as if he had just vanished, but that was impossible. Eyebiter was an even more improbable scenario.

The legend of Eyebiter, a supernatural entity that roamed the streets of Brownsville, was something every child grew up with. Well before the school was shot up, the children of the town were raised to fear this creepy ass woman that fed on kids. It was claimed she had a special affinity for eating their eyes, though Pete never knew a single kid in town that was missing an eye. After the tragedy at the school, the rumors grew to include her taking up residence in the school. Which, of course, was impossible because she would've been at least two hundred years old.

Avery pulled out her phone and pressed a button.

"What are you doing? We don't need the cops here," Pete said. A streak of panic raced up his spine. A moment later, he felt something vibrate in Doug's backpack. He opened it and realized what Avery was doing. It was Doug's phone.

"I really hoped he had it on him. This is messed up," Avery said, ending the call. Pete stared at Doug's phone and wondered his friend had gone. There weren't any missed calls on the screen other than Avery's.

"Oh, gross," Pete said. "Look, there are maggots in here." He opened the backpack wider to show everyone else. Ray let out a soft whistle. Avery feigned vomiting.

"Unless anyone needs to piss, let's get the fuck out of here," Pete said. He stuffed Doug's phone and flashlight into the backpack, then gently nudged Tom and Ray until they all got the hint to leave.

Back out in the hall, Pete ran a hand through his thick brown hair. Cut short on the sides, the volume on top added at least an extra inch to his height, making him appear almost six feet tall.

"If he didn't come this way," Avery said, "then he had to have gone further down the hall." She headed to their right, with Ray right behind her. Tom and Pete followed.

The next door down from the bathroom was wide open. They peeked inside and Pete realized it was an office. A metal desk faced them from the back wall. A toppled lamp and scattered papers lay on top, all covered in thick layers of dust. Right behind the desk on the cinderblock wall was another bullet hole, but this one was surrounded by a large faded brown stain. Pete swallowed. It wasn't brown. It was blood.

"Fuck," he said. "Who was the kid again?"

"Jimmy Lendway," Avery said. "He mentioned Eyebiter, too."

"Shit, he did, didn't he?" Pete replied.

"It was in the journal they found after the shooting," Tom said. "Didn't it say something like 'Eyebiter' made him do it?"

"That's what my mom told me," Avery said. "She studied the case quite a bit after we moved here." Avery's mom was a history professor at the nearby university and had her own supernatural experiences. Pete wasn't surprised that she'd researched local lore as well.

"That's all made up," Ray said. "The kid was fucking crazy, that's all. The Eyebiter story was fake. Someone mentioned it online, and it became part of the stupid lore of a make-believe ghost."

"Why are you so quick to dismiss it?" Avery asked.

Ray extended his hand toward the desk. "A gun and a crazy kid. He was fucked up in the head. He was bullied and didn't have a mommy or daddy to wipe his ass when he needed it."

Pete cleared his throat, trying not to lash out at him.

"Sorry man, I didn't mean anything by it. I know you lost your dad here, and that was awful," Ray said. "But the kid wasn't influenced by anything other than a warped mind and easy access to guns."

"Whatever his real motive was, he ruined a lot of lives," Avery said. She adjusted her pink hair tie, making sure a curl of hair extended perfectly down the side of her face. Pete had been her friend since she moved here, always wanting to make a move but too afraid of rejection. He opted to be "the friend" in hopes that one day she might see him like he saw her. In the dim light given off by their flashlights, she looked beautiful. He turned away and glanced back at the bullet hole.

"He caused a lot of damage," Pete added.

Avery stepped close to him and slipped an arm around him. "Are you sure you want to stay here? We can leave the school. I know this has to be hard for you."

Her calm sincerity caught him off guard. He was so used to her smart-ass comments that he was tongue tied at first. He finally broke through his stupor.

"We can't leave. We have to find Doug."

Avery gave him a gentle squeeze. "Of course," she said, then let go.

"Let's keep going down the hall," Tom said, then led them out of the office.

The musty odor they encountered when they entered the school now carried a hint of something else, something rotten.

"Do you guys smell that?" he asked. "It's like boiled eggs or something."

"I doubt anyone has eaten in here for years," Ray said.

"I know that. It's just . . . different, I guess," Pete said.

"I bet Eyebiter has eaten something," Avery said.

"Not that shit again," Ray said. "It's not real!"

"Then why did you come with us?" Avery asked, her eyes narrowing and her lips tight.

"I just . . . I wanted to . . . you guys are my friends. I didn't want to be left home alone tonight. Besides, it would be my last chance to check out this place." Ray shuffled his feet and avoided looking at Avery. She relaxed her anger and shook her head, as if in disbelief at Ray's words.

"When is demo? It's next week, right?" Pete asked.

"It's supposed to be," Avery said. "But I haven't seen any equipment brought in for it. Maybe they got delayed."

"I don't care what's been planned. We gotta find Doug and get the hell out of here. This was a mistake," Pete said.

"Agreed," Tom added. "I thought we'd get a great story to tell, but this place is creepy as fuck. We shouldn't have come here."

"Doug?" Pete called out. His voice echoed in the hall. "Doug, are you here?"

Ray nudged him. "Dude, not so fucking loud. We'll get caught. I can't have another strike on my record."

"I don't want to get caught in here either, but our friend is missing. We get him and we can go," Pete said.

Avery seemed to agree as she ignored Ray's plea and started calling out for Doug. Tom joined them. Ray grumbled, but then added his voice to the cause.

After several minutes of them calling out for Doug, Avery held out her hand for them to be silent. They listened for his reply, but all Pete could hear was his blood rushing in his ears. The prolonged silence rattled him and the hairs on his arms stood on end, brushing against the inside of his long-sleeved t-shirt.

"We're gonna need to try something else," Pete said. "What if we split up to cover more of the school?"

"I'm not going through here alone," Tom said when they all looked at him. "It's got bad vibes, man."

"We can go in teams of two," Ray said. "I'll go with Avery—"

She cut him off with a laugh. "The fuck you will. I'll go with Pete. You and Tom can go together." The disappointed look on Ray's face was not hard to miss, and Pete forced himself to hold back his laughter.

"Yeah, ok then," Ray said in a low voice.

"Does everyone's phone have service? How much power do you have left?" Pete asked. They all pulled out their phones.

"Yeah, and I'm at ninety-eight percent," Tom said.

"Shit," Ray said. "It works, but I'm down to twelve percent."

Avery shook her head like a disappointed mom. "Maybe charge your shit before you go out. Mine works and I'm at seventy-nine percent."

"I'm good and I'm at eighty-three percent," Pete added. "If you find anything, and I mean anything, call the other group."

"Maybe not Ray, since his phone will probably die out here," Avery said. A smirk crossed her face.

"Fuck, whatever. Let's find Doug and get the fuck out of here," Ray said.

"We'll go to the second floor. You two take this one," Tom added. He nudged Ray's arm and the two of them headed down the hall in search of the stairs, their flashlights bobbing as they walked.

CHAPTER 3

"**H**e really likes you," Pete said to Avery as their friends left.

"I know. But I've never thought of him that way. He's just not my type." She winked, and they crossed the hall to inspect the room.

"Woah," Pete said when his flashlight illuminated a two-foot-tall clown doll that was leaning against a small wooden chair. He took a few deep breaths to calm himself. The clown's once white face was now covered in a grimy patina and the paint on its red lips melted and dripped as though it had a mouth filled with blood. It wore a dark blue outfit with white polka dots that had yellowed over time. It was seated at a small wooden table with three other chairs, one of them toppled over. Stacks of wooden blocks and notecards littered the table.

"Clowns are freaky as fuck," Avery said. She entered the room, giving a wide berth to the creepy clown.

The two of them shined their lights around the room. "Doug? Dude, are you here?" Pete asked. Across the top of the black chalkboard were a series of posters depicting the alphabet and each letter was accompanied by images like animals and objects that started with the same letter. Below the letter 'J,' the chalkboard was damaged. Pete gave it a closer look and realized it was a bullet hole.

"Damn, how many shots did Jimmy get off?" Pete asked.

Avery stopped and looked up as though trying to find the answer. "Hmm, I think it was like fifty or something like that. It was a lot."

Pete shook his head and flashed his light around the room once more. The tiny desks were jumbled up in a heap in the back corner. Papers and books lay strewn about the floor. If Doug was in there, they would've noticed him.

"Next room," Pete said, careful to stay clear of the clown. He had a feeling that if he were close enough, the damn thing might jump out at him. He knew it was impossible, but he'd seen enough movies and read enough books to make him think twice about it.

Someone shouted and the two of them froze. Pete turned to Avery and her eyes widened. As they listened, they heard it again. It was a muffled "Doug" coming from upstairs. Pete let out a breath he'd been holding in, and Avery's eyes relaxed.

"Shit, that scared me," Pete said.

"Same."

The two peered into the next room. It was a small storage room with an old Ricoh copier, yellowed and covered in dust.

"Why do you think they never tore this place down?" Pete asked. "I know they wanted to preserve the scene for evidence, but that was so long ago. Why leave it up? Why leave it like this?"

"My mom told me once that the mayor and city council wanted to but that some of the parents protested, calling this place sacred or some shit," Avery said.

"Sacred?" He turned from the copier room, clearly empty of people. "I never thought that. I hated that they left it. It's just a constant reminder of what I'll never have."

Avery grabbed his hand and held it close to her chest. "I'm sorry Pete. I know this is hard for you."

Pete's heart raced in his chest. He'd made it to his senior year as a virgin. His hand had never been that close to a girl's boob before and of all girls . . . Avery? A flood of conflicting thoughts raced through his head. They were shattered when they heard another scream, but this one wasn't like what they heard moments ago. Someone was clearly in pain.

"Doug?" Pete called out, taking his hand back from Avery. "Doug, dude, are you ok?"

"Where's it coming from?" Avery asked.

Pete cocked his head so he could hear it better. "Upstairs, I think."

Another horrific scream and the two of them darted toward the stairs at the end of the hall. They climbed upwards, Pete taking two stairs at a time, until they exited out onto the second floor. It wasn't hard to see where their friends had gone, their footprints easily visible in the thick dust covering the floor though it looked like they went in different directions. A light shone inside a classroom to their right, where the tracks had gone.

"That way," Avery said, following the path on the floor.

A loud, blood-curdling wail came from inside the classroom. When Pete entered the room, he yelled out, and stopped in his tracks, Avery running into him.

"What the fuck?" he said.

Ray was the one yelling, but it wasn't him that worried Pete, it was Tom. Or what was left of him.

Leaning against the metal desk facing the entrance to the classroom was a headless torso. Blood gushed from the neck and oozed down his black shirt. It pooled around his body. One arm hung loose from the body. The only thing holding it in place was a thin strip of flesh.

"Oh my God! What the fuck?" Pete said.

Ray pointed at the body. "His head! Holy shit, where is his head? It's Tom. Fuck. What? Tom?"

Avery screamed when she saw the body. When she did, her flashlight fell to the floor, and the light illuminated something to their left.

"Oh fuck," Pete said. He shined his light on it too. It was Tom's head, his mouth frozen in a surprised expression, but even more sickening than the tendrils that extended outwards from the neck portion like a bloody octopus were his eyes, or lack of. Empty, bloody sockets leaked crimson.

"His eyes!" Avery said. Ray glanced toward Tom's head and when he saw the eyeless face, he bent over to puke. Vomit splashed on the tile floor.

"What happened up here? I thought you two were together?" Pete asked.

Ray answered by puking again, whatever was in his stomach lurching out.

"Eyebiter," Avery said. "It's true. She really exists. She's here."

Ray stood up, wiping his mouth but avoiding looking at Tom, either part of him. "No fucking way is that true."

"Then who did this? Was it you?" Pete asked. A flush of heat cascaded across his cheeks. Could his friend have done this? He didn't want to think it was true, but what else could it be?

Ray took a step closer to him. Pete smelled the rancid vomit on his breath.

"Are you accusing me of something, Pete? Come on out and say it then. You think I did this, don't you?"

Pete took a moment to compose himself. It was difficult to turn his thoughts away from the mangled corpse of his friend next to them, but this needed to be addressed.

"I think you know more than you're saying."

"Fucking idiot. All of you guys are my friends. How could you even assume I had something to do with this?"

"Doug," Avery said, breaking into the conversation. "What about Doug?"

"We hadn't found him. I don't think he was ever up here. Tom mentioned something about the dust not being disturbed when we came up here. Unless there's another way up, I don't see how," Ray said.

"No. What I meant was . . . could this have been Doug? Do you think he did this to Tom?" Avery asked.

She and Pete turned toward Tom's head. Ray refused to look in that direction.

"Shit, what if he did?" Pete asked. "I mean, I never would've pegged him to do something like this, but I guess it's possible."

"That or Eyebiter," Avery said.

"Or Eyebiter," Pete echoed. A chill ran down his spine. They came here to investigate the legend of Eyebiter, even bringing candles to do a seance to reach out to the malevolent spirit or witch or whatever the fuck the legend was. Could it be their friend they needed to fear instead?

"Fuck, fuck, fuck, fuck," Ray said. "What are we gonna do? We've lost one friend and now . . . now Tom."

"We need to call the police," Pete said. "We'll catch shit for being in here, but it's better than dying." He tried hard not to think of Tom's last moments and what it was that attacked him, but the freshly mutilated body was hard to ignore. "Let's get out of the room to begin with. I'm starting to feel sick."

The three shuffled into the hallway. A queasiness settled on Pete and a chill ran through him. A vomit and blood scented odor stuck in his nostrils and no matter how much he wiped it with his sleeve, it wouldn't go away.

He pulled out his phone to call the police, dialing 911. Nothing happened. Then he noticed the tiny text at the top of his phone that stated NO SERVICE. "What the hell? I don't have service. What about you two?"

Ray pulled his phone out. "Mine's dead."

Like Tom, Pete thought. *And maybe Doug, unless Doug is the one—*

"No service for me, either," Avery said.

A knot of worry grew in Pete's gut. This was bad. Something was seriously fucked up about this, and they were all in trouble.

"Then let's get out of here," Ray said.

"But what about Doug?" Avery asked. "He could be trapped in here, too."

"Or he could be the one that killed Tom," Ray countered. "I don't want to be the one to find out."

Avery gave Pete a sad look, her large eyes pleading with him.

"Sorry Avery, Ray's right. The three of us have to leave and let the police handle this. I want to find Doug too, but there's too much at stake here. We don't know if we can trust him."

"But he's our friend," she countered.

"I know." He tried to grab her hand like she did with him, but she pulled away.

"I'm gonna look. Screw it. If he's the killer, I'll take my chances. We always got along pretty good."

Avery brushed past them and headed into the dark hallway, calling out Doug's name. Pete exhaled loudly.

"Man, I'm gonna regret this," he said to Ray, "But I'm gonna stick with her. Come on, we can all stay together."

"It's a dumb fucking idea," Ray said.

"I know, but it's Avery. I'd hate myself if something happened to her."

Ray rolled his eyes and grunted. "Ugh, fuck. Ok, let's go."

CHAPTER 4

PETE AND RAY hurried after Avery, following the beam of her flashlight. Pete didn't want to spend any more time in the school. It was a mistake to think they could contact the spirits of the children or even Eyebiter herself. The mistake cost the life of one friend, maybe another. Losing Avery wasn't going to happen if he could help it.

"Avery, wait up," Pete said.

She stopped and glanced over her shoulder, adjusting her pink headband. "You guys didn't leave me. How noble of you. I'm not a stupid damsel in distress. I can handle myself."

"We need to stick together, no matter what. No more splitting up. The three of us will finish checking the school and get the hell out of here. I don't like being around all this death," Pete said.

Even without Tom's mangled body and eyeless head staring at them, Pete wasn't sure coming here was a great idea. To be clear, it was his idea, but once they stepped inside, he'd regretted it.

He'd never been inside the school after they closed it. He never stepped through the halls of where the terrible tragedy and scene of his father's death occurred. Standing inside the boarded-up school doors brought a dreadful sensation unlike anything he had experienced before. The only reason he didn't turn around to leave was that he was the one who got them all together to begin with. How much shit would they have given him had he backed out of something he organized?

Slowly walking through the second floor of the abandoned school, he regretted not listening to his inner fear. If he had, Doug wouldn't be missing, and Tom would still be alive.

"Did Jimmy ever make it to the second floor?" Ray asked.

"Jimmy?" Pete asked, but then knew it was a stupid question.

The gunman. The sick fuck that killed all those kids, along with his dad and four other teachers.

"From what I've read, he didn't get past the first floor because there were plenty of targets," Avery said. "Sorry Pete."

He waved her off. He knew she didn't mean anything by it.

"Why do you ask?" Avery said.

"No reason. The thought just came to me. I wasn't sure about it, that's all."

They poked into a classroom on their left. Unlike the others, it seemed barely touched by time. If it weren't for the layer of dust on everything, Pete thought it would appear like it was still in use. Nothing was toppled over. There were no stray papers lying everywhere. The math questions the teacher was using were still written on the chalkboard, the yellow color barely contrasting with the board.

"It's like a time capsule or something," Pete said. "It's weird. It feels like they just got up, walked out, and never returned. Look," he said, pointing to one of the tiny desks. A lightweight red jacket was draped over the back of the chair, the owner no doubt thinking they were coming back for it someday. They were unaware they'd never return to retrieve it.

"It freaks me out," Avery said. "It's crazy how quickly things change. Like, one minute these kids were bored out of their minds learning about math or vocabulary or whatever and the next, their friends were dead."

"Like Tom," Ray said. "That's fucked up shit."

"That's why we need to find Doug. It's too late for Tom, but we might still have a chance to save Doug," Avery said.

"Assuming he's not the one that did it," Ray added.

"And that," Avery said. "I really don't think it was him. But then again, I have no idea what happened to him. How does someone vanish when they go to the bathroom? We were all there and there was only one way in or out."

"The ceiling tiles weren't touched, either," Pete said. "It's just weird as hell."

They moved on from the pristine classroom and headed across the hall to another. Inside, it was much the same, but a little more chaotic with the trashcan tipped over and one of the desks on its side.

"This place gives me bad vibes," Ray said.

"Same here," Avery added. "The sooner we find Doug, the sooner we can get the hell out of here."

"Hey, the lunchroom is up ahead," Pete said with a touch of giddiness to his voice. The other two stared at him as though he had two heads.

"Sorry, I've never been there, and lunchtime was always my favorite in grade school."

They headed toward the entrance. When they did, Ray entered first. He turned back to the others and froze.

Pete heard something shuffle behind them and spun. Pointing his flashlight down the hall from where they came, a small cloud of dust hung in the air as though someone had crossed from the left to right, heading into the room opposite of where Tom's body lay.

"What the hell was that?" Pete asked.

"I saw something," Ray said. His flashlight quivered in his hand and the erratic beam of light bounced all around the hallway.

"What was it?" Avery asked.

Pete shuddered. His heart hammered his ribs. All he could think of was Eyebiter, whatever the hell that was.

"I have no idea. But it was someone. I think," Ray said.

"Doug?" Pete shouted. "Doug, dude, is that you?"

"Doug!" Avery and Ray shouted in unison. Then all three of them called him, trying to coax him into joining them.

A moment passed, and they went silent. The dust cloud settled and nothing else stirred.

"Fuck this," Ray said. He then pushed past them and scrambled down the hall, headed for the room where the strange figure entered.

"Ray, no!" Pete shouted. He and Avery froze. Every bit of courage within Pete dissipated as they waited for Ray.

"We should do something," Avery said.

It took all of Pete's will to force his foot to move forward. The second followed. He and Avery slowly crept down the hallway. Ray's light bounced within the room, pointing outward, and then went still, until it finally went out.

CHAPTER 5

PETE WORRIED THAT something was wrong. There was too much silence. The air felt dead, as though the violent act from fifteen years before had melded with whatever calamity they were now dealing with and sucked the energy from around them. He didn't want to lose another friend, another life. This building housed far too many deaths already.

Next to him, Avery's breathing broke the silence. She smelled of sweet perfume with a hint of anxiety. Her cheerful pink headband did nothing to lighten the mood. She swallowed hard and turned her large eyes toward him. He fumbled in the darkness until he found her sweaty hand, then held it tight in his, giving it a gentle squeeze. As afraid as he was, he wanted to assure her that it would be alright, even if he didn't fully believe it.

"Ray? Hey man, are you ok?" Pete called out.

"Ray!" Avery added.

Pete wondered what it must have been like to face the gunman, to know that you faced certain death. The kid was only a few years younger than he was now. What possessed him to murder a bunch of innocent kids? Though the reports didn't explicitly state it, he always thought of his dad as a hero in the situation. Jimmy shot his way through the school until he came to Pete's dad and three other teachers. They were found dead as though they'd created a human wall across the hall, blocking the gunman from advancing any further. Was his father as afraid as he was now? He tried to muster the same courage he always imagined in his dad.

"Ray, come on, let us know you're not hurt," Pete called out.

Pete and Avery were within a few feet of the door when the stark silence within the room was cut by loud, piercing cries.

"Ray!" Pete yelled. He moved quickly to the door but was forced to stop before entering when Avery pulled him back.

"Oh God, do you hear that?" she asked.

Ray's horrific cries went quiet. A sickening sound assaulted them. Flesh ripped, wet and meaty. Bones snapped like branches. Ray cried out again.

And then everything went oddly silent.

Pete froze in place, with Avery at his side. Both were breathing heavily. He felt Avery's heartbeat through her hand. Panic raced through Pete. He'd wanted to be brave like he imagined his dad was, but he lacked the conviction. The fleshy sounds replayed in his head, and he closed his eyes to try to force them out.

"Come on. We can't stay out here. We have to look," Avery whispered.

They moved closer to the door. Pete shook. If someone hurt Ray, that person was still in the room. There was only one way in or out and no one had left. They inched closer, Avery pressing closer to him, her body radiating heat. At another time and in another place, Pete would've enjoyed the touch. But now it was a reminder that they were in a terrible situation.

Side by side, the two of them turned to look into the darkened classroom. Pete shined his flashlight within. A massive streak of blood crossed the floor from the doorway toward the inner darkness. He swallowed hard, fighting back the tears that threatened to fall from his eyes. His breathing grew shallow and quick. He then raised his flashlight and gasped as the cone of light settled on their friend.

"Holy fuck," Pete said. Avery squeaked, words seeming to fail her.

Ray hung from the ceiling, the clothesline from his bag wrapped around both wrists, suspending him from the ceiling in a Christ-like pose from the metal crossbeams of the drop-down ceiling. His head drooped forward, blood spilling out onto the floor.

"Oh my God!" Avery said. She covered her mouth with her hand.

"Is he . . . is he alive?" Pete asked. He raced to his friend, trying to hoist him off the floor to relieve the pressure of the ropes digging into his flesh. "Avery, help me," he grunted. Ray was barely taller than himself but was far skinnier. Still, Pete struggled to lift him. She joined him and they elevated Ray, the clothesline going slack.

"Guys," Ray mumbled, his voice so unexpected that Pete and

Avery both jumped back, letting him fall. He groaned as his arms were pulled taut once more.

"It hurts," Ray said. "I was wrong." His voice was soft and muffled. Ray barely lifted his head, and Avery let out an ear-splitting scream. Both of Ray's eyes were missing, leaving bloody pockets that dripped down his cheeks. Life was rapidly fading from him. The way he spoke and the weakness in his voice told Pete they didn't have much time if they weren't too late already.

"Oh, shit!" Pete said. His stomach twisted and fear bloomed within.

"Who did this?" Avery asked.

"It's true," Ray said. He coughed and spat up blood. He struggled against his bindings, but with his feet unable to reach the floor, he had no leverage. Pete stared in disbelief.

Then he remembered the knife in his backpack. He swung it around and dropped to one knee in one smooth motion.

"Don't worry, man. I'll get you down." Pete's hands shook, and he struggled with the zipper. "Come on, damnit," he grumbled. He finally unzipped the bag and thrust his hand inside. Then he jumped up with the knife in his hand.

Ray's head fell backward, and he let out a loud breath. His chest went still, and his body shifted so that the clothesline tightened against the dead weight. Piss dripped from his pants and a strong stench of shit filled the room.

"He's . . . dead," Pete said in a quiet voice. Realizing that the killer must still be there, he spun around with the knife held out. Avery shined her light in all directions.

They were alone.

"This can't be real," he whispered. Avery sniffled, and he expected she was crying, but didn't turn to look. His throat went dry, and he couldn't find the words to speak, to express his confusion. Nothing made sense. Everything was screwed up, turned inside out and upside down in a wild, deadly twist that he wasn't ready for.

"Avery, do you see anything in here?" Pete finally said.

"No," she mumbled.

"I don't understand. It was only a minute or two, if that. It would take that long just to string him up. And then his eyes, oh God," Pete said. He turned to the side and, like Ray earlier, vomited all over the floor. The unease in his gut manifested itself into bile and stomach acid, which burned on its way out. It splashed on the blood-stained floor.

Avery pulled him from the room and the smell of death drifted further away. It was too much. They should've left earlier. Now another of their friends was dead. Pete couldn't take his gaze off the darkened room where their friend Ray now hung like an animal ready for processing.

"Eyebiter," Avery said. "Ray was telling us that the story is true. Eyebiter exists and is here. It's stalking us."

They came to the school to find ghosts, the spirits of the innocent whose lives were brutally ripped from them. Pete didn't want to believe that a deadly supernatural being was now hunting them, but the evidence was too much to dispute. The legends had to be true. Wherever Doug was, he would have to fend for himself if he wasn't already dead. Considering what happened to their other two friends, the chances that he was still alive were pretty slim.

"We can't stay," Pete said. "We gotta get the hell out of here."

Avery nodded, the conviction in her manners from earlier all but gone.

"Stick with me and we'll get out together."

"I'm so sorry I made you guys stay," Avery said. "I just thought that we could work together to find Doug. I didn't think he was the one doing this."

"It's not your fault. We made the decision to stay."

Avery gently placed a hand on his shoulder and kissed his cheek. "We get out of this together," she confirmed.

The two of them turned to leave when something shuffled down the hall and into the cafeteria.

"What the fuck was that?" Pete asked, the hairs on his neck stiffening. "Did you see it?"

"Uh huh."

It took Pete a second to decide that whatever it was, he didn't want to find out. There was no sense in risking Avery's life, or his own. They were leaving and getting to some place safe so they could call for help.

CHAPTER 6

PETE FOLDED THE knife closed and shoved it in his pocket. He grabbed Avery's hand and led them to the stairwell to their right. Once there, a child screamed from the bottom of the stairs. It sent shivers up Pete's spine.

"What is it?" Avery said, turning to him. Even in the darkened building, he could see the whites of her eyes.

The screams grew louder and more frequent, almost as if there were several children crying out.

"We can't go down there," Pete said, backing away from the stairway. The horrific sounds ended, but their echo remained.

"The cafeteria," Avery replied. "There's another stairway there. It goes down to just in front of the principal's office."

Pete didn't realize there was a second set of stairs. How did Avery know? The school was closed for years before she moved to Brownsville. Now was not the time to question her, not while ghosts or something else were blocking what he thought was their only path of escape.

"But what about that thing we saw go in there?" he asked.

"It's our only way out," Avery said. "We have to try."

Pete ran a hand through his hair again. Every option seemed like a bad one, but they had to choose one.

"Ok," he said. "Let's do it." He patted the knife in his pocket to make sure it was still there. It was the only weapon he had and would have to do if they needed protection.

Shrill laughter bubbled up from the stairwell, setting off alarms within Pete's head. He imagined little children laughing at his distress. Nothing seemed impossible in the abandoned school.

The two of them hurried back the way they came, trampling through their footsteps and heading toward the cafeteria at the end of the hall. One of the two doors was slightly opened, a bloody

103

handprint on the heavy wooden door where someone had pushed their way through.

Pete's heart pounded harder in his chest. Was this really the only way out? Maybe they could escape from a window or something?

At the opposite end of the hall, it sounded like several people were running, as though children were playing in the hall. Pete shined his light in that direction and the beam of light faded before it reached whatever was down there as though the darkness created a shroud that the light couldn't penetrate.

"Now this place is eating light," he said. When Avery scrunched her face at his comment, he nodded down the hall and she noticed it too, her eyes growing wide again.

"That's impossible," she said.

"Everything we've experienced has been impossible, but it keeps happening."

Pete wanted to curl up into a ball and close his eyes until the horror passed. It was too much, and his sanity was slipping.

When told about how his father was shot in the school and didn't make it, Pete slipped into a similar state of mind. His body shut down. He lay on the floor of his bedroom with a blank stare. It took his grandmother hours to convince him to break out of it and come out of his room. It took another couple of days for him to speak. Had his mother still been alive then, maybe things would've been different. But losing his last parent at such a young age, and in such a brutal manner, broke something inside of him. What was happening now was similar, but with a significant difference.

It may be the same place as his father's tragedy, but this wasn't some deranged kid with a gun. It was an evil force they knew little about that had already murdered two of his friends, if not a third one. Now it had children helping it?

Avery let out a heavy sigh, then gently nudged him into the cafeteria, closing the door behind them.

Inside the large room, darkness prevailed. There were windows along the wall to their right, but they were boarded up years ago. There had to be at least twenty tables, all comically short with attached circular chairs lining both sides of the tables. Two serving windows built into the cinderblock wall ahead of them were closed, shuttered with what looked like small metal garage doors. A metal rolling cart was filled with brown plastic trays. Many had fallen off and lay scattered on the floor. Posters about how milk would do the body good or admonishing students to eat their veggies hung from the walls. Some of them had started to peel away and hung loosely from the tape that had been used years ago, its strength fading.

"Where's the stairway?" Pete asked.

"Back this way," Avery said.

They hurried through the cafeteria toward the wall with the boarded-up windows. As they did, Pete noticed a flickering glow come from a doorway. Because of the angle of the room, he hadn't noticed it earlier.

"Avery, look," he whispered. He pointed his flashlight in that direction, and she gasped when she saw the glow.

"What is it?" she whispered back.

"Do you think there's a fire in there?"

"If there is, maybe we ought to let it burn this place to the ground," Avery said.

"What if Doug is trapped somewhere in here? We can't let him die."

"We're all on our own now. I honestly don't think he's still alive. You've seen what's happened to Tom and Ray. It's safe to assume he was killed as well. Something sinister is happening here, something more terrible than the shooting," Avery said.

"We still can't leave it. If the place is on fire, it'll burn up our friends. The police need to find their bodies so they can go after whoever did that to them," Pete said.

"We both know the cops can't do a damn thing to a witch."

"I'm not convinced it's Eyebiter," Pete said. "Not yet."

Pete stepped closer to the open doorway.

"Pete, what about what's out there? We don't have time for this," Avery said. Pete understood why she'd be worried, but he was compelled to investigate. Something was drawing him to the glow. He had to find out what it was.

When he reached the doorway, his eyes shot wide open. "Avery, come here!" She whimpered but crossed the cafeteria until she stood next to him and peered over his shoulder.

"Holy shit!"

"Doug, are you ok?" Pete asked.

CHAPTER 7

A MIX OF RELIEF and fear filled Pete. They'd been looking for their friend ever since they stepped foot into this awful place. Seeing him alive sparked hope that maybe now the three of them could escape . . . alive. But the hope that so quickly bloomed was just as easily crushed.

Seated in the middle of the barren kitchen was their friend Doug. Stainless steel tables had been pushed to the side, leaving an open space that was about ten feet wide. In the center of that, five black candles burned. A circle had been crudely fashioned with clothesline, with the candles set evenly apart around it. Doug sat cross-legged in the center with his eyes closed, facing them.

His eyes. Oh no, are they gone? Pete thought. A shiver ran through him.

"What is this?" Avery asked. "Was he in here the entire time?"

"Wait, look at the floor," Pete said, flashing his light on Doug and the floor around him. In what looked like flour or sand or something similar, lines crossed from one candle to another. "It's a pentagram," Pete said. The candles were placed at five points of the star.

"What the fuck is going on?" Avery asked. "Did he summon the devil?"

Pete wanted to dismiss the notion the moment Avery spoke it, but everything they'd seen that night indicated something odd was happening. Could it have been caused by Doug's dealing in the occult? He had no idea his friend was into that stuff.

"Doug, dude, are you ok? We were worried sick about you. Tom and Ray . . . they're dead, man. You gotta come with us," Pete said. "We need to get out of here."

Pete froze in his spot, unwilling to cross into the kitchen and come near the demonic symbol. That wasn't their plan when they decided to come into the school in search of ghosts. Honestly, Pete hadn't looked up any kind of ritual. He only chose black candles because it felt like the creepy thing to do, a way for him to amp up the scariness of the place. He never expected they'd have a true, hellish purpose.

"Yeah Doug, come on," Avery added. "We need to get you out of here. Bad shit is going on."

Doug shifted in his spot, the first reaction he made acknowledging their presence. He slowly opened his eyes, and Pete took a step back. Doug's eyes were still there, but they were a milky white, as though someone placed a sheet over them. A faint outline of his iris was visible behind the cloudy haze, but they were far different than ever before.

"Oh, fuck!" Pete said. "Dude, what's wrong with your eyes?"

Doug shifted his head from one side to the other, his neck cracking as he did so. Then he spoke.

"He commands and I obey. He needs his fill. He needs it all. I obey and live."

From behind his back, he pulled out a small cloth bag. Its opening was untied and something dark and stringy hung over the lip like spaghetti. Doug reached in and pulled something out. When he did, Pete felt a sickening feeling tighten in his chest.

It was an eye.

"Joseph commands," Doug said. His voice had taken on a dull monotone quality, nothing like his normal self.

Avery pointed at him. "Where'd . . . where'd you get that?"

Pete shined his light at the bag. The cloth lip had rolled down, and he realized there were more eyes inside.

"Who the fuck is Joseph? Are those from Tom and Ray?" Pete asked in a shaky voice.

Doug smiled. It was a sickening gesture, something like a madman whose scheme was figured out. A brief flash of a memory tickled Pete's brain. One of the reports about Jimmy, the school shooter, was that he had an eerie grin on his face when he opened fire. Almost every survivor who saw him reported the same thing. A wicked, haunting smile crossed the killer's face. Much like what Pete was seeing on Doug's face.

Doug held out the eyeball. Thin sinewy strands hung from the backside of it, all covered in blood. "This is his. They all belong to him. My life is in Joseph's hands. He will be set free. The sacrifices are all for him. Blood and death. Eyes. All the eyes. For him."

"You aren't making any sense," Avery said. "Joseph? We don't know anyone by that name. Doug, please, snap out of it. We can all get out of here alive."

Something thudded against the doors to the cafeteria. The sudden disturbance made Pete jump. He turned that way but didn't see anything.

"It's gotta be those things from the stairs," he said. A sudden urge to evacuate his bowels struck him and he fought hard to keep everything intact.

"Doug, what the hell, man? How'd you get in here? We lost you in the bathroom and never saw you leave," Pete said. "We can talk about that later, though. We have to get the hell out of here. Something is coming after us, and I don't think they're friendly."

The grin on Doug's face grew impossibly wider, his lips stretching to their limits. It made Pete shudder.

"Joseph," Doug said. "Joseph is back."

"Who is that?" Avery asked. She tilted her head upwards as though in deep thought. No doubt she'd scoured the local legends with her mom, the history professor. Pete tried to connect the name as well. The legend of Eyebiter was that she was a woman named Sarah, a distant relative of Nathaniel Browne, the founder of Brownsville. But who was Joseph? The only Joseph he knew was his father, but he went by Joe, and he'd been dead for fifteen years.

Doug moaned, stealing their attention. His eyes fluttered. The candles flickered.

"I don't like this," Avery said.

"Doug, come on, snap out of it. Whatever is going on, we can get help for you," Pete said.

Something pounded on the cafeteria door again and Pete spun around. The doors were slowly creaking open, but from where they stood, he couldn't see what it was. Haunting giggles followed. Pete dropped his flashlight, and the light winked out. He snatched it off the floor and shook it, but the light was dead.

"Damn it," he mumbled.

Doug let out a demonic howl. It was so sudden and so powerful that Pete clapped his hands against his ears to block out the sound, though it didn't help much. Avery had done the same.

"He's lost," she said, indicating Doug. "Whatever this thing is, it has him in its grips. We have to leave him behind. We gotta save ourselves."

The decision paralyzed Pete. Doug was their friend. How could he condemn him to his death?

Doug groaned again, the voice so deep and unlike him that it sounded like it came from someone else. The cafeteria door creaked again. Despite his misgivings, Pete's decision was made for him.

"Sorry Doug. I don't know what happened to you, but we can't do anything for you." It stung like hell, but Avery was right. They had to leave or face horrific consequences like Tom and Ray.

"Let's get to the stairs," Pete said. They rushed to the open doorway, and he looked back at his friend, who sat still in the diabolical circle, his white eyes fluttering in the candlelight.

They stepped into the cafeteria and, half expecting to find a demon or wicked creature, they found nothing. Avery scanned the area with her flashlight, and it was empty.

"I don't like this," Pete said. "We both heard it, right?"

"Yeah. It's like those dead children are after us."

"Fuck it, we aren't waiting around," Pete said. He nudged her toward the stairs, and they ran across the room with the tiny tables, avoiding them and crossing aisles when one was in their way. When they got to the stairwell, Doug let loose a bloodcurdling scream.

"Oh no!" Pete said. He looked back and didn't see anything other than shadows moving in the candlelight. The angle wasn't good, and he couldn't see what exactly was going on inside the kitchen.

"Doug!" Avery screamed.

Doug howled again, pleading for mercy.

"Please don't!" he screamed. "I'm yours!" Then his pitch rose higher, his screams more agonizing. It was punctuated by a loud plop. The visual in Pete's head made him sick. He couldn't see what happened, but his imagination ran wild.

"He killed him," Avery said. "Whoever this 'Joseph' person is killed Doug, even though he helped him."

Pete fought back the tears and turned toward the stairs. "We can't stay," he mumbled, then headed downstairs.

CHAPTER 8

WHEN PETE AND AVERY stepped out into the darkness of the first floor, a cold sensation made his skin prickle. Doug had fallen silent, but a heavy thud upstairs was followed by what sounded like something being dragged across the floor.

"Which way?" he asked. He was turned around and didn't know what hall they were in or where the exit was. The emergency exits no longer illuminated after years of neglect.

They were at a t-shaped crossing with one hall extending straight ahead. Avery used her flashlight to look down all three paths. Above them, the unmistakable sound of something being dragged grew louder, closer. Pete was ready to dart down any of the halls, just so long as it got them away from that sound.

Then it stopped.

Pete cocked his head. A heavy splat followed, spraying them both with a hot liquid. He and Avery jumped and spun around. When her flashlight shone on the source of the awful sound, Pete screamed.

It was Doug. Or rather, what was left of him. His body had been shredded. Long ribbons of flesh hung loose from his arms. The way his body fell from the second floor, they extended outwards like bloodied tendrils. His head had cracked open, and his face was turned toward them. Gray matter spilled out onto the floor.

"His eyes," Avery said. "Fuck, he got his eyes."

Just like their other two friends, Doug's eyes were plucked out. Pete imagined they were added to the bag with the others, but for what purpose? A collection of stolen eyes held no value. At least, not that he knew. To one called Eyebiter, maybe they held a sacred meaning.

Pete stumbled backwards and, without waiting for Avery, ran

down a hall. He had no idea which one. It was just a means to get away from the madness. He screamed the entire time, letting loose the terror that had been building within him. Fuck Eyebiter. Screw the wicked man, or whatever the fuck it was. He couldn't stay silent any longer. Something snapped inside of him, and he was powerless to stop it.

Avery called to him, but it was like he was in a dream and the voice was distant and disembodied.

Pete faced the need of the hall and stopped, his hands on his knees. The terror of the night raced through his mind, and he fought hard to push it back.

A light bobbed closer to him, and he shielded his eyes from its brightness.

"Sorry, I didn't mean to do that," Avery said. She turned her light toward the floor. "Pete, don't run off like that. Not without me. Hold it together so we can get out of this alive."

"Doug," he said between breaths. "He just tossed him over the stairs like he was nothing. I can't take this anymore. It's too much."

"We can make it out, but only if we stick together. We can do this," Avery said.

Pete took a few calming breaths.

He focused on her words, trying to maintain his composure. It wasn't like him to snap like that. There was just too much going on, and when Doug was tossed from the second floor, he couldn't hold it in any longer. Avery would need him to maintain his sanity, and he clung to that thought. It was tenuous, but it was enough to push away the fear, if only for a moment. She was right. Together, they could figure out how to get the hell out of that place and never turn back.

"The bad news is that you went down the wrong hall. This one is a dead end," Avery said. "That's how Jimmy was able to kill so many. They ran this way and didn't have any way to escape."

She did a quick check of the walls with her flashlight and the cinderblocks were littered with pockmarks, the remnants of the gunman's rampage.

Pete swallowed hard. "This," he began in a weak voice, "this is where my dad died."

He knew little of the events of that day, but the one thing he'd been told over and over again was that his father led a class down this hall and all but one of them died. He was criticized in the newspapers and vilified for his actions, with some people even accusing him of leading them to their deaths on purpose. It was too much for Pete to bear at the time and soon afterwards, he was in therapy five days a week instead of two.

"Oh damn, it is," Avery said. "This must be awful." Avery wrapped an arm around him and pulled him close, offering her best sympathetic hug.

A loud screech echoed through the school. The two of them clutched each other and faced down the hall.

"Avery, we're gonna have to go that way, aren't we?"

"It's the way out. We're dead if we stay here."

The screech intensified, growing darker and undulating in pitch.

"Shut up!" Avery said.

Pete clutched her head, covering her ears with his arms. But that meant he was forced to listen to the hellish sound, and it made his blood run cold.

The screams stopped, and he let Avery go. She was breathing heavily, as he was.

"Ready? Tell me which way to go. I'll lead. I couldn't stand myself if something bad happened to you," Pete said, mustering the courage he'd lost earlier.

"Back. We go back to the intersection and follow the hall directly across from the stairs. At the end of that, turn left and the entrance should be there. Unless I have my bearings all screwed up."

Pete pulled the knife from his pocket. The small blade wouldn't do much damage, but it gave him a sense of security he sorely needed at that moment.

"Shine the light ahead of us. We'll move slowly."

Avery did as he asked, and then he walked ahead.

The terrible screams stopped; their echo left ringing in Pete's ears.

"Thank God," Avery said. "I couldn't think with that going on. Pete, if we don't make it out of here, I want you to know that I really like you. I never realized how much until tonight."

He stopped. That was not what he expected to hear. "Umm, so I, uh . . . thank you." He felt his cheeks flush.

Slowly, they worked their way back to the intersection, keeping some distance away from the stairwell. Avery's flashlight landed on Doug's broken body and she let out a squeak. They pushed themselves against the wall opposite the stairs. Pete kept his hand on the rough block walls, feeling the grooves within. At one point, his finger slid into a jagged hole. Without looking at it, he knew it was a bullet hole. His heart sank. Was it done before or after his father was killed? To be so close to where he was murdered unsettled him, and he yanked his hand free of the wall.

They got to the intersection of the halls, and Avery shined her light ahead of them.

"I don't see anyone," she said.

"Let's get out," Pete answered. His overworked mind and raw nerves had had enough of the school. It was a mistake to have come here.

They entered the hall and moved slowly. There was still something lurking in the school, and it maimed and killed their friends.

Halfway toward the exit, a deep and menacing growl echoed in the darkness. At first, Pete thought it was a dog, like a Rottweiler or a pit bull.

"Avery, what is that?"

She swung her flashlight around, searching the shadows for the source of the sound. "I don't know. I think it's coming from that classroom." Her flashlight landed on an open door across the hall from them.

The sinister growl continued, and Pete felt a chill race down his spine. "Do you think that's her?" He didn't need to say the name. He knew Avery would know exactly who he meant.

Avery ran her free hand over her headband, her eyes darting back and forth from the room to the exit. "Maybe?"

"We need to run for it. We're almost to the door," Pete said.

The growl turned into a wild, high-pitched shriek. Pete shuffled away, his heart racing and his eyes growing larger.

The darkness in the hall grew darker, a phenomenon Pete didn't think was possible. The air suddenly turned frigid, and his flesh prickled.

"Avery, it's her," he whispered, afraid to speak any louder for fear of capturing Eyebiter's attention.

Avery lifted her flashlight, so the beam pointed at the sudden darkness blocking the hall from where they came.

A figure shrouded in shadows stood with its head nearly

touching the ceiling. It covered its face with arms dripping in thick strands of shadow, obscuring its face. Pete froze, and his bladder almost gave out.

"What is that? Is that . . . "

Avery clung to him, her earlier bravado slipping away in the presence of the malevolent creature.

A low growl escaped the thing, and then it dropped its arms. The shadow dissipated from around it and it shrunk in size. What was left made Pete gasp. Words failed him, but deep inside, he screamed. It was impossible.

It was his dad.

CHAPTER 9

PETE WAS ONLY three when he was killed in the shooting, but he'd thumbed through photo albums for hours at a time, attempting to connect with a man he barely knew. It had only been the two of them since his mother's unexpected death when he was just a baby. Memories of his dad tucking him into bed were all that he had and even then he wasn't sure those were real or manufactured by a traumatized mind.

But the man standing in the hall was the man from the photos, though with significant physical differences. He had no doubt it was his father, Joseph Speight.

"What's wrong, son?" he asked. His voice sent chills through him. He'd heard recordings before, but there was always a metallic timbre present. His words now sounded smooth and dark. He held something in his hands, but he couldn't tell what it was.

Pete's words refused to form, the shock of the moment tightening his throat.

The person before him was an emaciated version of his father. Taught, ashen skin was draped over his skeleton. His thin lips were cracked. His hair was nearly gone, exposing a bone white skull. He wore tattered clothes, his shirt in ribbons and his pants shredded. But despite all the changes, it was something in his eyes that reminded Pete of the memories he had of his father. There was no doubt that this creature staring at him was his dad.

"Son," the eerie man said. Shadows drifted from him in curls of smoke. Avery's shaky flashlight made them even more menacing. "It has been so long. You've grown into a fine young man."

The man, his dad, shuffled closer, shambling across the tile floor unsettling the dust underneath him.

"This isn't real," Pete whispered, words finally escaping his lips. It was impossible. How could his father be here?

He smiled wide, his black pit of a mouth growing larger and his lips cracking worse than before. "Come now, is that how you greet your father?"

"You're not his father!" Avery yelled. Pete glanced at her and then back at the creature.

"Your eyes will be a delight," his father said.

Pete's legs grew weak, and he almost fell down. "Eyes?" he asked.

His father cackled. It was a wicked sound that dripped with evil. "My son, isn't that why you came back? To see me, to see the one you call . . . Eyebiter."

Pete stumbled backwards. Avery grabbed his arm and held tight.

"No," he said. "No, it can't be true. You aren't . . . no, please dad, tell me it's not true."

"That's not your father," Avery muttered. "Don't listen to his lies."

Pete was thrown into confusion. All the legends said Eyebiter was a woman, a witch from the earliest days of the settlement. How could this thing in front of him be the legend and his dad? It was impossible.

"You will understand the truth, but that will be the last thing you do," his father said. He held out what was in his boney hand. A brown cloth bag, the one Doug had in the cafeteria. The one filled with eyes.

"I hated these little children," his father said, extending his sickly looking arms, indicating the school. His shirt hung from his skeletal frame. "They drained my energy, made me weak, but I soon discovered they could help me."

Help you? Pete thought. He wasn't sure he wanted to know.

"Jimmy did as I commanded, but he was reckless. He destroyed the source of my strength like a brute. The eyes must be harvested with their souls attached. His methods were too quick, too final for me to extract what I needed. I asked him to maim, but the killing frenzy took over. When I brought him more children, he turned the gun on me." His father inhaled deeply, continuing his awful speech.

"Ever since that day, I've waited for freedom. My spirit lives within these walls, but I need to escape. In death, the children taunt me worse than in life. Their sickening laughter reminds me how much I loathe them. But these," he said, holding up the bag, "these are what bring me life. These will break the bonds which tie me here. And Doug was more than eager to fulfill my needs." He poked into the bag and plucked out an eye, thin bloody strands dangling from it. He inspected it like he was choosing a diamond. "His gift," he said, then held the eye to his lips. And bit.

It popped like an overripe grape. Blood and gore dripped down his chin. He chewed with his eyes closed, his head back in ecstasy. Slowly, his jaw moved as he savored the soft bite. He slurped up the thin strand connected to the piece he bit off and licked his dry lips. He took a couple deep breaths and let out a soft moan.

"Have you ever tasted the soul of another?" he finally asked.

Pete was shaken to his core. His feet refused to move, frozen in place. Was that truly his father and did he just eat Doug's eye?

His father poked the other half of the bloody eyeball into his mouth and gazed at Pete as he chewed with his mouth partially open like it was scalding hot and he needed relief.

"The final bite is always the best," he said.

Pete's stomach twisted into knots.

"Fucking gross," Avery said.

"But oh, so necessary, little one," he said.

Avery grabbed Pete's arm and pulled him away from his father, Joseph. "We have to get out of here!"

Pete's fear intensified as his father's face twisted and contorted in on itself. Deep fissures creased his flesh and peeled back, his thin skin tearing away. He plucked another eye from the bag and popped it into his mouth, chewing loudly on the bloody orb. It splashed on his teeth, and they dripped a thick crimson liquid. But as he did so, his face returned, and the deep gashes closed on itself.

"He's healing with each bite," Pete said. None of it made sense. How could the spirit of his dad be doing all this?

Avery let out a whimper. "This really is the witch or . . . or . . . something."

Joseph raised a boney finger at her. "You would do well to join us. Your mother knows all too well the dealings with the dark one. Come, join her."

Pete faced Avery; her eyes bulged.

"No! Please don't. It's not . . . it's not true!"

"Avery, what does he mean?"

She shook her head, her hand covering her mouth.

Pete spun her around and pulled her along. He wasn't staying one more second in this place. Father or not, the creature facing them was dark and disturbing. "Come on, let's go!"

CHAPTER 10

THEY RACED AWAY from Joseph. Pete glanced back, but with the light gone, he saw nothing but an open maw of darkness. The thing that claimed to be his father could be anywhere behind them.

A rumbling growl echoed in the hall. Pete's heart thumped harder, his adrenaline kicking in, and his muscles screamed from exertion.

They made it near the end of the hall where the final corridor crossed, revealing the exit to their left. He had no idea where his father had gone to, but Pete was thankful for finding their way out. He yanked Avery in that direction, and she was ripped from his arms.

"No!"

Avery's ear-splitting scream jolted him. She was pulled back into the darkness, and she dropped her flashlight. It clattered on the tile. In a sliver of light, he caught a glimpse of a black shadow escaping into the nearby classroom. Which is also where Avery's scream came from.

Pete snatched the flashlight from the floor. He had to hurry. If his father was as quick as he thought he was based on what he'd done to Tom and Ray, he didn't have a second to spare. He needed to save Avery from whatever fate awaited her. It was not supposed to be like this. They were only here to commune with the dead, not die themselves.

Pete ran to the room and lunged inside.

The flashlight shined on a frightened Avery. She floated in front of the desk at the back of the room with thin wisps of black shadow swirling around her like living bindings. His father was next to her. A dusty wooden nameplate on the desk had the name "Mr. Speight" engraved on it. Pete's eyes grew large.

"This was your class."

He was too young to remember where his father's classroom was. Because he was killed further back in the school, he always associated his class with being back that way. It was only now that he remembered the rumors about his father's actions in the shooting, despite his death at the hands of the killer.

The news reported he assisted Jimmy, that he somehow let him in the building, but he always thought that was crazy. He often wondered why his father would let him in to kill all the kids. It never added up but was a constant source of embarrassment for him. Until now. Until the words his father shared moments earlier shattered his hero worship.

"This was your class," he repeated. "Why?"

His father grinned and stepped closer to Avery. His friend didn't seem like she could speak, but her wild eyes and convulsions gave away how frightened she was.

"I never wanted children. You were your mother's idea. When she selfishly died, leaving you with me, I burned with a hate so deep. Working around children reinforced my disgust with you."

Pete's eyes filled with hot tears. How could his father be saying such awful things?

"Then it became all about the eyes."

A deep gash opened on his father's face again, but this one wept black blood. Things crawled out of it, wiggling out of the wound, and landing on the floor. Another gash crossed his forehead and black worms worked their way out from inside and crawled down his nose. They fell to the floor. When he spoke, more of them fell from his face.

"I wanted to be rid of you long ago, but I couldn't bring myself to do it. Not personally. That's where Jimmy came in, but he failed me and when I tried to stop him, he turned it on me."

He smiled, more worms falling from his face. Then he produced the bag of eyes that was sitting on the desk and plucked out an eye. He set the bag back down and slowly savored an eye, slurping on the nerve attached to it.

"You brought him in . . . to kill me?" Pete said. The revelation shook him to his core. How evil was he? All those kids died because he wanted his own son dead, and he was incapable of doing it himself. Pete's face darkened, and he glared at him. Hate boiled within. Ever since his death, he had a longing for him, a deep chasm inside his soul that could only be filled with his love, but this? He'd never have guessed this.

His father smiled, then bit down, severing the orb in his mouth. Pete heard a soft pop through his closed lips as he chewed. The moment he did, the cuts on his face closed up and he was healed from his grotesque wounds.

Avery struggled against her shadowy bonds, but couldn't escape from the force holding her. Pete's stomach was doing flips, the grossness of his father eating an eye and the truth of his revelation unsettling him.

How was he going to stop him? If this was an evil spirit or a witch or something like that, how could he do anything to him?

His father placed a gnarled hand over Avery's face. Avery opened her mouth to scream, and nothing came out, her face a mask of pure terror. His father dug his black nails into the eye socket on Avery's right side.

Pete lunged forward, but his father was too quick. He heard the sound of Avery's eye plucked from her skull, a disgusting, wet, sucking sound. Pete slammed into Avery. He hadn't expected his father to let her go, but he released the bond and the two of them tumbled onto the desk. Pete fell face down and stared at the bag with the remaining eyes. The idea struck him like lightning. The eyes. He said it was all about the eyes.

Avery cried out and clutched her now empty eye socket. Sympathy welled up inside Pete, but the time to console her wasn't now. Not when he had someone to stop.

He grabbed the bag and the thin wooden nameplate from the desk, spinning around to face his father. If these are what gave him strength, then destroying them was the only way he could think of to stop him.

CHAPTER 11

PETE'S FATHER WAS inches from him and held out Avery's bloody eye, the green iris looking back at him from between her fingers. A storm of anger and confusion raged within Pete. Facing the monster that was his father shook him to the core.

"Recognize this one?" his father said. A stench of rot and decay invaded Pete's nostrils and his stomach lurched. He held his breath, trying to avoid tasting it.

His father backhanded him, the blow coming unexpectedly. Pete flew across the room and the bag slammed against the wall, the eyes inside falling out. The wooden nameplate flew in the opposite direction.

"My eyes!" his father screamed. Before he ate Avery's eye, he dove to the floor and felt through the dust for his prized possessions.

Pete stood on shaky legs. Avery was on her knees with her face in her hand. The faint light from the fallen flashlight illuminated angry streaks of blood that raced down her arms, evidence of her missing eye.

Fueled by rage, Pete lunged at his father. He slammed into his corporeal body, the physicalness of him a shocking surprise. The two of them hit the wall and Pete thrashed, trying to disengage himself. His hand slammed down on something wet. It crushed underneath the force and his hand was covered in a thick, sticky substance.

His father roared. "No!" he bellowed. Rising up on his haunches, he flung out his hands and tried to grab Pete. His nails scraped Pete's skin. The wounds he left were hot and stung like a thousand bees.

Pete fought through the agonizing pain to search for the other eyes. With Avery's eye, he expected there should be three left.

His father flung his hand out and Pete was tossed back several feet, even though he never touched him. Pete crumpled to the floor and slowly uncurled himself, ready to destroy the eyes. In the darkness, he just barely saw his father shove an eye into his mouth and eat, a deep groan escaping from him.

Two more. He had to destroy the last two if he had any chance of escaping.

His father cackled and rose to his full height. Pete flashed the light on him. With a wicked grin, his father held out a skeletal hand with two eyes in his palm, one brown and one green. *Avery's eye*, Pete thought.

"You were an embarrassment once. You're not any better now. At least you will serve a purpose before you die." His father lifted one of the eyes to his mouth, but Avery had recovered. Pete's dad didn't see the girl as she dove into him. The force of the impact made him drop one of the eyes and reflexively crush the other as he braced himself.

Avery screamed wildly. Pete's dad howled at the loss of his precious stolen eye. The two of them struggled on the floor, with Pete's father threatening to eat Avery's remaining eye right out of her skull.

Pete had to do something. There was no way he'd let his father kill Avery. If it was the last thing he did, he'd save his friend. This was not her fight. It was between him and his dad.

That's when he spotted the last eye. It had rolled against the wall and was covered in dust. A glimmer barely caught his attention in the faint light, but he knew what it was.

Hurrying toward it, he snatched it from the floor and held it up.

"Joseph!" he yelled, ditching the formality and refusing to call the monster his father. "Let her go."

Avery scooted away from Joseph, who was distracted by the appearance of the eye.

"Give it to me," he snarled. "You don't know what kind of powers you are dealing with."

Pete held the sticky orb between his thumb and forefinger. For a second, he wondered which one of his dead friends it belonged to. If he ever escaped this madness, he vowed to make sure their memories were never forgotten.

"Leave us. Go back to wherever the hell you came from," Pete said.

Joseph rose to his full height. He snarled, then a crack opened on his cheek. Maggots and worms wriggled their way out. He tried to cover it up with his hand, but the insects still squirmed through his thin fingers.

"Give that to me!"

"You need the power, don't you?" Pete asked. All the rumors of an eye eating witch were true, and much to his horror, they involved his own father, this thing in front of him named Joseph.

Flashes of gunfire erupted in his head. Screams. Children crying. People shouting. Bullets ricocheting off the concrete. Memories he hadn't accessed in years assaulted him.

Across the room, Joseph grinned. Worms crawled in and out of his mouth. Maggots inched down his cheeks. More cuts erupted on his flesh, which had now taken on an even more pale gray hue.

"Give in to the fear. Remember your past. Let go of the present and abandon hope," Joseph said.

"Fuck you," Pete said. Against the backdrop of his past racing through his head, he narrowed his eyes and glared at him. "Fuck you and your evil ways." He then wrapped his hand around the last eye and squeezed.

Joseph wailed. It was an awful, demonic sound.

The eyeball popped and gushed into Pete's hand. It felt like a ball of puss had burst. Like a giant blister filled with sickening fluids. The inside of the eye coated his hand in a sticky substance.

Joseph's face turned upwards. Worms and centipedes and maggots crawled out of his skin. His head shook violently, and the creatures sprayed all over the room. Pete covered his face with an arm. He felt tiny things fling against him and he backed up several steps.

"Avery!" he called out. He felt a tug on his shirt, and he turned to the side. It was her. He wrapped an arm around her and the two of them clung to each other as Joseph continued to howl and cry out.

More of the bugs escaped his flesh. They clung to Pete. Frantically, he brushed them off as though they might infect him with Joseph's evilness. Whatever ate away at Joseph's decency would never infect him. The wickedness would end with him.

Joseph screamed again. Pete and Avery were both locked on to him, their eyes unable to turn away.

The shadows that had circled him started moving like a violent storm. They swirled around his head until they closed like a noose around his neck. Then the shadows crept upwards, snakelike, slithering up his neck and chin. It split into several tendrils, each one stabbing at the wounds on his face. Another strand broke free and slid into his nostril. His eyes grew large. There was a slight pause. An unsettling silence followed.

Joseph grinned. The worms in his mouth dangled from his teeth.

"It's not over," he hissed.

Then the shadow shoved itself into his mouth. His face expanded like a wicked balloon. Veins bulged; their dark lines visible under his translucent flesh. His wounds wept blood, the insects no longer pouring out. Then, just as Pete thought it couldn't get any worse, Joseph's head exploded.

Black blood splashed the wall behind him. It sprayed Pete and Avery. Its rank odor was like nothing he'd ever experienced.

While the two of them watched, the black shadow consumed Joseph's body, devouring it. He screamed a high-pitched wail. Both Pete and Avery covered their ears until the horrific cries ceased.

Within minutes, the room fell silent.

Blood rushed in Pete's ears. Avery's breathing grew shallower, and she whimpered. He turned the light on her.

It took everything he had not to jump away in revulsion. A couple maggots crawled around her empty eye socket, feasting on the fresh blood. Without thinking, he brushed them away, and she yelled as he touched exposed nerves.

"Maggots," he said, trying to explain his action. He thought he saw another one deeper within, but he was not about to touch it. Hopefully, she'd feel it and take it out herself.

"We have to go," he finally said, recovering from the moment. "Can you make it out?"

Avery nodded without replying. She covered her exposed eye socket with one hand, and he led her out of the room. At the door, he glanced back at the empty room. All that was left of Joseph was the stain on the wall and the wooden nameplate. He grunted and then led Avery out of the school.

CHAPTER 12

PETE TAPPED HIS fingers gently on the wooden table. He had asked Avery to meet him at Coffee Haven, their local coffee shop. She had yet to arrive, and the waiting was eating at him. They hadn't spoken in days, and she wouldn't text him back until after the fifth try, when she finally relented and agreed to meet.

When she arrived, he grimaced at her. She wore a black eyepatch over her one eye. He imagined it hurt like hell and a touch of guilt settled within him. Without his insistence on finding ghosts, she might still have an eye. And his friends might still be alive.

"Hey," he said, breaking from his thoughts.

"Hi," she replied in a neutral tone.

"You want any coffee?" he asked.

She shook her head. "No, I'm fine."

He gestured with a hand for her to sit. They were at the back of the shop, far from the door. Black and white photos of bags filled with coffee adorned the wooden slat walls. Pete waited for an older couple next to them to leave before speaking.

"Are you ok? Have you spoken to the police?"

She nodded. "I said what we agreed on."

When the police questioned Pete and Avery about the incident, they both agreed to blame it on their friend, Doug. No one would believe they'd actually come up against the legend known as Eyebiter, so they did the only thing they could think of.

Neither one of them fully understood how Doug was involved and how he escaped the bathroom that night, but after all they'd seen and been through, both could believe anything.

"Good. I hate that we had to, but . . . " He trailed off. It didn't need to be said aloud.

Avery barely looked at him with her good eye, instead her focus was on the table, as though she were inspecting it.

"Speak to me," Pete said in a soft voice. "I want to help. I know you've been through hell, and not just with, well, you know who."

Avery had gone missing not long after her and her mother moved to town and her mother had a mental breakdown, blaming spirits or wraiths. She didn't deserve another tragedy in her life, and it broke his heart that she'd been put through another terrible trial.

"It's fine, I promise."

"When do you get your eye?"

His question invoked a slight smile on her face, the first sign of life yet. "In two weeks. The doctor said it'll take me some time to adjust to it, but after a while, I won't know it's there."

"How's your vision?"

"It still throws me off. My balance is all out of whack, but I manage."

"Avery, I'm so sorry this happened to you. It was me he was after. I know that now. I wish we'd never have gone there that night. It was dumb."

She blinked and gazed into his eyes with her one remaining eye. "I'm not sorry."

"What?"

"I mean it. I'm not sorry we went."

"Avery!"

"Things happen for a reason. I'm not the same anymore, and I'm thankful for that."

Pete didn't know that to say. This was not what he expected. Sleep eluded him the past few nights, haunted by the memories of that night and the horrible deaths of his friends.

As he stared at her, a small maggot crawled out from under her eyepatch. She noticed it, plucked it off of her skin, and tossed it to the floor.

"If that's all you have to say, then I think I need to go," Avery said. She stood, and Pete jumped to his feet.

"Avery?"

She smiled, and when she did, it was like looking at Joseph. He couldn't explain it, but there was something in the way her lips curled back. A sickening feeling settled in his gut.

"See you around," she said, then tiptoed out of the shop. A

shiver ran up Pete's spine. Something was wrong with Avery, and he felt sure Joseph was behind it. The thought slammed into his mind like a lightning bolt.

"Oh no," he whispered. He covered his mouth with his hand, the truth dawning on him.

Eyebiter was still alive, and now he lived in Avery.

VOLUME 3: EXPIRATION OF SENTENCE

JOHN LYNCH

CHAPTER 1

"**MR. MURPHY**, you sit here before the parole board today and present yourself well. You've taken every class recommended to you, volunteer in the mentorship program, and aside from a few scattered incidents here and there, your discipline record within the institution paints you in a favorable light," said Mr. Doyle.

"Thank you, Mr. Doyle. I understand I can't change what I've done, but I know that every day I have a new opportunity to put my best foot forward and work on becoming a better me. Each day is one day closer to going home, and I think I am ready to reintegrate into society. I'm glad that . . . "

Sean Doyle cleared his throat, cutting off inmate Richard Murphy, identification number 115374, mid speech. "Mr. Murphy, please, I'm not finished speaking. Before you count your chickens, maybe you should listen to *everything* the board has to say."

Murphy swallowed what felt like a meatball sized lump. His prison jumper was soaked in sweat despite the meat locker like chill in the room. His heart felt as if it had sunk deep into the pit of his stomach. He'd been hopeful, but he was no dummy and he could already tell which direction this conversation was headed. It was a done deal, the board members' minds made up. He tuned Doyle out. There was no need to listen to the fucking toolbag lecture him. Listen to him take a shit on his hopes and dreams. Whatever the man said to him was nothing more than a long winded, roundabout way of saying two words.

Parole Denied.

Even with the outcome a forgone conclusion, he couldn't just get up and walk away, he had to stick around and let this asshole talk down to him and take it like a bitch. If he were to behave in any other manner, they'd have it out for him again the next time parole consideration came around. Murphy learned long ago that while in prison, the easiest way to do your bid was to avoid making waves. Whether good or bad, leaving an impression on someone rarely led to anything good around here.

Doyle continued. "As I was going to say, you *present well*. But I know that you're a smart man, Mr. Murphy. You aren't like many of the other inmates around here. You admit what you've done. You appear to show remorse for your crime. But you'll notice the key word there. You *appear* to show remorse, Mr. Murphy. I believe that a smart man such as yourself is simply playing the game. You aren't remorseful for your crime. You killed a man. And not only did you kill another human being, but you plotted and schemed with meticulous detail what you were going to do and when you were going to do it. And what you did to that man, regardless of the crime that *he* committed against your family, takes an especially twisted mind to carry out. This was no heat of the moment situation, were that the case special consideration may be granted. But Mr. Murphy, when I look into your eyes, I see a man who, if given the ability to go back in time and change his actions, he would instead choose to behave the same way. And enjoy doing so."

Murphy slammed his fists on the table, shaking the large rectangular piece of furniture. Doyle looked as if he shit his pants, surprised at the outburst. Who knows, maybe he did. Suits like him talked tough, but at the slightest sign of trouble, the bitch in them appeared.

"You're right," Murphy said. "I would do it again. That scumbag molested my son. He did it multiple times. My son's life is ruined because of that fucking monster. And what did the state do? What did they consider *justice*?"

The two officers stationed in the room approached Murphy in case things spun out of control, but let him keep speaking. Everyone knew what he was in for. Most of the correction officers would have done the same thing if placed in his shoes and readily admit as much.

"The judge gave that piece of shit a light sentence on a plea deal. Five years to serve with 15 years suspended. And you all on this very board let that fucking scumbag out two years early for good behavior? He raped a fucking child and served *three fucking years*. There are guys doing more time in here for selling weed.

EXPIRATION OF SENTENCE

Guys in here doing more time for bullshit theft charges, yet diddlers get soft sentences and parole for good behavior when what they really deserve is to be dragged out back and shot, for the good of society. Every single one of you should be ashamed of yourselves. I did what the state would have done if our lawmakers had a set of balls between them."

The room was silent. After a moment Doyle started to speak, but Murphy had heard enough. If they remembered this outburst the next go around, so be it. He'd serve the full sentence if that's what it took. Murphy didn't have to go to bed at night knowing some scumbag he let out early might rape another kid, but these boards members would. The man he'd murdered had hardly been the first piece of shit they let out, and he sure as shit wouldn't be the last, either.

Hands gripping the edge of the table, he pushed himself up from the chair. The two officers monitoring the hearing reached for their cuffs and pepper spray but didn't immediately react. Murphy shook his head. "I'm all set, guys," he said to the officers. "You're not gonna have any problems with me. I'm just done with this bullshit hearing. I'll go back to my cell now."

He strolled out of the room calmly, although he felt anything but. His blood boiled in his veins, and he felt ready to snap at the slightest provocation. The rage simmered underneath the surface. The last time that happened, Murphy had killed a man. That was the real reason he excused himself from the parole meeting. Not because of the mic drop he'd just performed on the parole board, but because in his mind he pictured himself hopping across the table and choking the life out of Doyle. Squeezing his neck until his beady little eyes popped out of his fucking skull like the scumbag he was. He saw himself pounding the man's face over and over until it was broken and battered. Teeth shattered, eyes swollen shut. Nose twisted and mangled. Being carried away in handcuffs while Doyle's face lay bleeding, looking like raw ground beef. Images that had flashed before his eyes in a few brief moments.

He smiled, thinking about the visions. He liked what he saw.

But a cooler head prevailed. Murphy knew it better to leave the room on his own accord, lest he end up facing an assault charge, possibly even an attempted murder. The threat of new assault charges was not one Murphy took lightly, but the thought of being pepper sprayed and dragged out of the hearing in handcuffs by the two meathead officers in the room was even more of a deterrent.

***

Murphy was alone in his cell. He'd stuffed a towel in the narrow window frame, blocking sunlight from getting through. The environment matched his mood, and he was ok with that. Sometimes he liked the dark, felt at home in it. It would be some time before his cellmate, Lewis, returned. He was enrolled in community college classes in the education area and wouldn't be back for at least another hour, possibly two. Murphy was thankful for the alone time. He wanted to stew in his thoughts, unbothered. Physically, he ran through his daily cell workout routine as if he'd never had a hearing to begin with—business as usual. But mentally, his mind raced as numerous scenarios and what-ifs swirled about his mind. Parole was out of the question.

Not only had he been denied, but after his outburst he'd been given a two-year review, rather than the standard one. A big fuck you to Murphy for speaking his mind. And two years from now when he was up for review again? Well, common sense told him it would be nothing more than a formality. He'd blown any chance of the parole board *not* having a poor impression of him at the next meeting. It was never a smart move to piss in the Cheerios of those who had the fate of your future in their hands, and he'd done just that. If he was lucky, maybe there would be new parole board members at the next hearing. At least that way it would be like having a fresh start. A new chance to show everyone how *rehabilitated* he was.

All roads led to one conclusion: there was no chance in hell he would be leaving Glenwood Correctional Institute in the near future.

Murphy paced back and forth in his cell in between sets of his workout—push-ups, body weight squats, jumping jacks, and sit-ups. Those forty-five seconds were supposed to be a respite from the intense workout he put himself through, and while it allowed his body a moment to breathe, those few moments of rest were when his mind ran rampant. He completed fifteen sets of his circuit, five more than usual. After completing the circuit, exhaustion took over, and he collapsed on his bunk, too tired to change or shower.

Murphy slept like the dead, only stirring from his sleep when the area officer kicked his door during his nightly count.

CHAPTER 2

MURPHY AWOKE THE next morning to the sound of watery shit splattering in the toilet. The stench of human feces threatened to choke Murphy in the confines of the small cell. He gagged and struggled to not vomit.

"Man, what the fuck?" Murphy said to his cellmate, Darius Lewis.

Lewis laughed. "My bad, man," he said, "you know those spicy chicken patties they give us in the chow hall give me the bubble guts."

"You call that bubble guts? It smells like something died in your ass, resurrected, and died again. That's fucking putrid."

"I've got IBS, asshole, I told you that. Now you can either deal with me shitting myself every so often, or I can let the C.O. know that you're watching me shit. You know they take that prison rape shit serious now. I bet you'll get a week in segregation if I tell them you were scoping out my hang down."

"It's not that serious man, besides you know I left my electron microscope at home. I couldn't see your baby dick if I tried. And not for nothing, the feds give a shit about the prison rape elimination act, but this place has gotten far worse since I've been here, and I don't think anyone gives a flying fuck what we do here as long as we do it quietly."

"You want to find out? Maybe we will get single cells out of it, at least until the next new commit comes in and that shiny, empty bunk gets an occupant. So, you can deal with bubble guts, or I can tell the officer you're making sexual comments to me. Who knows, maybe when you get out of seg, the next guy they stick you with will be some nasty fuck that doesn't shower. Or a thief. Or some fucking sex fiend. Or . . . "

"Lewis, I get it. You're the best cell mate I'm ever gonna have.

Please, just wipe your ass man, I need to call my wife and tell her the bad news."

Lewis finished wiping his ass, flushed the toilet, and washed his hands. He shook his head in disbelief at the revelation that Murphy had yet to tell his wife the bad news. "Bro, you better call that woman. She's gonna fuck you up if she hears from someone else that they denied your parole. You should have told her that last night."

"Yeah, I know. I just didn't know how to break it to her. I'm gonna go eat breakfast when they call chow. Give myself some time to figure out how to break it to her. I'll give her the bad news on a full stomach."

***

Murphy sat on the metal stool at the far end of one of the dining tables in the mess hall. The tables and stools were uncomfortable, unforgiving. Bolted to the ground, they were nothing more than solid, unmovable pieces of steel. Most things that were large and heavy enough to be used as either weapons or escape tools were bolted down or kept locked behind cages.

The overpowering smell of onions wafted through the mess hall. For whatever reason, onions were used in damn near every meal and the disgusting funk of them spilled out of the exhaust vents in the kitchen's roof, but that didn't stop the aroma from making its way into the dining room and assaulting the olfactory senses of every person in the area. It was disgusting. Murphy couldn't stand onions. Who the fuck would think it was a good idea to use them in so many recipes? It had to be some kind of cruel prank on the inmates.

There were plenty of inmates who'd love to work in the kitchen. It was a position that came with the luxury of being away from the general population most of the day, preparing your own food, and eating plenty of meals the rest of the inmates didn't get. But the tradeoff was that the stench of the kitchen seeped into your clothes and skin. The result was a funk that followed you wherever you went, no matter how clean you were. Murphy didn't think the pros outweighed the cons, so he never bothered requesting a job in the kitchen or the dining room.

He shoveled runny scrambled eggs into his mouth, washing the slop down with a carton of milk that was set to expire today. Best not to dwell on whether or not the chunks laboring down his throat were from the food or the milk. *Nothing but the best for us.* Murphy didn't bother with the hard slab of charred bread they had the balls to call toast. The hunk of bread was hard enough to break a window, but even if it *weren't* burned to a crisp, the assholes in charge of the menu didn't even bother serving it with the usual slab of butter. Who the hell eats dry toast? Either the kitchen stock was running low, or someone had pissed off one of these officers this morning—likely his wife—and he decided to take it out on the inmates.

Though he believed it should have been impossible, somehow over the years he'd been locked up, the food had gotten worse. Not that it was ever *good,* but there used to be the occasional decent meal. Prisons weren't known for the quality of their cuisine, but Jesus Christ, the food should at least be edible. Things could be worse, though. If the inmates who'd done time in southern states were to be believed, there were some real horror story meals out there. Prisons where the entire menu comprised nothing but low-quality deli meat sandwiches and hard-boiled eggs.

Maybe I shouldn't complain about the food.

With most of the edible parts of his meal finished and the garbage left untouched, Murphy reached across his tray to grab the one thing he'd actually been looking forward to eating: the blueberry cake. It was nothing special, but the cake was usually moist, and the blueberries had real flavor. He considered this pastry the one *good* item on the current rotating menu, and had it not been included in this morning's breakfast he likely would have remained in his housing area and waited until the horrid stench of Lewis' ass dissipated before throwing a breakfast together out of his commissary purchases.

As his fingers gripped the cake, lifting it from the tray, a large, tattooed hand closed over his, squeezing the bones together.

Murphy's heart pounded, threatening to burst from his rib cage as adrenaline spiked through his system. A situation like the one he found himself in was undesirable in a correctional institution, but he recognized the tattoo adorning the massive bear paw enveloping his own hand and knew *undesirable* was an understatement.

The hand belonged to Jason Reese, the 'heavy' of the housing block Murphy lived in, and the piece of shit leader of Glenwood's white supremacist gang.

Reese wrenched Murphy's wrist, flipped his hand over and snatched the blueberry cake from Murphy's grasp. "You weren't gonna eat this, were you?" Reese asked.

"Nah, you can have it, man."

"Yeah, I know I can. But I want to make sure *you* know I can."

"Must be nice to have juice like that around here."

"It *is* nice, having whatever you want. *You* can have whatever you want, too. You just gotta stop being a race traitor and pick a side."

"Pick a side? What side? I'm on *my* side. I want to do my bid and get out."

"Do you remember we just established I get what the fuck I want? I'm giving you some leeway here because we respect what you did to that piece of shit that fucked with your kid. That's the type of motherfucker I want to roll with. I'm guiding you to the right decision, just in case you're too fucking stupid to make it on your own. You know, lead a horse to water and shit. In this scenario, you're the horse, so take the fucking drink." Reese paused for dramatic effect before continuing.

"So when you leave this dining room, you're gonna walk back to the block and you're not even gonna go to your cell. You're gonna stop right at the officer's desk and tell him you don't want to live with anyone but whites from here on out. You're done hanging with anyone who doesn't look like us, you understand? I don't ask twice, so believe me when I tell you this is as far as my grace extends. Like I said before, I respect what you did, but I'll be more than happy to make you my bitch if you keep acting like one."

Pontification over, Reese took a mouthful of Murphy's blueberry cake and then tossed the rest at Murphy's chest. Murphy said nothing in response, sat in silence and watched as Reese stood, brushed his hands on the front of his jumper. He pulled at the bottom of the shirt, straightening the wrinkles in the orange uniform before sticking his chest out and strutting from the mess hall. Reese always made it a point to peacock anytime he entered or exited a room. He was the baddest man in the entire prison, and although everyone from inmate to officer knew it, Reese still liked to bring extra attention to himself any time he could.

As Murphy watched Reese leave, Ralph Adams, the disgusting excuse for a human that sat diagonally across from Murphy, in the seat next to where Reese had sat, cleared his throat and asked,

EXPIRATION OF SENTENCE

"You gonna eat that, buddy? I'm still hungry." Before Murphy could respond, he reached his filthy hands—stained with years of grime—across the table and snatched the remnants of cake from Murphy's tray. As he brought the blueberry cake to his mouth, crumbs of cake sprinkling from between his disgusting digits, another skinhead came up behind Adams, whispered something in his ear, and stuck a blade in the man's back. Adam's body went rigid. The food crumbs mixed with blood dribbled from between his lips. He coughed, spraying the mixture across the table. Dotting Murphy and the inmate next to him with little crimson droplets. The skinhead locked eyes with Murphy and winked at him as if to say 'see, nobody fucks with one of us' before dropping the shank to the ground and placing his hands on his head, signifying to responding officers he was compliant, no longer a threat.

Murphy shook his head and remained seated until officers cleared the area so nursing staff could perform life-saving measures on Adams until the rescue arrived. If the man was lucky, he'd pull through.

Murphy didn't care either way, Adams was no friend of his.

He left the scene of the attack as instructed.

It was far too early in the morning to deal with this much fucking *excitement,* and Murphy still needed to break the bad news to his wife.

Today was going to be a long day.

CHAPTER 3

THE CALL WASN'T going well, which was exactly as Murphy had expected. His wife continued assaulting his ear, "I had to hear from my goddamn mother-in-law that you didn't make parole! How the fuck do you think that felt? At no point did it occur to you that maybe you should pick the phone up and call your fucking wife? Maybe let her know you *weren't* coming home? I waited around all day for you to call me, but no, you couldn't be bothered. That would have been the considerate thing to do. But Richard fucking Murphy doesn't give a shit about what's going on in anyone's head but his own. Instead, Marge called me this morning to tell me she spoke with your counselor, and they told her they denied you parole. You're a piece of shit, you know that?"

Murphy sighed. He listened to his wife berate him, offered no defense. What else could he do? She had a point. He twirled a pen around in his hand as he watched the inmates go about their business throughout the cell block. It was a habit of his to divide his attention between phone calls and his surroundings. Call it paranoia, or call it survival instincts, but when you're locked up and surrounded by razor wire, you never knew when someone might try you. Weakness was picked out much the same way a shark detected blood. Prey didn't last long behind bars.

The very first day he'd arrived in the block after his sentencing he'd witnessed a man smash another inmates head in with the phone, beating the man repeatedly with the handset until his face looked like raw hamburger. The handset was heavy duty to prevent it from being easily broken, which also meant it could do some real damage. When the handset eventually shattered, the attacking man wrapped the cord around his victim's neck and strangled him with it until correctional staff responded with batons and pepper spray. The attacker spent thirty days in segregation while the man

140

who'd been brutally beaten spent three weeks at Glenwood Memorial Hospital. The beating was so bad the inmate had lost sight in his left eye.

Glenwood Correctional Institute had never been the safest prison. In fact, the original facility had burned to rubble years ago, the result of years of turmoil ending in a catastrophic riot. Things took a severe downward turn immediately following the hire of a new, mysterious warden—a man that to this day is as much of an enigma as he was back then—after the previous warden turned up dead under questionable circumstances. Many of the senior officers were terminated following the warden's arrival and were replaced with new officers who had little to no experience in corrections. The termination of the senior staff members meant there was nobody around to teach the new guys the ropes, but what the new hires lacked in experience, they made up for with a willingness to put hands on inmates at any given time. Violence spiked across the board. Inmate on inmate, inmate on staff, and staff on inmate violence reached all-time highs until the place had gotten so bad the state kept an ambulance on standby in the parking lot.

The states financial woes, along with local political issues, meant that the situation went ignored and unchecked until it was far too gone to *right the ship*. When it was all said and done and the fingerprinting and blame placing ceased, the one thing everyone had agreed on was that Glenwood Correctional Institute was an 'evil' place.

But a necessary evil.

While the facility had been reduced to rubble, there was still a need to house members of the population who couldn't conform to the laws of society—Glenwood Correctional Institute had been rebuilt in record time, but the state's fiscal responsibility to the taxpayers meant drastic measures were taken to complete the project with a minimal budget within a record amount of time. There simply was nowhere to house the inmates, so the state made agreements with neighboring states to temporarily house the displaced inmates during construction of the new facility. The cost-cutting measures included the consolidation of the prison's satellite buildings into the new facility, and the reclassification of inmates to lower security status designations they had no business being classified as.

If that weren't bad enough, Glenwood's already decimated staffing levels mixed with the inability of law enforcement agencies nationwide to properly recruit and hire new staff meant that Glenwood, a department that low staff levels had always plagued, now approached crisis level. In prior years, recruitment classes previously numbered in the hundreds, but were now reduced to dozens. To combat this, issues that would have been grounds for disqualification from the hiring process were now overlooked in order to bolster the ranks. Corrupt officers were no longer slipping through the cracks, they were invited with open arms.

All of that meant one thing for Murphy—if the simple fact of being incarcerated meant he must always remain vigilant, then the deplorable state of GCI increased the need for vigilance tenfold.

"Are you there? Hello?" his wife asked.

Murphy snapped back to reality. Lost in his thoughts, he hadn't heard a word his wife said. "Yeah. Yeah, I'm here. I was just thinking."

"I need you. You need to appeal this decision, or something. Your son needs his father." A click on the other end of the line.

Murphy slammed the handset onto the cradle over and over until the earpiece broke off. He dropped the phone and let it hang, swinging back and forth like a pendulum.

Someone grabbed him by the shoulder. "Hey man, what the fuck did you break the phone for?"

After the morning he had, Murphy was a ticking time bomb and the intrusion into his personal space lit his short fuse. He turned around, swinging his fist wildly as he pivoted. A perfectly placed punch, Murphy's knuckles connected with the man's jaw, smashing his teeth together with an audible click. The skinhead dropped to the floor like a sack of shit.

One of Reese's henchmen, Spencer.

Seeing red and unable to control himself, Murphy jumped on top of Spencer. It didn't matter that the man was already out cold. Murphy pounded him, raining blows from above, pummeling the man's defenseless face and body. Blood and spit flew from his mouth. His nose pancaked and twisted with a sickening crunch. Each strike bounced Spencer's head off the ground like a basketball.

The beating continued until Lewis rushed in and wrapped his arms around Murphy, doing his best to calm the man down and keep him off of Spencer. Eventually, responding officers rushed into the housing unit, batons and pepper spray at the ready.

"Everyone take a fucking knee, nobody move!" One officer shouted.

Murphy was already face down with his hands over his head. He wanted no part of the department's fight response, but it didn't matter because these were the new breed of officer, the ones who were going to take their pound of flesh when called upon, regardless of if force was still necessary by the time they arrived on the scene. Murphy gave no resistance and complied with the orders being shouted to him, but the moment he heard an officer scream, "Stop resisting," he knew he was fucked.

Almost immediately after someone had screamed the words, a baton found its home across his shoulder blades with a loud, meaty thump. Even as the baton bruised his flesh, he heard the unmistakable *whoosh* of a trigger-happy officer painting his face orange with a can of pepper spray the size of a quart of milk. His day had gone from bad to worse in a span of seconds.

The wet spray burned every orifice and pore on his face. Not wanting to get more in his eyes, Murphy tried to focus on squeezing his eyelids shut, but it was impossible. All plans were out the window the moment that first taste of spray hit your nostrils and throat. He coughed and spit while the pepper spray wreaked havoc on his respiratory system and the baton strikes continued to find their home on various *non-lethal* points of his body.

Eventually, the officer with the baton grew tired of beating Murphy and placed him in handcuffs.

As bad as Murphy had gotten it from the officers, he was apparently in better condition than Spencer. He heard a radio crackle, and an officer called medical personal to the housing area for an inmate who'd been pummeled in a fight and needed immediate medical attention. Spencer was breathing, but unresponsive, they said.

The pepper spray burned Murphy's eyes, preventing him from opening them, so as the officers escorted him from the housing area, he never saw Reese standing in the corner.

Watching.

CHAPTER 4

THE SEGREGATION UNIT was set up in a *U* shape, three sections, with each area kept independent of the other by a large, steel door which allowed inmates to be housed together, while still keeping enemies or potential problems apart. Each of the three sections had two levels, one ground level, and one up a set of stairs. Murphy had been placed on the lower level at his discipline hearing and had been hammered with the maximum amount allowable under state law—ninety days. Ninety days locked up in a damp, dimly lit cell with no human contact aside from the occasional officer walking through the unit, and the one hour of day the inmates could leave the cell for *recreation,* if you could even call it that. For inmates placed in disciplinary units, recreation consisted of being placed in handcuffs and escorted to cages, which were essentially giant dog kennels outside the unit. The cages were not technically outside—they were in the middle of the area, and there was no overhead roof in that section, which allowed natural sunlight to seep into the rec area, but it was a far cry from actually being outside.

A prison within the prison.

Inmates could spend one hour a day, Monday through Friday, inside the recreation cage with a few other inmates, so long as they were well behaved. Further infractions within the segregation unit resulted in a loss of recreation privileges and, depending on the infraction, more disciplinary time.

Murphy didn't bother going to the cages. He didn't have any enemy issues with any of the other inmates currently housed in segregation, but that didn't mean he liked any of them, either. He was of the mind to do his time in the box by himself, reading and writing to keep his thoughts from wandering.

Murphy liked to remain optimistic, and the one up-side to

being housed in the unit cells were larger cells that only had one bunk. No need to worry about having a nasty pig for a roommate. The extra space gave him more room to do his cell workouts. It sucked, being in the box, but if you could figure out a way to pass the time without losing your mind, it wasn't nearly as bad as Hollywood portrayed it. That being said, some men simply couldn't compartmentalize their brains in a way conducive to passing the time and ended up going what Murphy liked to call *soft in the brain*. There was something a tad bit *off* with men who'd done too much time in the box and couldn't hack it.

Murphy had met a few men like that since getting locked up and didn't want to be one of them, so he did his best to occupy his mind.

A week had passed since the fight, and Murphy was getting a little stir crazy. He'd finished all the books he'd checked out from the library cart quicker than he'd expected and it hadn't come back around, so when it *did* eventually arrive, he was ecstatic. It stopped in front of his cell, and he slipped the books he wanted to return through the feeding tray slot. Once they had been removed by the inmate pushing the cart, he pointed out a few more he wanted to read. The inmate handed them to Murphy through the tray and continued to work his way through the area. With some new books to read, his mental state would improve, he was already feeling better. The ability to get lost in someone else's world made sure he didn't have to remain trapped in his current reality. He flipped through the pages of a book by a man named Aron Beauregard, *Wedding Day Massacre*. It had some sick illustrations in it, so Murphy thought he'd read that one first. As he went to place the book on the shelf, it slipped out of his hand and a loose piece of paper fell from between the pages.

With a grunt, he reached down and picked up both the book and the paper. He placed the book on his shelf and unfolded the paper. It struck him as odd, finding the paper within the pages as he had. Usually, an officer would flip through the books before the cart went around for the sole purpose of making sure no inmates were passing around correspondence through the books. He furrowed his brow, wrinkling his forehead. Murphy was no engineer, but to him, the paper looked like building schematics.

What were building schematics doing inside of a book?

Adding to the peculiarity of the situation—the plans were

labeled Glenwood Correctional Institute. But that couldn't be right. Something was off about them. The landmarks surrounding the building on the schematics appeared the same, but there were definitely some rooms on the schematics that didn't exist in the facility, as Murphy knew it. He also noticed there were rooms *not* included in the schematics that he'd seen for himself.

That sparked a memory, something he'd heard someone talking about, but it hadn't crossed his mind at first because the Murphy family hadn't been Glenwood natives, they'd moved to Glenwood a year after their son was born, in search of the perfect place to raise him. What a mistake that had been.

Hadn't the prison been rebuilt a while back? These must be the old plans, Murphy thought.

Initially, Murphy put the plans away. Finding them was certainly unexpected, but they were nothing worth keeping. They were contraband that would see him in further trouble. But his mind kept coming back to them. Something about the schematic called to him, and before he knew it, he spent days wracking his brain over the plans, stopping only for necessary bodily functions. Eating, bathroom breaks, and showers. But even those, he pushed aside until he simply couldn't wait any longer. It had become an unhealthy obsession, one that he couldn't explain. Everything else was put on the back burner, and Murphy spent his time studying the wrinkled sheet of paper, yellowed with time, like an ancient artifact. In some ways, that's exactly what it was. At least as far as things in prison went. And while it may not have been *ancient*, the more Murphy studied it, the more he became convinced his initial assessment had been correct. In his possession, he had the schematics for the old Glenwood Correctional facility, the building that had stood in this very spot prior to its destruction.

Eventually, he had the plans committed to memory. But still, he kept the paper despite knowing the risk of being caught with it. While the plans didn't match up completely with the prison as it stood today, there were more than enough similarities they would likely charge him with possession of escape paraphernalia. Being caught with something like that could mean years in segregation, and likely being classified to a super-max facility once his seg time was served.

Any time Murphy knew he'd be leaving his cell, he folded the plans as small as he could, wrapped them in toilet paper and stuffed the wad between his ass cheeks. The last thing he needed was for an officer to toss his cell searching for contraband while he was at an attorney visit, or next door in the medical unit. It was a great deal of trouble for a piece of paper, but if what he saw on that sheet of paper was correct, the schematics showed something that would be worth a great deal to the inmate population of Glenwood.

A way out.

After pouring countless hours into studying it, and committing it to memory, he came to the realization that there was a basement in the old facility, one that had been built over when the new facility was constructed.

What if that basement were still there? They couldn't have possibly filled it up, could they?

The basement presented an entrepreneurial opportunity for Murphy. Information like what he possessed was unheard of and would fetch quite the prison retail value. No more smoking cigarettes that had been smuggled in through someone's asshole. Filters cut off to make the bundle smaller. He could be the "richest" inmate in the facility if he discovered a way to monetize this escape route. Murphy could only imagine what some inmates would pay to learn about this route. To learn that if someone were to find a way to dig into the basement, they could follow a large drain tunnel that appeared to empty about a mile and a half east of the complex. The more Murphy thought about it, it wasn't a matter of *if* the basement was still there. It had to be. It was a matter of what was the best method of breaking *into* it.

Murphy continued studying the piece of paper. The possibilities were endless.

CHAPTER 5

MICHELLE MURPHY STOOD in front of the kitchen sink, absentmindedly staring out the window with tears carving streaks down her cheeks. Water poured out of the faucet. She hadn't even noticed that she'd dropped the plate. Jagged shards of dish littered the stainless steel, teetering on the edge of the drain. The stress of day-to-day life was becoming too much to bear. The pressure had been steadily building for years, starting before they'd discovered the horrors committed against their son, continuing long after. A never-ending perpetual loop of life beating the shit out of the Murphy family.

Before they'd learned the truth of what happened to their son, Billy, there were warning signs that something wasn't quite right. There usually are, with such atrocities, but warning signs can be easy to miss when you aren't actively looking out for them. And why *would* you be on the lookout for signs that something horrific had happened? Because nobody *ever* thinks it can happen to their family until it does, at which point it's too late and everyone is left scratching their heads, asking themselves, *why us?*

But hindsight is 20/20. Their sweet Billy had suddenly become secretive and much less inclined to talk. He'd always been a motor mouth, so she blamed herself for not noticing right away when that had changed. But sometimes a shift in behavior like that isn't something you pick up on right away. The therapist had even told her as much. Told her it wasn't her fault. It wasn't *anyone's* fault other than the predator responsible for taking his innocence. Still, she couldn't help but feel guilty. It took a while, but eventually she noticed. But even then, Richard had told her it was 'probably just a phase.' Told her she 'worried too much.' For as much as Michelle blamed herself, she blamed her husband more. Motherly instincts told her something was wrong, but she allowed her concerns to be downplayed by her husband until she submitted to him, falling into that old, outdated family dynamic. The misogynistic *father knows best* stereotype.

If only she had only trusted her instincts instead of acquiescing to his misogyny, maybe they could have helped Billy sooner. Things continued without any further changes to the status quo, until suddenly, further behavioral issues arose. When that happened, she really beat the drum that something was wrong. Suddenly her little boy had become a lit fuse, and would lash out at the drop of a dime. He became further withdrawn. Always a B student, his grades suddenly dropped off a cliff and he no longer wanted to participate in the town's youth baseball program. Michelle thought that especially odd, Billy had always loved baseball but seemingly out of nowhere he loathed the sport, had even ripped the posters of his favorite players off his bedroom wall.

It soon came to light Billy's love for the game had soured because his coach was a monster disguised as a human, hiding in plain sight. A man who had seemed like the perfect role model for a young boy, dedicating his spare time to teaching local youth how to play America's favorite pastime.

A man who gained the trust of families before ruining their children's lives.

The monster was eventually apprehended and sentenced to prison, which should have ended the ordeal. But wounds like those inflicted on the Murphy family don't heal properly. The scabs begin to itch until someone picks them and rips the wound open again.

Richard Murphy ripped their scab off, bleeding their family dry.

The criminal justice system decided the monster had learned his lesson, granting him an early release on parole for good behavior. He'd taken a sex offender class and completed it without issue and somehow, they had decided that upon completion, magically, he had been reformed and was no longer a threat to society. Just like that, a few classes and some asshole in a suit and tie gets to decide a child predator's sickness healed, as if there wasn't something irreparably broken inside of a person who got off on children.

Michelle was too emotionally drained to feel anything, but the same couldn't be said for her husband. Richard was furious. He petitioned the parole board, sent letters to the state, spoke on local news channels trying to spark awareness in hopes that the decision would be overturned, but it made no difference. The predator was once again a free man.

So, Richard took matters into his own hands.

He hadn't been thinking about the ramifications of vigilante justice, hadn't considered the consequences of his actions. In his mind, he was simply out to correct a mistake made by the arm of the state.

Michelle couldn't say she disagreed with her husband that the bastard didn't deserve parole, but that was as far as their beliefs ran parallel. She didn't think it was any man's decision to take matters into their own hands. The monster had served his time, and whether he should have served more wasn't something that Michelle had any input on, so she let it go and focused on what was important. All that mattered to her was taking care of Billy.

Richard couldn't cast the past aside, though. He hadn't even bothered hiding his intentions, but Michelle thought her husband was speaking from a place of frustration. She thought it would blow over, like his anger had on so many prior occasions. And if it didn't? She'd talk him off a ledge. It wouldn't be the first time she'd have to calm her husband down, and it probably wouldn't be the last.

Despite her willingness to move on, there was still a part of her that wanted the predator to suffer, but in the end, Michelle was smart enough to know how that one would end. Billy needed his parents to be there for him, not avenge him. Taking action would do nothing but reopen the scars.

What Billy needed was stability from the two people whose job it was to provide such a thing.

What Richard Murphy decided on was revenge.

With the deed done, Billy was fatherless, and Michelle was forced to play the role of Mother, Father, and protector. But now, she wasn't so sure about playing protector. Shortly after her husband was convicted of first-degree murder, Michelle began to experience unease. A sense of impending dread that she couldn't seem to shake. She saw potential catastrophe everywhere. In her mind, simple pranks had nefarious intent. Ding dong ditches were attempts at home invasions. New cars driving through the neighborhood were relatives of the monster out for a little revenge of their own, or another diddler looking for a child to molest. Every man seeking a woman to assault and rape.

Michelle wanted to tell her husband what the stress was doing to her. How being alone, forced to carry the full weight of the consequences of everyone else's actions, along with her duty to Billy, made her feel paranoid, helpless to defend their son. She felt depressed and hopeless. At times, suicidal. But Richard hadn't called her since she'd gone off on him about his delay in telling her about the denial of his parole. At first, she thought he must be upset about the way she'd spoken to him, so she waited a few days to give him some space to clear his mind. But she soon got bored waiting and decided it was time for a face-to-face conversation. Michelle made the two-hour drive to Glenwood Correctional Institute, hoping to pay her husband a visit, only to be turned away at the door.

Inmates in segregation weren't allowed phone calls or visitation rights. The only contact she'd have with her husband for the next few weeks would be good old-fashioned snail mail. *What had gotten into him?* She'd never known Richard to be a violent man, but here he was, in prison for first degree murder and now for what she was told was a brutal assault on another inmate. Clearly, the man she'd married had changed, or had pulled the wool over her eyes, masking his true nature from her.

There were some days—more frequently as of late—where she regretted saying "I do."

Above her, she heard a laugh track from some sitcom Billy was watching. It brought her back to the present. She'd gotten lost in her thoughts, finally allowing herself to drown in the emotions she'd pent up for so long trying to be strong for Billy. With the onslaught of emotion behind her, she could focus on her son once more. He'd been let down too many times and she wouldn't fail him again. Even if it meant putting her own mental and physical well-being aside. Once Billy healed, she could heal.

She had to tell her husband how she was feeling. It would be good to get it out, to write the words down, bleed on the page. Michelle wrote her husband a letter. She withheld some of her feelings, still wanting to speak with him. Some things were better said, not written, allowing her to more easily express her feelings, making sure they weren't lost on the page. Hopefully, he'd call her when he was released from the disciplinary confinement unit. If not, she'd make the drive again.

Michelle's loneliness caused conflicting emotions to battle for dominance. She loathed him for what he'd forced his wife and son to endure, but she was tired of being alone, tired of feeling like everything was up to her. She missed having a partner to deal with life's curveballs.

CHAPTER 6

THE SOUND OF the food tray slot being yanked open startled Murphy awake. He couldn't remember falling asleep. His body was so exhausted he'd simply laid down for a moment and nature took its course. His body ached, stiff from sleeping on a shitty mattress. It screamed for proper nourishment and sleep, but how could he sleep when he had chanced upon such a fascinating discovery? The more he thought about the old, dirty paper, the more it wriggled its way into his brain like a parasite invading a host.

The officer that slammed the food slot open shoved a plastic tray across it. The tray slid across the slot, stopping at the edge of the slot where it hung, dangerously close to flipping over and spilling its contents across the floor. Murphy leapt off the bed, ignoring his body as it screamed at him and rushed across the cell to retrieve the tray before it toppled over. Not that the food was anything special, but he was starving and had no desire to play janitor in his cell so soon after waking. Besides, without a mop and cleaning chemicals to do the job properly, the scent would attract pests. Roaches and mice already ruled the night in the segregation unit. Murphy saw no need to further entice them. He didn't need any unwanted roommates.

He reached for the tray just as gravity worked its magic, snatching it from the air before it splattered. As he rescued the tray from catastrophe, the officer that had shoved it through the slot tossed a single piece of mail through the same opening. The edge of the envelope struck him in his bare chest, leaving a small dimple where it poked the flesh. Murphy placed the tray on the small writing table that was bolted to the wall and bent over to retrieve the letter. He stopped before picking it up. The handwriting on the envelope was that of his wife. Seeing an unexpected letter from her caused him to freeze. How long had it been since they'd had communication of any kind? Murphy didn't know. Off the top of his head, he couldn't recall how many days he'd been locked up in segregation.

Fuck, I forgot to write to her this entire time. I've been so wrapped up with the schematics. She probably thinks I'm dead. Once she realizes I'm not, she's gonna kill me herself.

Murphy slid the letter out of the envelope. There was no need to tear it open. The mail room officer did that to every single piece of mail prior to delivering it. It was the only way to ensure contraband didn't come in through the mail, and even then, drugs still found a way in all the time. He sniffed the letter. Usually Michelle sprayed it with perfume, but this one had no such accouterments. Unfolding the letter, he noticed the usual long, looping script of her handwriting was replaced with quick scratches of a pen. Some points in the letter were almost nothing more than a scribble. Something was clearly wrong; this letter had been written in haste or under duress. Murphy sat on his bunk and, as he took in the contents of the letter, his heart sank steadily into his chest.

Richard,

I just found out you're in disciplinary confinement. A fight, they tell me. At first, I was pissed because I thought you were blowing me because of our argument, I can't help the way I feel, my only regret is how I said it, but you'll need to excuse me for my lack of tact, I'm hanging on by a thread and you'll never understand just how bad you fucked us. I've tried to hold things together. I've been a faithful wife and caring mother, but I don't know how long I can do this. I'm lonely, and I don't feel safe. Everywhere I go, I see a pedophile waiting to snatch our son or a would-be attacker out for revenge because of what you did. Some family member who believes in an eye for an eye, much the same way you do. I've considered getting a gun, but what would be the point? I don't know how to use one; I don't want to kill anyone. I'm not a monster like you are. Even if I learned how to shoot, there's still a chance that I accidentally kill someone if I'm constantly jumping at shadows, assuming the worst of every stranger I come across. Every day is a struggle to take care of our son, make ends meet,

and keep my shit together. Why did you have to leave us? Why?
The more I'm here alone, dealing with the consequences of your
actions, the angrier I get. I don't know what to do anymore. Billy's
childhood was ripped away from him, then his father was ripped
away from him and I'm here by myself, trying to pick up the
pieces of the mess that everyone made of our lives. Call me. Please.
If you care about Billy, find a way to call me. Tell me how we fix
this. I don't know that we can.

Michelle

Murphy stared at the letter. So many thoughts swirled through his mind at once.

Hurt. Anger. Sadness.

He knew he fucked up bad when he killed the diddler, and as much as he'd plotted and planned to take that piece of shit's life, as much as he couldn't see a past where he *didn't* put a bullet in that piece of shit, he had never once considered the repercussions it would have on his family. Maybe he wasn't the illustrious father he had always thought he was. If he was even *half* that good, at some point he would have considered the impact his actions could have on his family. But he didn't. Instead, he had been consumed with revenge, neglecting to think about the ramifications on his family until he'd acted.

Murphy laid down on his bunk and tried to go back to sleep, tried to shut his brain off, but he couldn't. Not now, not after reading the heartbreaking letter from Michelle. Clearly, she was going through some shit, and it was his fault. He couldn't blame that piece of shit child molester for all of his family's troubles. The man had made his mark, that's for sure, but Murphy couldn't put all the blame on him. This one was all on him. *God have mercy on my soul.*

He lay on the bunk for hours, unable to think of a plan. What could he say? What could he do to make his wife feel better? She was right. For him, every day was groundhog day, but for his wife and kid, time had continued its breakneck pace. Bills didn't stop for them simply because Murphy was locked up. Doctor appointments, parent-teacher conferences, preventative maintenance on their vehicles—all routine things in daily life that continued to be necessary, and while he was here feeling sorry for himself, his wife was at home getting shit done. His own mind wouldn't give him a break, reminding him what a fucking idiot he was. Yes, a monster had upended the lives of the Murphy clan, but it was Richard Murphy himself who'd replaced their boogeyman by becoming a murdering monster himself, ensuring they would never recover from the damage done.

That was something he would have to live with for the rest of his life.

Eventually, exhaustion claimed victory over the restlessness of his mind and Murphy passed out.

***

When Murphy woke, he had no clue the time, or how long he'd been asleep for. The overhead lights in the hallway were off, as were the lights in his cell. The officer in the segregation control unit could turn the lights in each individual cell on and off, as well as the lights in the hallway with just a few button presses. Midnight was usually lights out for the unit, the only source of illumination from that point on were the "night lights" within each cell—nothing more than a dimmer version of the main light in the cell.

But not tonight. Even those were off, and Murphy could hardly see his own hand when held up in front of his face. It was possible the facility had lost power, but even then, there was a backup generator that ran on diesel and kicked in automatically in the event of an outage.

Something was wrong. Different. In a place like this, different was never good.

Heavy footfalls echoed down the hallway, reverberating off the walls, the sound amplified in the darkness. Drops of water dripped from the open-air shower next to his cell, pinging off the hard cement floor. The noise was torturous when trying to sleep, but here, in the dark, it set the small hairs on his neck on end. Murphy listened closely, trying to gauge where the footfalls were headed. It had to be late, or early, depending on how you looked at it. Even with all the lights off, if daylight hours there would be *some* ambient light coming through from the small crack at the top of the cell wall that constituted a window.

The footsteps grew louder before eventually stopping in front of Murphy's cell. He heard a voice whisper, "You've got 10 minutes," followed by another hushed voice, "Not gonna take that long."

The first voice, "Don't forget, you owe me."

"I don't owe you shit. Don't forget who runs this motherfucker. That badge doesn't mean shit around here. It would be a shame if little Jimmy didn't make it home from school, don't you think?"

"You fucking piece of shit. I did what you asked . . . "

"Relax fuck face, get me in that cell and nobody is gonna touch him."

Murphy had no clue what was going on, but he knew enough about Glenwood to know the number one way inmates got correction officers to do fucked up shit was to threaten their families. It sounded an awful lot to him, like someone was about to enter his cell and there was no way in hell anything good could come from that.

He hopped off his bunk, slipped on his shoes, and put his back against the wall, all within a few seconds. The cell door slid open as he raised his fists in the air, ready for anything. The cell door slammed shut as quickly as it had opened, the loud metal clang deafening in the otherwise silent area. Someone was here, but who? It was still too dark to see across the cell, even after his eyes had acclimated to the absence of light.

The sound of footsteps came once again as the intruder stalked forward. "Hey there, Richie. You mind if I call you Richie? You think you're a real bad mother fucker don't ya? You must have lost your goddamned mind if you think I'm gonna let you put one of my boys in the hospital the way you did and you just get to stay in segregation like a bitch and not get what's coming to you. You like being a bitch, Richie? Because I'm about to make you mine. From now on, your new name is Richelle, and you're my bitch, so bend over for daddy, Richelle."

Reese's words set Murphy over the edge. He charged at Reese, ready to pummel the life out of the racist, bigot piece of shit.

It was the last thing he should have done, all things considered, but Reese must have been smart enough to know what Murphy lacked in stature compared to him, he made up for in brains and cunning. Poking the bear, angering Murphy enough to throw caution to the wind, effectively removed Murphy's biggest advantage.

Murphy closed the gap with a few quick steps and launched himself through the air, throwing a superman punch at Reese. The bigger man easily sidestepped the blow and Murphy sailed past him, landing on the ground with a thud. He tucked his knees at the last second, using his momentum to roll forward, narrowly avoiding Reese's counter-attack—a well-aimed kick that would have otherwise connected with the back of Murphy's head.

Murphy stood up, reorienting himself, squaring up with Reese. Staying on the offensive, he made the first move again. But this time, he did so in a calculated manner, not letting his temper overwhelm him. Any mistake could cost him his life. A left-handed jab, a quick flick of a punch, connected with Reese's nose. Blood ran from Reese's nostril. The punch wasn't meant to do significant damage, but to distract Reese from defending against the straight right hand that followed the quick punch. And it would have worked, but Reese was an experienced fighter, he'd been to this rodeo far too many times to *not* expect punches in bunches, so after getting tagged with the first shot he immediately moved his head off-center, slipping the follow up and countering with a left hook to Murphy's ribs.

The counterpunch landed on the money.

The meaty slap of flesh on flesh echoed through the small cell and the impact of the blow forced the oxygen to rush out of Murphy's lungs with an *oof* sound. It felt like someone had hit him with a baseball bat. Murphy did his best to mask the pain, aside from having the wind knocked out of him. He didn't want Reese to know when he caught him good; the man was a predator and if he knew Murphy was a wounded animal, he'd surely go in for the kill.

Following Reese's clubbing blow to his ribs, Murphy dropped his right elbow slightly in order to better defend against another body shot, which is exactly what Reese followed up with. The blow, thrown to the same area, landed hard against Murphy's elbow, crushing the ulnar nerve against the humerus bone. A sharp, tingling pain shot through his arm. It was horrible luck that the punch landed in that exact spot, but he didn't have time to think about it. Instinctively, he shook his arm out, trying to shake off a pain that would burn bright for moments, but quickly dissipate.

Reese pounced on Murphy's momentary lapse of defense, throwing two more left hooks to the body that landed flush, right in the spot Murphy's arm had been moments before. He followed them up with an overhand right haymaker. It connected flush on Murphy's chin in a downward arc, driving him to the ground.

Reese jumped on Murphy, throwing punch after punch. Many of them didn't land clean because Murphy covered up like a turtle in his shell. But Reese was a large man and each blow from his swarming attack chipped away at Murphy's defense and stamina until he was too exhausted to even shell up any longer.

The attack ceased, but if Reese was winded, he gave no indication. His breathing was normal, no wheezing, as if he hadn't just rained hellfire down on his opponent. Murphy lay on the ground bleeding, blood bubbling from his mouth as the heavy, labored breaths passed through his lips. He tried to crawl away, but moving even a few inches was too much for his battered frame.

Reese grabbed Murphy by his long, dark brown hair, squeezing tight. He dragged Murphy to the corner of the cell and dropped him in front of the toilet. His fingers hovered momentarily at the waistband of his orange jumpsuit. "I told you I was going to make you my bitch, Richelle," Reese said as he dropped his pants and boxers to his ankles in one smooth motion. His long, thick cock stood at attention, and he licked his hand before sliding it up and down, helmet to shaft, lubricating his weapon with saliva and pre-cum.

With one hand stroking his member, Reese grabbed Murphy by the hair once more and hefted him over the toilet. Reese's upper chest lay across the bowl, the hard surface crushing Murphy's sternum while supporting his weight.

Murphy struggled to get free, but he'd been beaten too badly to muster any real resistance. He wouldn't beg for Reese's mercy. The man had none. He was a monster, and Murphy wouldn't give him the satisfaction of begging. Sick fucks like him fed on the power, it made them feel important. He'd take what Reese had as quietly as possible and, if luck was on his side, live to fight another day.

Reese pressed hard on the back of Murphy's head, keeping him in place as he thrust, ramming his huge cock—slick with saliva and pre-cum—into Murphy's virgin asshole. A hot poker of pain pierced his anus as his rectum tore. Reese pounded away and Murphy's entire body went rigid from the searing pain brought on from the beating his anus was taking. The pain and exhaustion he had felt moments before couldn't hold a candle to the pain, fear, and shame overwhelming him as he was violated.

Too battered to resist, Murphy tried escaping from the moment mentally, tried to force an out-of-body experience, but he couldn't bring his mind to his happy place—the water park with his son. It was his favorite memory and when times got tough, he reminisced, retreating into the memory. Not now though, Reese's animalistic grunts as he raped Murphy kept him anchored in the moment, rendering him unable to escape.

He no longer wanted to live to fight another day. He wished Reese would kill him, waited for death's cold embrace.

"You like that, you little bitch?" Reese grunted.

Behind them, the cell door slid open with a grinding metal sound that momentarily halted Reese's fevered thrusts. "Time's up, Reese," a hushed voice said.

"Gimme a second."

Reese started pumping away again, quicker this time, pounding Murphy's asshole until he abruptly stopped, gripping Murphy tightly while his ejaculate spurted out.

"I said, let's fucking go," the officer said as he took his baton in a double fisted grip, bringing it over Reese's head and lowering it to his throat. The officer yanked Reese backward, strangling him as he dragged the skinhead across the ground, pants at his ankles, heels sliding across the floor.

Reese tried to talk but the only sound that escaped was garbled nonsense, the baton crushing his trachea as he was extracted from the cell by the same man that had permitted him access earlier.

The cell door slammed shut once more, locking Murphy away in the dark with nothing but shame to keep him company. With nobody around to keep a facade for, Murphy broke. He wept on the floor until he passed out; the darkness dragging him into a restless sleep.

***

The days turned into weeks, and Murphy hardly knew of their passing. He stopped taking showers, refused any recreation time. Following the assault, Murphy didn't eat for the first few days, and he even held his bowel movements for fear that taking a shit would open up the wound, physically and mentally. He tried so hard to forget the pain, he couldn't risk experiencing it again. Eventually, he could hold it no longer. Nature took its course and Murphy was relieved to discover the bowel movement was pain free. Still, he only ate one meal a day. The sexual assault took something from him mentally and it took everything he had to not end it right then and there. Staff noticed the odd change in his behavior and placed him on suicide watch, but after a few days passed with no attempts at self-harm, they interviewed Murphy, clearing him of suicide watch. He never mentioned the assault. Rats in Glenwood Correctional Institute had a short life expectancy and although he had wished for death the night of the assault, he didn't want to bring further trouble to himself.

Footsteps echoed down the hall and Murphy went rigid. Blood coursed through his veins, and he clenched his fists. He was ready to fight, but when the footsteps stopped at his cell, it turned out to be an officer passing out dinner trays. A clear, plastic tray slid through the opening in the middle of his door and the officer spoke. "Time's up buddy. You're going back to population tomorrow. Hope you had a good time," he said, chuckling to himself and continuing down the line of cells. Murphy's blood boiled. *Was that the piece of shit who let Reese in?* It didn't matter. He couldn't do anything about it, anyway. Better to not know the truth because he might do something he'd regret later on.

He stood up, making his way to the cell door and grabbed the tray from the slot, lifting the lid as he brought it to the small desk welded to the wall. Spicy chicken tenders on the menu tonight. The smell stung his nostrils, and his stomach growled. He'd eat this meal, although he'd regret it. Murphy could never turn down spicy foods, despite the acid reflux he was guaranteed to experience later, and the way it would burn coming out the other end after his body digested it. Thank God for the cartons of milk they pass out with dinner. He'd need it to tame the acidic burn that would be sure wreak havoc on his esophagus. Murphy devoured the entire tray in minutes and placed it back in the slot where it would sit until the inmate working the area collected the trays.

Murphy lay back down on the bunk and closed his eyes, willing sleep to come. Better to sleep the days away than live like an animal locked in a cage.

***

The squeaking wheels of the library cart echoed through the dark corridor, waking Murphy from his sleep. He sat upright, unaware of how much time had passed. It had to be late; the nightlights were on. *Why would the library cart be making rounds now?* It made little sense. The cart always made its rounds during the morning shift. They'd already eaten dinner, and all inmates returned to their cells by 8:30 each night.

Whether or not it made sense didn't change the fact. It *was* the library cart, and that for some reason it was stopped right in front of his cell.

The inmate pushing the cart stepped in front of the cart, placing his body right against the door. A shit-eating grin smeared across his face. Murphy didn't recognize the inmate. Not only could he not place a name to the face, but he was positive he'd never seen the man prior to this moment. The inmate was tall, slightly chubby, and had pale skin spotted with freckles. The longer Murphy observed him, the more the man's complexion didn't seem just pale, but looked flat out unhealthy, like he hadn't seen the sun in decades. A generous mop of curly orange hair adorned his head. It made Murphy immediately think of the comedian, Carrot Top. The name tag stitched across Carrot Top's chest read *O'Rourke*.

Now, Murphy was positive he didn't know the man. Realistically it was impossible for Murphy to know every inmate housed in the facility, but he knew most of them and O'Rourke looked so sickly he was sure he'd have remembered meeting the man. And that name, so stereotypically Irish, he'd have remembered hearing it around. He supposed O'Rourke could be a new commit, but if that *were* the case, how had he gotten a cushy job like inmate librarian so soon? A job like that was reserved for men doing big time who'd proven over the course of their sentence that they could be trusted as much as staff could trust an inmate, at least. With a position like librarian, it would be far too easy to pass contraband within books and hide them away within the shelves of the library—a place the officers rarely went, never mind searched.

"Gonna need that reading material back now," said O'Rourke.

"I'm not finished with the book, though."

O'Rourke smiled again. "I didn't say anything about a book. I said that reading material."

Murphy's blood ran cold. *He couldn't be talking about the plans, could he?*

Feigning ignorance, Murphy said, "All I've got is this one book. I've had it most of the time I've been in here. I've been reading slowly, as of late."

"Don't play with me, Murphy. I know everything that goes on here. I'm the librarian of this place. I deal with nothing but knowledge. As I said, it's time to return your reading material," O'Rourke said, waving a familiar slip of paper in front of Murphy's cell door.

"What the fuck? How did you . . . " Murphy picked the book up and flipped through the pages. The map was gone, but how? He flipped the book on its side, shaking it so the pages flapped, expecting the map to fall out.

No such luck. It had vanished.

Murphy crossed the cell, pressing against the door. "How did you get that?" he hissed.

"Like I said, kid, you're done with it. Your time is up. It goes back in the cart."

"Where did it come from?"

"It came from here. Things have a funny way of disappearing and turning up around here. This is a very, very old place. The original building stood for hundreds of years before they torched it in the riot. Imagine, if you will, the amount of pain, suffering, despair, and death that happens in a place such as this over the span of the facility's lifetime. By default, prisons are terrible places, and when you put enough bad in one spot, it becomes a magnet for evil. If that map found you, there's a reason for it, and you've got to think that maybe whatever set you on the path to finding it didn't do it for altruistic reasons. It can take you where you need to go, yes, but why would it *want* you to get there? What's the toll on a route paved in blood?" O'Rourke turned around and began pushing the cart away.

Murphy pounded his fist against the cell door. O'Rourke was talking in riddles. What the fuck was this guy's deal?

"Listen, man, I don't need a damn map out of this place. I'm not going anywhere until they let me out. So why the cryptic shit? I don't *need* to go anywhere. What the fuck does that even mean?"

O'Rourke spun around and grabbed the bars, pressing his face into them. He was now eye to eye with Murphy.

Murphy jumped back, his heart jack hammered in his chest, and he cried out. O'Rourke's features had undertaken a macabre transformation. Half of his skull was caved in, brain exposed. Maggots wriggled along the chasm in his skull, feasting on dead, rotting brain matter. A few of them fell from their perch, plopping onto the food tray flap of his cell. The hideous creature that had been O'Rourke was missing its left eye. Where the eye should have been was an empty socket filled with more insects—millipedes, beetles, cockroaches. His skin still screamed of pallor mortis, but was now covered with deep purple bruises. One side of his mouth was sliced open from the corner of the lips to the jaw hinge, exposing the few decaying teeth left in the corpse's mouth. Strands of connective tissue seemed to be the only thing holding the jaw in place.

Through its mangled face, O'Rourke spoke in a harsh, whispered rattle, "It means exactly what it fucking sounds like, Murphy. When they rebuilt this place over the ruins of the old facility, the *evil* didn't just go away. The warden was a manifestation of that evil, of darkness. When the warden's physical vessel was destroyed in the riots, the few remaining inmates and officers that knew what was really going on thought they had stopped the darkness. But they stopped nothing. Evil doesn't die. It can't die. It can dissipate, it can move on, you can even take away its strength, but you can't kill it and its strength always comes back, eventually. What they did all those years ago was cap a pipe. Eventually the pressure will build up and the pipe will burst, Glenwood will be a much worse place once that happens. Evil is a funny thing. It latches on to people, on to things. Have you ever heard the stories of the Maniac of D Block, correctional officer Lee Harris? He was a real son of a bitch. A no good piece of shit correction officer. He'd earned that distinction even before the darkness arrived here in the form of the warden. Even the nickname, *The Maniac*, was a moniker he'd earned before evil had truly arrived. The Maniac had a penchant for beating the shit out of inmates. He'd even killed a few and gotten away with it. And when the darkness here grew, it fed on him, and he fed on it until they both grew stronger. What people don't know about the riot is The Maniac was responsible for more deaths, inmate and officer alike, than any other person who'd had the misfortune of being at Glenwood Correctional Institute when shit popped off. He'd used the riot as his opportunity to kill, unchecked. When the building went up in flames and crumbled around him, Lee was presumed dead."

O'Rourke stopped talking, turned around and pushed the cart down the hall, leaving Murphy to digest what O'Rourke had told him.

Murphy called out, "What do you mean, presumed dead? They never recovered a body?" He thought about what O'Rourke said. *Evil doesn't die.*

The walking corpse, O'Rourke, was gone. Vanished without answering Murphy's question.

EXPIRATION OF SENTENCE

His head spun. He felt nauseous. Clearly, he'd spent too much time locked in this cell and was losing his mind. That had to be it. What other explanation could there be? He'd been locked up, stuck in his own head, and now he'd become a statistic. Another number for the studies on inmate mental health. One more person to add to the list of names lawmakers would use as ammunition in their pushes to get rid of disciplinary confinement all together. Murphy didn't think that was going to happen. He'd been in prison long enough to know that there were just some men who couldn't be around other people. They were a danger to themselves, and a danger to others. But sitting here in the dark, talking to dead men? Maybe they had a point. Maybe segregation really did make men go crazy. Either that, or he was having one hell of a nightmare.

He lay back on his bunk, scared shitless. There would be no sleep the rest of the night.

CHAPTER 7

THE SUN ROSE high in the sky the next day and Murphy was awake to watch the sliver of light through his tiny window, eyes burning with fatigue. After his encounter in the middle of the night, he'd been unable to sleep, try as he might. Every time his eyelids grew so heavy, he couldn't keep them open, visions of O'Rourke flashed before his eyes. His mind conjured images of a correction officer gone mad with power, brutally murdered in a riot, yet somehow the body gone missing. The viciousness of the assault he pictured was likely a consequence of the man's own malicious conduct. Something about that story bugged Murphy. He couldn't be sure what he'd seen. He'd spent too much time locked away in segregation to be confident it wasn't a hallucination. But the idea of evil lurking within Glenwood sent shivers up his spine that were difficult to ignore.

None of it added up. The appearance of O'Rourke, for one, meant Murphy was probably certifiable. And this Lee Harris guy, The Maniac, how was it possible they never discovered his body? Even if the faculty burned to the ground, shouldn't there have been *some* sort of remains? Bones? Clothing? Hell, dental fillings?

Murphy should have been excited, knowing he was about to be released to general population. Instead, he was depressed, exhausted, and terrified. He couldn't close his eyes or his mind, but who could blame him? When you were surrounded by fences, razor wire, and massive steel doors, even the most beautiful day was dreary. You woke up each morning and, if you were smart, attempted to make the most of a shitty situation. But you could only polish a turd so much. You were still locked up. And if that weren't bad enough, Murphy had been isolated for weeks with almost no human contact.

He was a caged animal in the land of the free.

EXPIRATION OF SENTENCE

It was something Murphy thought about often.

In a book somewhere in the prison's library, Murphy had read some crazy statistics that had opened his eyes to the country's criminal justice system. America, the country with the most total number of inmates, along with the highest incarceration rate in the world. Roughly twenty-five percent of all incarcerated inmates worldwide were housed in the United States. *Experts* could argue until they were blue in the face about the *how's* and the *why's*, but in the end, it didn't matter.

In life, rarely do things *really* matter. Stats were stats. For as many ACLU types as there were fighting for better conditions and policies in America's criminal justice system, the hard truth was that most people simply didn't give a shit how people locked up lived. *It's prison. Nobody forced you to commit a crime* was the prevailing attitude. But as bad as Glenwood Correctional Institute was, it was common knowledge it had been even worse in the months and years before the riot that ended in the destruction of the entire facility. And Murphy knew as bad things were at Glenwood, there were prisons across the country far worse.

Objectively speaking, Murphy could understand why the vast majority of American citizens didn't give a shit what went down in prisons, how inmates were treated. Why would anyone care about the living conditions of murderers and rapists? If he were honest, some amenities they received would probably shock the average person. Tablets with email and FaceTime access, video game consoles, cable television. Hell, that they were wards of the state meant that many inmates received lifesaving medications and procedures that they simply wouldn't have received had they not been incarcerated. Medications, equipment, and procedures that plenty of law-abiding citizens simply didn't have access to, either. Murphy understood why that would upset people. But was that a prison problem? Or maybe Americans had simply put up with being raped by the medical industry with no help from the government for far too long and accepted that as the standard.

Whether the inmates deserved that level of care, Murphy couldn't say for sure. Sometimes he felt they should have access, and other times where he felt most of the guys in Glenwood deserved every shitty thing that came their way. It was a tough call to make after meeting some of the men here. Men who made the crimes Reese committed seem like nothing more than detention worthy stunts. Men who had committed crimes so despicable, calling them atrocities was an understatement. The type of shit that would make a person lose hope in humanity. Sick things that Murphy thought would cause even the most avid true crime fan to pause.

As far as Murphy was concerned, *those* guys deserved a bullet, not a PlayStation, three warm meals, and access to life saving healthcare.

With his mind preoccupied with O'Rourke, The Maniac, and the United States criminal justice system, Murphy forgot to eat his breakfast. It sat on the edge of the tray slot, untouched, until it was taken away. A few hours after the tray was removed and the sun was at its peak in the sky, they finally released Murphy back to the general population. They'd even sent him back to the same housing unit he'd been in prior to the fight that had landed him in segregation.

Normally Murphy would have considered that a good thing, but Reese lived in the same unit. Now more than ever, each day he was trapped in Glenwood was another day Reese or one of his goons might make an attempt on his life. He'd need to be extra vigilant and do his best to not provoke the skinheads. Living in the same unit would not make that a straightforward task. He tried to look on the bright side. At least being housed in the same unit as Reese would make it easier to monitor the man. Maybe keeping his enemy close would allow him to be better prepared for the inevitable.

Murphy walked up the pathway in the yard all the way back to the housing unit with all his belongings packed into the cart he was pushing. The trek was more difficult than Murphy would have thought, the wheel on the cart broken and spinning sideways.

When he arrived, he was instantly disappointed. The officer had given him his new cell assignment, and it disheartened him to learn that Lewis had a new cellmate. He wasn't surprised. In fact, he'd expected it. With the new commits to Glenwood every day, the population was rapidly expanding, and it was almost for a single occupant to remain in the cell with no roommate for more than a few days. That luxury was reserved for inmates with mental or physical health issues that made having a roommate either improbable, or impossible. Even Reese—a man with half the staff in his back pocket—was forced to double bunk with someone.

EXPIRATION OF SENTENCE

Still, a part of him had hoped that Lewis would have somehow convinced the block officer to hold a bunk for him until they released him back to general population.

Entering his new cell, Murphy quickly realized he'd pulled the short straw. The first thing he noticed was the putrid funk permeating the air. The cell stunk like absolute shit, the funk so overpowering it made him wonder if his new cell mate took showers. Hopefully, the man wasn't one of the crazies that refused to bathe. There were a few guys like that around Glenwood. Men so disgusting, and so averse to personal hygiene that staff were forced to physically place them in a shower for their own health, and for the health of the inmates forced to house with them. The cell was practically barren aside from his cellmates' few belongings—food scraps and dirty laundry. The nasty fucker had even left a fefe—a homemade flesh-light—lying on the floor in the middle of the cell. As for the slob the mess belonged to, he wasn't in the cell. Murphy gave the housing unit a cursory look, scanning for a man who looked trashy enough to live in the filth Murphy was standing in. He didn't see anyone that fit the bill.

A large, red cockroach skittered across Murphy's beat up Timberland work boot. He kicked the roach out of the cell, careful to scoot his foot so he didn't crush the nasty fucker. He shivered. Nothing grossed him out more than the vermin and pests that infested the prison. It was impossible to avoid them no matter what lengths you went to to keep your cell tidy, but a roommate like the nasty bastard he was stuck living with attracted them like flies to shit.

Murphy unpacked his belongings and, just as he finished making his bunk, a haggard, dirty man entered the cell. He stood there watching, unnoticed, as Murphy did his best to organize his belongings. After a few moments of Murphy not noticing the man behind him, the slob coughed, trying to get Murphy's attention. Murphy turned around and locked eyes with the nasty little fucker. Red splotches and dry, flaky pieces of dead skin littered the man's face. He smiled a mostly toothless grin. Murphy could practically see stink lines straight from an illustration wafting out of the man's sewer hole of a mouth. The walking Irish Spring advertisement held out a dirty, grimy hand—a rather disgusting greeting. There was no way in hell Murphy was touching that man's hand. Scabies weren't on his list of things to experience in prison.

Far from a match made in heaven, this living situation simply would not work. The man was every disease wrapped up in a human shell and something needed to change ASAP, and he was pretty sure it wouldn't be the man's personal hygiene. There were only a few ways this scenario could play out going forward. Best-case scenario, he'd find a new cellmate, hopefully Lewis. If that wasn't an option, he'd strongly suggest to his soup sandwich of a roommate that it would be in his best interest to practice good hygiene. Brushing his teeth, wiping his ass. The basics. If the implied threat of serious bodily injury wasn't enough to convince the slob to shower more often than Murphy would simply beat the shit out of him, do another stint in the box, and when he was released to general population again, he'd be assigned to a new, hopefully more desirable cell.

Murphy looked around the cell block once more. He hadn't seen Lewis since he reported back to the unit and was excited to check in with his friend to see how things were going. Truth be told, he was a bit bummed out that Lewis hadn't stopped by the check in with him. Maybe he was busy at a class or something. After looking around for a bit, Murphy eventually spotted Lewis in the back corner of the housing unit. He was standing next to the phone sipping a plastic cup filled with shitty mix and stir coffee.

Murphy approached Lewis, a grin splitting his face from ear to ear, arms spread in the universal gesture of a hug. Lewis looked him dead in the eyes and said nothing. He didn't return the smile, didn't reciprocate the gesture. Murphy's shoulders slumped; his mood soured at Lewis' lack of excitement.

Lewis nodded his head but broke Murphy's gaze. "What's up?" he said, after it was clear the reunion was going to be an awkward one.

"What's up? That's all you've got to say? I've been locked in a cage for all this time, and you can't even pretend like you're happy to see me. What's up with *you?*"

"Nothing's up with me, man. I'm good, I just don't want to be bothered is all."

Murphy wasn't buying it. Lewis was acting weird. They'd been close since the first week Murphy arrived at Glenwood. It wasn't like his friend to brush him off the way he had. Wasn't like the man to be *bothered* by his closest friend's presence.

"I was hoping you'd have gotten one of the officers to get me back in the cell with you. I don't have a problem with a top bunk, you know that," Murphy said. "Now, I'm stuck with that gross motherfucker, and not for nothing, but you're acting like you don't even know me. What's the fuckin' deal, man?"

Lewis scratched his head before answering, seemed to think a bit too long about how he wanted to respond. "Yeah, about that. I was thinking maybe I shouldn't fuck with you anymore. Reese is right, you should just keep away from me. Those skinheads, racist fucks don't like me, and I know they're giving you shit about it."

Murphy's face turned red; his ears warmed with shame. Did Lewis know about what happened in segregation? Did Reese tell everyone? Word traveled quick behind bars, but had it spread that quickly?

Lewis continued speaking, made no indication whether or not he knew about the assault. "Reese isn't happy about what you did to his boy," Lewis said. "You know people talk. I heard what happened when you were in the box. You look healed up. I don't want to cause more problems for you, man, that's all. I don't want to give Reese another reason to target you after what you did to his boy."

So, there it was. Lewis knew about the beating. Did he know about the rape, too?

"I get what you're saying, and I appreciate it, but I'm not gonna let those dickheads control my life. Reese and his dogs can get their faces fucked." Murphy said with a stone-faced expression.

"If you say so, man, but don't get mad at me when they come looking for you. Those white boys don't like any of their own to talk to the rest of us."

"I'm not one of them. That's my word."

"I know. You're good people, Murphy. That's why I wanted to keep some space. I know where this goes from here."

"Me too. It is what it is. I'll deal with it when the time comes. So, what do you say? Are we good?"

This time Lewis opened his arms, the only response necessary. They embraced.

"So, what was it like doing that much time? How the fuck did you *not* go crazy in there?" Lewis asked.

Murphy laughed. "Who said I didn't? You ain't gonna believe this shit man, I almost don't believe it myself. Maybe I snapped a bit. Check this shit out," Murphy said.

He motioned for Lewis to follow, and as the two men paced back and forth through the block, Murphy recounted the strange tale. How he'd found building plans tucked away in a book, and how an inmate named O'Rourke that he'd never met before just showed up one day with the library cart and somehow the plans were gone from his cell and reappeared in the man's possession. He even told Lewis the story O'Rourke had told him about the old prison, The Maniac of D Block, Lee Harris, and how O'Rourke had suddenly turned into a festering corpse.

When the story was over, Lewis seemed to have taken the whole thing in stride.

"As bat shit crazy as it sounds, I believe you. I've seen enough creepy shit go down around this motherfucker to *know* this place is haunted. And why wouldn't it be? How many people have died here over the years? Murders, suicides, natural causes. Nah, you couldn't convince me it's *not* haunted. Truth be told, I've met both O'Rourke and Harris. Not recently, of course, that was decades ago. I was maybe eighteen at the time. But you described O'Rourke how I remember him, before the whole being dead thing, and anyone who'd ever met Harris would remember The Maniac of D Block until the day they died. Hell, I met him before he started doing the *real* fucked up shit he eventually got a rep for, and even back then he was a real son of a bitch. So yeah, it's nuts, but I believe you. And if "evil" was gonna latch on to something, or someone around Glenwood, The Maniac is about as perfect a candidate as you're ever gonna find."

"That's it? Just like that? You don't want proof; you don't want an explanation? You just believe me?"

"Yeah. I don't need any proof. The fact you know about O'Rourke and Harris is pretty fucking telling. Like I said, way too many people have died here, and way too much bad shit happened in this facility, and on the grounds for it to be anything *but* haunted."

"Right, but you're not even a little put off about some psychotic correctional officer somehow fusing with some sort of evil that had been feeding on everything bad that happened here in the old building? It sounds like some shit out of a Bentley Little novel."

"Man, pull your head out of your ass. Of course, I'm put off by that shit. I'm scared to death of some shit like that. But you know what? If that motherfucker has been stuck in the basement this whole time, or wherever the fuck he's at, that means he's not near me, and that's enough to let me fall asleep at night. I'm gonna sit right here in this block, eat my three meals, jerk off to the penthouse forums books I bought, and count the days until I get up out of this bitch again. And when I'm out? I ain't ever coming back, that's for damn sure."

Murphy laughed. "How many times have you said that before?"

Lewis punched Murphy on the shoulder. "Fuck off, man, I mean it this time. Fifty is too old to be fucking around with all these young kids in here. And last time I said it, I didn't have your crazy ass telling me these fucked up stories."

"Shit man, you've got that old man strength, huh?" Murphy rubbed his shoulder. "So, you're really gonna make me live with that smelly ass bum, huh?"

"I'll consider asking the officer if he can move us. Maybe I'll wait until tomorrow, though. I wanna make you really appreciate how clean I keep my area."

"You're a real piece of work, you know that, right?"

The intercom sounded, interrupting their conversation. *All inmates return to your cells. It is count time. All inmates return to your cells and stand for the count.*

"Shit, I didn't realize the time flew by that quick. I'll see you in a few hours," Murphy said.

"Alright. Don't go beating anyone up now. Especially not that fucking gremlin you're living with. It isn't his fault his ass stinks."

"Fuck you, man. If it's not his fault he doesn't wipe his ass, who's fault is it?"

Lewis laughed as he walked into his cell, closing the door behind him. Murphy returned to his own cell, mentally steeling himself for the stench of the old bastard they forced him to room with. Hopefully, he'd be moved in with Lewis by the end of the night. He knew his friend would come through.

CHAPTER 8

Richard,

I've tried my best to keep everything together while you've been locked up, despite the fact that I have barely been able to hold myself together. I know that what you did, you did out of love for our son. But what you did was wrong and has caused further irreversible damage to our family. Not only was his innocence taken by a monster, but his father was taken from him by that same monster. He's constantly bullied at school. The kids all call him all sorts of nasty names. They tease him about the horrific trauma he was forced to go through. We all know children can be cruel, but that is beyond fucked. Maybe that's why he tried to kill himself last week. Imagine going to school every day when all the other students know what happened to you. I can see why he might have felt like it was his only option. But you didn't know that had happened, did you? Because once again I haven't gotten phone calls or letters from you. Are you in disciplinary confinement again? And if not, why are you avoiding me? Do you have a side chick? I'm starting to think you might be looking for another young, gullible girl dumb enough to believe what you tell her. When I came to visit you that day, they turned me away because you were in segregation. The officer that gave me the bad news also told me you guys have been known to do that when you're locked up. Play the field with young women with low self-esteem. Is that it? You have your wife at home, holding it down, and a little side bitch that talks dirty to you? Sends you nasty letters and naughty pictures? That's cheating, too, you asshole. It's called emotional cheating. You don't have to stick your little pecker in someone to cheat. You men and your games, you try to play us like chessboards, and now the more I think about it, the *more I believe you've got another woman lined up to give you some ass on the side when you get out, because nothing else about your behavior makes sense to me.*

So, what's new with your wife and son? Well, for starters I can't even afford the rent anymore now that the savings is dried up. Mr. Vega told me he wouldn't start the eviction process, and I could pay the back rent, along with next month's rent, if I sucked his cock. I told him he can suck MY cock and go ahead and start the process. There's no need for that though, because I won't be here by the time it goes to court, and neither will your son. We're leaving. We're going to find a place somewhere far away and get a fresh start. I don't feel this is a safe place to raise my son anymore, and frankly, I want to start a life for myself and my son that doesn't include you, because I don't think you're safe to be around him, either. Consider us the family you left behind. Don't write. Don't call. We don't want to hear from you.

Michelle.

Murphy screamed. He threw the letter to the floor, picked it up, and read it again. And again. And again.

He couldn't believe the words scrawled across the page. Tears streaming down his cheeks, he crumpled it into a ball and threw it in the corner of the cell. It was a sick joke; it had to be. Someone else had written the letter, a fucked-up prank. Reese. Reese was fucking with him.

He picked the crumpled letter up, unfolded it, and read it once more. Who was he fooling? Reese hadn't pranked him. The handwriting was clearly that of his wife. The words were still there; he hadn't imagined them. Daggers of ink drawing blood as if made from the sharpest metal. His wife had really taken his son and left. When did they leave? He picked up the envelope and checked the date on the post office stamp. It had been postmarked a week ago. They could be anywhere by now. Michelle never mentioned a destination. And why would she? She had made it clear in the letter that they were through, and he wasn't welcome in their lives anymore. But she couldn't do that, could she?

There had to be laws against it. Even if he were incarcerated, there had to be some kind of laws protecting his parental rights. Was this a kidnapping? Maybe, but how was he supposed to get ahold of an attorney on such short notice? With his trial long over, he no longer had one on retainer. There hadn't been a need for it. He'd even thrown the guy's phone number away, not expecting to have use of him again. He could send the attorney a letter through snail mail, but that would take forever, and even if he could get ahold of him, he didn't have the funds available to put him back on retainer.

Off the top of his head, the only thing he could think to do was put in a request form to make an appointment with one of the prison's counselors and hope they could help. If he were lucky, a supervising lieutenant could get him in with a counselor sooner, but if not, it could be another week before he spoke to someone. With a week having already slipped by before he'd received the letter, tracking her would prove difficult, but if he had to wait *another* week? He may never see his son again.

The only limitation Michelle had was money. Did she have enough saved up to travel far? In her letter, she had mentioned not having money to pay the rent, but that didn't mean she hadn't set aside emergency cash for a situation like this. Murphy thought that might be the case, because this didn't seem like a spur-of-the-moment decision, and he knew his wife wasn't an impulsive woman. No, she had to have been plotting this, or at the very least if she didn't have an entire plan ready to go, she had the bones of one in place. Something to get her started that would allow her to hammer out the details as things progressed.

His head swam. Suddenly he was sweating bullets. The urge to vomit was difficult to suppress. Jack hammering behind his ribcage, his heart threatened to burst from within. His chest felt heavy and had tightened up so much he gasped for air, hyperventilating. Murphy dropped to the floor, flat on his ass with his head between his legs, arms resting on his knees. Was he dying? The dam burst and tears streamed from his eyes. He tried to keep the display of emotion in check, but failed. He knew if he were to be caught crying in his cell, it would make him ripe for the picking. Being caught in such an emotionally compromised state would see him branded a bitch, and from that point, it was only a matter of time before the violent, sexual predators of Glenwood paid him a visit. There were plenty of them around, guys who'd been locked up for so long. All they saw was a hole to fuck. If you happened to be the owner of that hole, you could either play ball or you were in for the fight of your life.

EXPIRATION OF SENTENCE

It had happened to him once already. If this got out, too, he was fucked.

A fat, bald, tattooed man had been standing outside of Murphy's cell, watching as he lost control. He observed in silence, and as Murphy snapped out of it, he cracked the cell door open and tossed a small object into the cell. The item hit Murphy in the head, snapping him back to reality, anchoring him in the present. Surprised, he scanned the floor. At first, nothing seemed to jump out at him, but then his eyes settled on a white object on the floor. Something that hadn't been in his cell a few moments ago.

Murphy knew what it was the moment his eyes crawled over it

A mark. Small tokens, carved in the shape of a swastika from a Domino game piece.

Reese used them to place a hit on his enemies, or people who'd crossed someone with enough money to pay Reese and his men to do the dirty work.

When delivered a mark, the receiving individual had two options: Carry out the hit, or find your name attached to the next mark. One week to complete the task, no excuses.

"Darius Lewis," said the man known to the inmates of Glenwood as Bic—a name he'd earned when one of the officers who'd taken him out on a hospital trip discovered a lighter in Bic's asshole when returning from the furlough.

"No," Murphy whispered, but Bic hadn't heard, or didn't care. Either way, it didn't matter. Marks were final.

Murphy couldn't kill Lewis, didn't have it in him. Even in a place like this, he still had honor. Friendship meant something to him and he wouldn't sway, even with his life in the balance. In a facility where Darwinism was a way of life, the friendship that had made him stronger also put his life at risk. The fact that Lewis had been chosen as the mark and Murphy tasked to complete the deed was no coincidence. It had to be payback; it was the only thing that made sense.

Payback for befriending a black man rather than siding with the skinheads. Payback for beating the shit out of one of Reese's lapdogs. Reese had to know that Murphy wouldn't kill his friend. No, this was simply a letter of intent. A way for Reese to let Murphy know his transgressions hadn't been forgotten and his days were numbered. He could fight back, maybe even successfully defend himself and live to fight another day. But locked behind bars, it didn't matter if he stopped an attempt on his life, because the attempts on his life would never stop.

Eventually, the reaper would come for him.

There had to be another way. But what? He had to think, come up with a plan. Bartering wouldn't work, Reese had unimpeded access to just about anything he wanted and there wasn't a damn thing on this planet that Murphy could get into the prison that Reese himself wouldn't be able to. Food, drugs, sex, you name it.

Things just kept getting worse. How was he supposed to get Reese off his ass *and* stop his wife from leaving with his son? He wasn't sure he could do either of those things, never mind *both*.

Think, Murphy, think.

The plans!

That was it. Murphy had studied the plans long enough they burned into his brain, and while he couldn't stop Reese from coming after him, escaping Glenwood meant escaping Reese. *And* if he was lucky, he could find a way to stop Michelle from taking his son. By no means did being rid of Glenwood mean that he'd be able to track his wife down or stop her from calling the cops even if he did, but it was a foot in the door. If he could find her, maybe he could appeal to her senses.

She wanted an escape from her current life. Maybe they could escape the country as a family. Flee to somewhere where nobody knew their names. Where nobody would be searching for them. Murphy remembered a story about a woman accused of killing a cyclist who'd fled to Costa Rica and, for a while, had gone undetected. Murphy wasn't anywhere near as high profile as that case. Maybe they could remain hidden and start over again as a family.

But that was something to think about later. First things first. He needed to get the fuck out of prison.

Murphy knew he would need to speak to Lewis about this, get him on board. Now that they were rooming together, it would be impossible to accomplish without involving Lewis. It's not like his friend could claim ignorance to a tunnel in his cell once a staff member discovered Murphy missing. And on a selfish but practical note, Lewis held a job in Glenwood's industrial work area, meaning he had access to tools and equipment that would make tunneling through the floor far easier than doing the work with a spoon or some other primitive object.

EXPIRATION OF SENTENCE

Murphy sighed; he didn't like his options. If any of the *many* moving parts of the plan forming in his mind failed to come together, he was as good as dead.

CHAPTER 9

ALL WEEK, everything went smoothly and according to plan, though the act of tunneling through a secure facility like Glenwood was both physically taxing, and time consuming. Their secret project was coming down to the wire. Luckily, Lewis had agreed to become a co-conspirator alongside Murphy, because without his help, it would have been impossible to do in a week. Even with his help, they'd barely make it. Murphy never really doubted his friend would leave him hanging, and there were two main reasons. First, Lewis was a ride or die friend and even when their friendship had seemed as if it had evaporated, it had only been because Lewis was trying to keep Murphy out of Reese's crosshairs. Second, if Lewis refused to help, both men were as good as dead. Better to take the risk and fail than to do nothing and be murdered. At least if they were unsuccessful, they'd most certainly be moved to a new, higher security facility, one where Reese's influence held no weight.

Lewis' contributions to the cause were invaluable. His job in the industries department, and his reputation for being a good, trustworthy inmate worker, meant that not only did he have access to tools which could aid the escape, but he generally avoided suspicion of staff members. They were simply too busy, and too complacent to notice a few missing items, and by the time that someone eventually *did* do the job correctly and conduct a proper visual inventory, Murphy and Lewis should be long gone.

The two men had worked tirelessly since the first evening they discussed the plan, scraping away at the cement around the toilet day and night, only stopping at the various times of the day they knew an officer would walk around. For staff, complacency kills, but for inmates, it made their lives a whole hell of a lot easier.

All of this hard work could be destroyed in an instant. It would only take a simple cell search to discover what the two had been up to. But luckily for them, this was another area where the department's staffing crisis played into their hands. It had been years since the staff members of Glenwood had conducted a detailed search of an entire housing unit. The act of searching one such unit was both time and labor intensive and required a full complement of staff. A luxury that Glenwood, like most law enforcement agencies in America, no longer had. These days, the staff were so burnt out from mandatory overtime you were more likely to catch them sleeping on the job than searching a cell. Murphy knew as long as they kept their noses clean and did nothing to draw unnecessary attention to themselves, the chances of someone discovering their little project were as likely as Jesus Christ appearing in the middle of the weight pit in the yard.

Still, one couldn't be too careful, so without divulging what they were up to, they paid a few of the more trustworthy inmates to keep an eye out and give warning if any staff or inmates were getting too close for comfort.

Day six and the coast remained clear.

On the eve before their deadline, the two men finally scraped through the last bit of concrete holding the toilet in place.

They tossed their tools aside and sat there for a moment, neither man ready to break the silence, worried that speaking about it would jinx the operation. Everything hinged on what Murphy had seen on the map. If his interpretation of the plans in relation to the current facility were correct, after removing the large, steel toilet housing, they should be able to drop into what had been bowels of the old facility. If Murphy was wrong, and the plans had simply been the hallucinations of a man's mind stretched to the breaking point, or if the basement were otherwise inaccessible from where they'd dug the tunnel, they were dead men walking.

As if on cue, Murphy and Lewis stood up and took position on each side of the toilet. They looked each other in the eye and nodded when ready, lifting the toilet and moving it, careful not to slide it—the last thing they needed was the obnoxious sound of metal dragging across the floor to alert someone this late in the game.

With the toilet out of the way, Lewis handed Murphy the flashlight he'd stolen. "Let's hope this works, brother. For both of our sakes."

Murphy closed his eyes and said a silent prayer. He'd once heard someone say *there are no atheists in a foxhole*, and since getting locked up, he'd discovered prison was much the same. All of a sudden rapists, murderers, drug dealers were devout religious practitioners. They walked around the building wearing kufis, yamakas, and rosary beads. Men who were the worst of the worst, monsters who'd never given a second thought to a higher power, now converted, worshipping with every fiber of their being—their immortal soul. All within the view of staff, of course. Because most of the newly converted behind bars had had a change of heart for one of two reasons—they'd committed a crime so heinous society couldn't forgive, and now sought forgiveness from a divine entity, or simply because federal laws mandated inmates must be allowed to practice religion, which ultimately led to inmates receiving special religious meals at certain times of the year, depending on what faith they were currently subscribed to. But when those men were released from prison, the sudden discovery of religion disappeared as quickly as it had come about, much the same as soldiers when they returned from an overseas deployment.

There were many gods for a hopeless man to choose from. But when that man's sentence was up and salvation was no longer vital to their sense of self preservation, they cast aside their god of choice. Forgotten, like their victims.

For the entirety of his time behind bars, Murphy had resisted the temptation to seek a higher power, laughed at the men who clearly didn't believe but maintained a facade.

Until now.

His life was on the line, and if there was a deity in existence who could nudge the odds in his favor, he'd sure as shit like to have them on his side.

He opened his eyes and exhaled. He'd been holding his breath for so long without realizing it that his head swam. The anticipation was too much and the vein above his temple throbbed in tandem with the jack-hammering of his heart against its ribcage prison. A wave of nausea washed over him, and his balls felt as if they'd ascended into his abdomen. Shaking the feeling off, he forced himself to act.

Murphy shined the flashlight into the brand-new hole created by the absence of the toilet. The beam of light sliced through the darkness like a scalpel through eager, waiting flesh. Beyond the plumbing of the toilet, Murphy saw only darkness where the beam wasn't strong enough to illuminate.

Relief overtook the nausea, although he knew they weren't out of the woods yet, not by a long shot. Still, that there appeared to be some sort of drop meant there was *something* underneath the floor of the prison. The real test was still before them. If things continued to go smoothly, Glenwood Corrections would soon be a thing of the past, putting Murphy one step closer to his son, and many, many steps away from Reese and impending homicide.

He tossed aside any remaining doubts, not because he genuinely believed success was now a given, but because a man at the end of his rope would seize any opportunity to cling to hope.

"Jesus Christ, bro, you were right," Lewis said, laughing as he spoke. In the face of the impossible, he broke into hysterics.

"You doubted me?" Murphy said.

"I mean, I believed you thought you saw something. I knew O'Rourke, and I know this place is haunted by its past. I believe in ghosts, and paranormal shit like that. But I guess part of me wasn't convinced, especially when you started talking about plans for the old facility appearing and disappearing. It seemed to me like the hallucinations of a man who's mind was on the brink of collapse, like your brain had created a fantasy in order to protect itself and hold on to whatever sanity remained."

"Really? Are you fucking serious, man? When did you become a therapist?"

Lewis laughed again. "Since I've been watching Dr. Phil every day in this bitch. But seriously, I don't think it would be unrealistic for anyone to assume that staying locked up in segregation took a toll on your mental health man. You did a lot of time down there, and that's not even taking into account all the other shit you've had going on with parole and your family. A man can only take so much, and I know you compartmentalize your problems instead of dealing with them. Eventually, that pressure is going to cause something to snap. I had a friend who'd served in the military, went overseas and saw some shit. When he came home, he never talked about it. One day, he decided enough was enough and suck started his AR15. I don't think you're suicidal or anything like that, but I think maybe you were getting close to your breaking point, and part of that story was a coping mechanism. Clearly, I couldn't have been anymore fucking wrong though, and this tunnel is going to save our lives."

"Yeah, maybe . . . " Murphy trailed off. He thought he'd heard something, but couldn't be sure.

"What do you mean, maybe? This is it. Once we get out of here, we just have to keep a low profile, make sure we don't get picked up again. Law enforcement all over the country are going to have our pictures, but if we can avoid pigs we're fucking free, man."

Murphy shook his head and spoke quickly. He was getting nervous, sitting around with a newly dug hole fresh inside of the cell. "That's not what I mean. That last night I was in segregation. When I saw O'Rourke, he said something odd. 'What's the toll on a route paved in blood?' or something like that. I forgot about it at the time, but lying in my bunk last night, it popped into my head out of nowhere, and I've been thinking about it ever since. Thinking about that, and about the entire situation. Why me, Lewis? Why now? This area has been abandoned underneath the prison for how long? And O'Rourke and the plans suddenly materialize after all the time? I couldn't be the first person to have flipped through that book. It doesn't make any sense. I don't know something about the way he emphasized all the shit about evil and latching on to people and places. It sounds fucking nuts, but I'm not gonna lie, that evil never dying, and the Maniac of D Block has got my skin crawling just thinking about it all again. This whole situation is like some shit out of a cheesy 80s horror movie."

Lewis chewed his lip. "Who knows, man? All of this seems too good to be true, but what choice do we have? The time to worry about all of that shit is long gone. We just tunneled through our fucking toilet. Even if we said, 'fuck it' and changed our minds, we've passed the point of no return. Someone is going to find this tunnel, eventually. It might take some time, but someone *will* notice, and when they do, we're absolutely fucked. *And* that's if we aren't already dead by the time someone discovers it. I don't think Reese is going to take his time proving his point with us. A guy like that is gonna want to make an example. I'll take my chance in the tunnel. What's the worst that could happen? We've got some food, we've got tools in case we need to dig some more, and we've got these," Lewis said, holding up a toothbrush with a razor blade melted to the tip. "You ever see what these do to someone's face? Any officer finds us and they're gonna need a plastic surgeon to fix them up. And if Lee Harris really is down there somehow, he's gonna wish he'd stayed dead in the riot."

Murphy nodded his head. Lewis hadn't calmed his fears, but he was right about one thing—they didn't have any other options. "Yeah, you're right. Is everything set for tomorrow? You took care of the arrangement with Ruiz?"

"Sure did. Ruiz has the hots for one of my girls, Trixie, so I had a little talk with him, and in exchange for a diversion Trixie has been sucking him off in the back of the law library for the past few days."

Lewis had been running a pimping operation out of Glenwood for a few years now. He was a savvy businessman and saw an opportunity to make money off sex in the facility. He offered protection to the gay and trans inmates who'd otherwise have been targeted in the facility. The men and women employed by Lewis were happy to work for him—better for the sex to be a choice they made under more favorable terms than to left beaten and abused, possibly killed.

Murphy laughed. "Offering them protection and pimping them out turned out to be a smart move, man. All that money you made, and now this, I wish I had your business sense."

"A day late and a dollar short, man. So, here's the plan. Tomorrow, Trixie is going to gobble the tube steak one last time, making our part of the bargain with Ruiz paid off. Once Ruiz shoots his load off, he's going to start a fire in the library. The aim is for that happen right around the time the education movement is going on. There's going to be so many inmates roaming around the building at that time, the entire place will be absolute fucking chaos. Plus, that early in the morning, most of the officers haven't gotten around to making sure everyone's cell doors are shut, so when all the staff goes running off with fire extinguishers and they're busy taking care of that whole situation, it's not going to look out of the ordinary for us to be going in and out of our cell. It's almost a guarantee that anyone monitoring the surveillance system is going to be too busy watching the action to notice what is going on in the housing units."

"I like where this is going," Murphy said.

Lewis clapped Murphy's shoulder. "I told you we'd be all set. By the time the officer gets back on post, we should have at least a twenty-minute lead, maybe more. I figure there are three ways this thing could go once he's here again. The first, someone rats us out. There are plenty of snitches around, and I'd be surprised if *nobody* saw us. The second, whatever officer working the area tomorrow, is a go-getter and decides to make a tour around the block after he returns from responding to the fire. I think this is the most likely scenario, especially if they end up calling an emergency count after the fire is taken care of. The third, and best-case scenario, whatever officer works this area tomorrow returns from responding to the fire and then parks his ass at the table and doesn't move until the *routine* morning count. Personally, I'm not counting on this happening, I think it's always best to plan for the absolute worse, and if it ends up being easier than anticipated, well then, we have something else to celebrate when we're on the other side."

Murphy let out a long sigh. He clapped his hands once and rubbed them together, psyching himself up. "Alright man, looks like there's nothing left to do but wait. Let's cover this hole up until the morning. We've already sat here way too long, bullshitting. Lucky for us, most of the staff around here likes to sleep at night instead of doing their jobs."

They grabbed the toilet and positioned it back in place, once again taking care to avoid scraping it across the floor.

Both men had been locked up for years, had spent plenty of time *waiting*, but with their freedom, and lives in the balance, it would be the longest wait of their lives.

◆

CHAPTER 10

THE NEXT MORNING after shift change, the cell doors opened promptly at 7:30 A.M. Glenwood corrections, despite all of its current problems, still kept a tight schedule. Although many of the inmates incarcerated at Glenwood were some of the worst behaved prisoners the facility had ever seen, and what little staff currently employed were simultaneously the least disciplined, and the most overworked officers to ever put on the badge, the daily schedule was one thing that operated like clockwork.

Coincidently, all of those things combined formed a perfect storm of conditions to plot and execute a successful prison break.

Shortly after the cell doors opened, their housing unit was summoned to chow. Both Murphy and Lewis made their way to the dining room. Neither man wanted to eat—nerves kept their hunger at bay—but they knew to make an escape attempt without first fueling their bodies would be foolish. It was a risk, leaving the cell for so much time, anyone could happen upon the tunnel they'd made, but neither man knew when their next meal would come and even if things went off without a hitch, it could be days before they were able to stop and rest long enough to eat something more than a quick snack.

By the time they finished eating breakfast and made their way back to the block, there was less than an hour remaining before their expected go time. There was nothing left to do but wait for the fire alert to be called over the intercom.

Officer Manning was in charge of the area this morning, a perfect hit as far as they were concerned. Manning was about as lazy as they come and didn't give a shit what went on so long as the inmates in his area weren't fighting. Most of the time, he didn't even bother touring his area. He simply sat in the large, safety glass enclosure overlooking the module, stuffing his face with

McDonald's breakfast sandwiches, washing them down with Ghost Energy drinks. Between the horrible diet, overconsumption of caffeine, and morbidly obese frame, he was a cardiac event waiting to happen. The same reasons Manning was a prime heart attack candidate also made Murphy and Lewis confident there was no chance he'd stumble across the hole before they jumped down it. They were looking at a few hours of lead time before being discovered, much better than the 20 minutes they were planning for.

Sadly, staff like Manning were no longer the exception. They were the rule. Since the old facility burned down it had become normal for officers to monitor the housing units from the control area, rather than from within the unit itself. There had been a time, years ago, when officers were required to remain in the housing units, and were even held liable in civil lawsuits put forth by inmates after getting into fights if it was discovered the fight happened and the officer *wasn't* in the unit. But when staffing became a crisis and Glenwood became a more dangerous place for both inmates and officers, the administrators changed the policy in order to keep workers' compensation claims to a minimum. Worker's compensation claims were a thorn in the warden's side and were another reason it was impossible to maintain a full complement of staff.

The result was a prison where officers spent less time on workers' compensation but did less work and were no longer on the hook for civil suits.

The same policy change was a large part of the reason Glenwood inmates had free rein of the facility, and the reason a plot such as the one Murphy and Lewis had concocted was even a possibility.

Murphy and Lewis sat at a table playing chess, waiting for the alarm to sound. Though there was nothing out of the ordinary going on at the moment, the housing area was so loud that Murphy had trouble concentrating on his next move. One hundred men congregated in an indoor space, carrying on dozens of separate conversations meant that even when things were quiet, they weren't really *quiet*. But if the room were dead silent, Murphy didn't think he'd be able to concentrate, anyway. His mind kept hopping to the various conversations happening around him, trying to pick out any sign that their secret had been discovered.

So far, it didn't seem as if anyone was talking about it, but that didn't mean nobody knew. There were plenty of rats running around Glenwood, and not all of them had tails.

Murphy was dressed for comfort and ease of mobility. He wore his black, state issued recreation sweatpants and a white t-shirt along with a pair of brown work-boots. Initially, he was going to wear sneakers, in case they needed to move quickly and quietly, but Lewis had convinced him otherwise. They were headed into an unknown underground area. A waterproof, heavy-duty boot made more sense than a thin sneaker protecting their feet.

Inside the housing unit, the temperature was bearable, if not comfortable. Often during the warmest months of the year, the module would become so humid the floors were soaked in water like a slip and slide. Officers had been known to go out on injury from slipping on the floor before they ever got a chance to break up the fight they were running to in the first place. Not today, though.

Today, the air conditioning was working as intended. Despite that, sweat trickled down Murphy's forehead, along his back, and down the crack of his ass. It was still early, yet his shirt was saturated with sweat. He fidgeted around, not only trying to get comfortable but also trying to remove the wedgie plaguing him without having to pick his ass in front of everyone. Murphy thanked God that there were no staff around at the moment because the amount of perspiration leaking from his pores made him look guilty as sin.

Lewis moved a piece across the board. "Relax man."

"I am relaxed."

"Yeah? Because your shirt would get you first place in a wet t-shirt contest. You're sweating like a hooker in church."

"I'm as calm as I'm gonna get, man. I'm just ready to get this thing started. What the fuck is taking Ruiz so long?"

"Chill, it's still early. He's gonna do it right when they call the movements, which should be," Lewis looked at his watch, "any minute now."

As if on cue, the crackle of the overhead speaker cut Lewis off.

Code red in the library. Code red in the library. All staff respond to the library for a code red. Glenwood fire department notified and en route.

Murphy remained seated at the table and watched as officer

Manning opened the control center door and took off running with a fire extinguisher as fast as his enormous frame could carry him, looking every bit like a soup sandwich on his way out the door.

With a bit of luck, the fire would be a good one and it would be a while before Manning returned. He hoped that the fire department already on the way meant the blaze was a good one.

The instant officer Manning left the area and was no longer in sight, a calm washed over Murphy, forcing his nervousness aside. It happened the same way before he killed the monster who'd ruined his son, nothing but nerves until go time, and then it was like someone flicked a switch.

Once again, it was go time.

They abandoned their chess game and made their way to the cell, trying to look as normal as possible. Murphy was eager to get going and could hardly contain himself. He knew Lewis had to be feeling the same. How could he not? Still, they kept themselves in check, making it a point to mask their eagerness and walk, rather than run. This close to the finish line, there was no need to draw unwanted attention to themselves.

They reached the cell, crossed the threshold, and closed the door behind them.

Neither man had seen Reese stick a paper towel in the locking mechanism earlier to prevent it from catching. And *had* they been paying closer attention to their surroundings, rather than trying to play it cool, they might have seen Reese and two of his cronies watching them like hawks circling prey.

By the time Murphy and Lewis closed the door, the three skinheads were already crossing the housing module, rapidly closing the distance between them and their prey.

***

Reese stood against the wall with one foot up, flat against the surface. His arms were crossed over his chest, hands clenching his prison jumper. He watched from afar as Murphy and Lewis sat at a table playing chess. The sight alone causing the blood to boil in his veins. He couldn't believe the nerve of that piece of shit Murphy. How dare he spit in the face of his white brothers in the joint? Clearly, he hadn't gotten his point across, but what else could he have done? He'd already taken Murphy in every way a man could take another man, and yet the fucker still dared to defy him.

Reese wouldn't allow that transgression to go unpunished.

EXPIRATION OF SENTENCE

The moment Murphy refused to carry out the mark, he'd signed his own goddamn death warrant. But Reese wasn't going to pass this off to someone else. This was a special occasion, and he was going to take care of both of those pricks. He needed to prove a point. Make sure that *nobody* forgets what happens when you fuck with Jason Reese.

But before that happened, he was going to have some fun. Reese had big plans for those two. If Murphy thought getting his ass taken was bad, he had another thing coming because he was going to be sucking dick like there was no tomorrow. His little fucking buddy's salty load would be the last thing he'd ever taste before Reese's blade ran across his fucking throat and sawed his goddamn head off of his shoulders. And when he was done? Lewis was going to get his own cock-meat sandwich when Reese chopped his pecker off and force fed it to him.

Looking at the two of them, Reese knew they were up to something. Murphy was drenched in sweat and fidgeting like a tweaker. Lewis whispered something to his friend and Murphy quickly settled down.

Yeah, those two fucks were up to something. Maybe he'd get a chance to handle these two cunts sooner than he'd anticipated.

He called over Bic and Kelly—two members of the gang who were always up for dirty work—and ran them through the idea that had been marinating in his brain. They were going to get those two ball bags cornered in a cell and take care of them for good.

Reese grabbed a small stack of paper towels and wadded them up. While the two cornballs sat at the table looking suspicious as hell despite their efforts to play it cool, Reese used their lack of situational awareness to his advantage and stuck the wad into locking mechanism before making his way back to his cronies. Now he simply needed to wait for them to enter the room and close the door. It would shut, but the lock wouldn't engage. As long as they didn't slam it shut hard enough for it to swing back open, they'd never be the wiser.

Then Reese and his boys would make their move.

He continued to observe the two men, silently stewing in his hatred. Beside him, his two cronies kept silent as well. They knew better than to chum the waters when the shark was hungry.

Suddenly, the crackle of a loudspeaker cut through the silence, announcing a fire in the library. All the inmates in the area paused to listen, but as the fire was nowhere near the housing module, they quickly went about their business as if nothing had happened.

Everyone except Murphy and Lewis, both of whom walked straight to their cell the moment officer Manning was no longer on his post.

Gotcha, Reese thought.

"Let's go," he said. The two overgrown lapdogs followed their pack leader. Reese didn't know what those two were up to, but it had to be major. Their poker faces gave them away, and if officer Manning wasn't such a shit bag, he'd have noticed their behavior right away. Besides, the timing of the fire and their immediate response to it was too big of a coincidence, and Reese didn't believe in such things.

Whatever the two of them were up to, he didn't give a flying fuck. All he knew was that their little scheme had tossed them right in his lap.

Reese and the gang stopped in front of the cell door. "You boys ready for this? They don't leave this cell alive; you understand me?" The skinheads nodded.

Reese swung the door open and said, "Surprise, you cock . . . "

The cell was empty. Murphy and Lewis had pulled a disappearing act, literally. The toilet no longer sat against the wall, but in the middle of the cell.

Where the toilet had once been—a hole.

"They're not getting away from me that easily. Once we kill those fuckers, the warden will thank us for cleaning up this mess," Reese said.

CHAPTER 11

MURPHY STOOD UP and straightened his shirt. He'd underestimated the distance to the ground and landed wrong, falling flat on his face in the process. Still, he'd been luckier than Lewis, who was now hobbling around in the dark like a wounded animal. If Lewis hadn't had the foresight to throw their mattress down first to create a landing pad, they might have both been fucked. If Lewis couldn't shake off whatever was wrong, they still might be.

"Hey man, are you alright?" Murphy asked.

"Yeah, I think so. I tweaked something, but I think I can walk it off. I don't think it's broken."

Murphy shook his head. "Fuck. Ok whatever you do, don't take your boot off. If you do that, it could swell up and then you're not going to be able to get it back on. We'll take it as slow as we can for the time being. That way, we can get our bearings straight and hopefully you'll be able to move quicker once we figure out where we are going. If we're lucky, nobody is gonna realize we're missing until we are long gone."

Lewis sucked his teeth. "What do you mean 'Once we figure out where we're going,' I thought you memorized the layout?"

"I did, but I've never been down here before. Have you ever seen blueprints? I'm not a fucking engineer man. Now imagine those blueprints were drawn by hand on an old, weathered piece of paper that was crinkled up and looked like it had been hidden in someone's asshole for two decades. And it's dark as hell down here man, that flashlight is a piece of shit. You couldn't have stolen one that works?"

"I didn't see you risking your ass stealing any of the equipment. That's the best I could do, so if you don't like it, feel free to get fucked."

Both men were stressed and were starting to take it out on each other.

Murray sighed. "Just chill out. I'll get us out of here. We can't be at each other's throats now. We're too close to the finish line. Getting out of here is gonna be the straightforward part. Not getting caught is gonna be the problem we need to solve. We never game-planned that far out."

"No, but we were working on a short timeline. There wasn't much in the way of choices. It was either escape or get murdered."

Murphy nodded. "Yeah, well, it's a little late in the game for that. We'll cross that bridge when we get the fuck out of here. Let's just keep moving. If you need to rest, I'll stop, but being down here gives me the willies. I can't get O'Rourke and The Maniac out of my head."

"Then let's just go. Don't worry about me, I'll be fine."

Murphy scanned the underground area with the aforementioned shitty flashlight. It was tough to tell exactly where they were, but Murphy thought they were in the mechanical room that had been marked on the plans. If he remembered correctly, there was some sort of tunnel at one end of the sizeable area that connected with a smaller passageway which spilled out underneath a highway overpass. It wasn't exactly a sewer, but it was the closest comparison Murphy could think of.

Overhead, water dripped from the ceiling, plinking off the ground. The surrounding walls were crumbling, and the stench of rot and mildew permeated the air. It was clear this area had been derelict for a long time. Who knew how long? Decades? By the looks of things, it was entirely possible nobody had set foot down here since the fire. None of the equipment seemed to be functional, and why would it? If they simply built a new foundation over the old basement, surely the power would have been disconnected. The water dripping from the pipes overhead led Murphy to believe the only thing still functioning were the PVC pipes from the toilets and sinks in the cells above.

The two men walked the room slowly, searching for anything that may be of use while also taking care to navigate through the rubble of the past. Piles of cement and stone littered the area, along with overturned shelves and even old metal bunk beds. After a short while Murphy eye's adjusted to the lack of light. In the distance, he thought he saw where the mechanical room spilled into the drainage tunnels.

"Look over there. You see that? That's where we need to go," Murphy said before sprinting to the end of the room. In his excitement, he'd forgotten about Lewis' injury, leaving his friend limping behind. Coming up on the tunnel, Murphy cartoonishly skidded to a halt, his feet slipping on the loose rocks beneath them.

Fear and anger fought for control over his emotions when he realized what he was looking at. A large fence which spanned the archway and climbed from floor to ceiling blocked the tunnel off. A heavy-duty lock kept it secured.

"Fuck!" Murphy yelled. "Lewis, it's fucking locked! You got anything on you to smash this?"

Lewis hobbled over, still trailing a good distance behind Murphy. His ankle clearly bothered him more than he was willing to admit. Shaking his head, he replied, "Nothing heavy enough to break that."

"Fuck," Murphy said. "Ok, we're gonna have to look around for a big stone or a piece of cement. Something heavy and solid. There's plenty of rubble around here. There's gotta be something big enough to smash the lock."

Lewis picked up a large piece of stone. The edges were jagged and sharp. He turned it about in his hand as he finally reached Murphy, presenting the stone to him with a smile on his face. "This should work."

Murphy grabbed the rough stone, gently tossed it up—the stone barely leaving his palm—before agreeing with Lewis. "Yeah, this should do the trick."

He held the stone over the lock, slowly bringing it up and down, mimicking the arc he'd take to smash it, making sure it lined up just right. The last thing he wanted to do was to crush a finger down here. Finally, when he felt comfortable enough, he raised the stone over his head and brought it down hard. The impact reverberated through his entire arm, a shockwave of concussive force from wrist to shoulder. He even felt a spike of pain in one of his tooth fillings. The stone's jagged edge bit into his palm, drawing blood. Ignoring the pain, he brought the stone up and down, again and again until the lock was bent and twisted. Despite his efforts, the lock held.

"It's no use," Murphy said. "These heavy-duty locks are built so guys like us can't get through them. We need bolt cutters; this isn't going to work. Any ideas?"

Murphy jiggled the lock, hoping maybe it would come undone after the beating he'd delivered to it. After a few moments of fiddling with it, he became annoyed by Lewis' silence and spun around. "Hey man, did you fucking hear me?"

Murphy's jaw dropped, as did the stone he was holding. Lewis had been unable to respond because one of the skinheads—a guy nicknamed Bic—stood behind Lewis, holding him with one large arm across the forehead and face. In the man's other hand was a long, sharp strip of metal. The rusty tip pressed into his friend's neck, dimpling the flesh. A line of blood trickled down his neck. Flanking Bic and his hostage were Reese and Kelly. Reese had the biggest shit-eating grin Murphy had ever seen plastered across his face.

Murphy couldn't believe it. All the meticulous planning they'd done. How could they be so stupid as to allow Reese and his goons to get the drop on them? He'd been too obsessed with breaking the lock open and now it was too late because, barring a miracle, they were as good as dead. Murphy only hoped he'd have an opportunity to do some damage, maybe take one or two of them along for the ride to hell. A 3 on 2 against men the size of the skinheads wasn't a fight they could win. Murphy knew that, but he wanted to make sure they never forgot him.

Reese spoke. "I've gotta say, I didn't see this one coming. I knew you had *something* in you, Murphy. That's why I gave you so many chances to do the right thing. But you had to force my hand, didn't you?" Reese and Kelly both stepped forward. Murphy backed into the heavy fencing. He turned his head side to side, looking for a way out, but the two assailants had already begun fanning out in order to prevent him from making a break in either direction.

"Don't try to run, asshole. You're just going to get your friend killed. Why don't you come on over here and we'll talk this out?"

"Yeah? Now you want to talk. You're gonna kill him no matter what I do. Go fuck yourself, bitch."

Reese laughed. "I'm the bitch? You've got that wrong, buddy. You were the one shitting out my kids after I fucked you, so wouldn't that make you *my* bitch?

Murphy had heard enough. He charged at Reese, but Kelly was ready for it and launched his body at Murphy like a missile, spearing him to the ground before Murphy got anywhere near

Reese. The two men hit the ground with a thud, rolling around. Punches flew from both combatants, but none of them landed cleanly. The men were too wrapped up to get any leverage behind the blows.

Reese stalked his way over to the two inmates scuffling like school children and picked Murphy up by the collar of his shirt, punching him in the gut with his free hand. Spit flew from his mouth as the oxygen was forced from his lungs.

Murphy was winded from the blow, but it was a life-or-death situation and the dog in him refused to quit. Murphy lashed out in retaliation but with the wind knocked out of him, all the pop had been taken out of his own feeble counterattack.

Reese responded with another strike of his own, this time a vicious head butt that shattered Murphy's nose, flattening it like a pancake and spraying crimson syrup all over both men.

Murphy choked on his blood, coughing globs of snot and plasma up. Reese dragged him to where Bic held Lewis's hostage and forced him to his knees. "Pull his pants down, Kelly. Since these two love to mix race so much, we're gonna let them have some inter-racial right now."

Kelly's face went slack. "What?"

Reese stared at Kelly; his eyes were dead serious. "Pull his pants down and fluff him."

"I'm not jerking anyone off, Reese. Are you fucking serious?"

"If you don't do what the fu . . . "

A geyser of blood erupted from Reese's neck and behind it, a long, black object pierced one side of his neck and protruded from the other.

A river of red poured from the wound, soaking Murphy as a large, hulking behemoth of a man yanked the object, ripping it from Reese's neck.

The lifeless corpse fell on top of Murphy, pinning him to the ground. A gloved hand wiped the tip of the long, black object—a Monadnock expandable button, the "safety tip" ground down to a jagged point, turning the blunt object into a twenty-one inch heavy-duty, heat-treated steel knife.

The man stood well over six feet tall, massive in both height and frame. A real life giant. Dressed in Glenwood Correctional Institute's signature dark black, military style BDU's, the man dwarfed Arnold Schwarzenegger in his prime. The uniform was tattered and worn, old. Underneath the rips and tears in the cloth, his exposed skin was scarred and burned. In other places, wounds still festered. The man's face was a horrific sight. Poorly healed scars ran from eyebrow to jaw line on both sides of his face. A milky white film covered the only eye in his head. The other eye was gone or covered with scar tissue and melted skin.

Murphy gagged, not from the dead body on top of him, but the smell wafting off the giant. Mildew and decay assaulted his nostrils. Grave rot mixed in, making a menagerie of putrid smells.

"Jesus Christ, it's fucking Lee Harris," Lewis said.

The sudden intrusion of Lewis' voice snapped Bic out of the trance he'd been in. He shoved Lewis away and devoted his full attention to The Maniac of D block. "I don't know any Lee Harris, but this fucker right here is a dead man. Let's get that son of a bitch, Kelly."

Kelly and Bic launched a joint attack at The Maniac. Bic dove at him, but The Maniac caught him mid-flight and tossed him like a rag doll. Bic's colossal frame sailed through the air and collided with the steel fence that had been blocking the tunnel with enough force to knock the fencing down. It clattered to the ground and Bic landed with a thud and a grunt on top of the steel fencing.

Lewis turned his attention to his friend and tried rolling Reese's bloody corpse off of Murphy, but the man was too large, his dead weight far too heavy. "You're gonna have to help me out here, man."

Murphy grunted as he worked in tandem with Lewis to shove Reese off of him. The two pushed with all their might and managed to free Murphy. Lewis grabbed his friend under the arms and tried to help him up, but Murphy shoved his hands away. He didn't need help getting up; he needed to get the fuck out of dodge while they preoccupied The Maniac with their uninvited company.

"Look, the fence is busted. This is our chance," Murphy said.

"Alright, let's go."

***

Behind The Maniac, Kelly saw the blurry forms of Murphy and Lewis as they took off running like the little pussies they were. He ignored them as he kept his focus on the abomination Lewis identified as Lee Harris, as if that name was supposed to have some kind of significance. The two chickenshits he'd deal with after he slaughtered the mother fucker who' done Reese in.

EXPIRATION OF SENTENCE

The Maniac stood as still as a statue as Kelly Maneuvered forward, closing the gap while slashing wildly in front of him with the shank that Bic had dropped when The Maniac tossed him aside.

Vacancy. That's what Kelly saw in the eyes of The Maniac as he approached, as if the thought of getting diced to ribbons by a shank was nothing to be worried about. If he cared, he made no indication, didn't budge an inch as Kelly approached.

When he was within an arm's distance, Kelly sliced again, this time the shank being met with resistance as it cut through The Maniac's correction officer uniform, parting the skin beneath it. Fetid, black sludge cascaded from lips of the wound. The Maniac looked down at the muck spilling from his body with indifference. He made no sound when the shank had opened him, nor did he make even the slightest expression of pain. It was as if the man felt nothing as his skin was ripped open.

Kelly continued carving The Maniac, Lee Harris, like a rotisserie chicken to no effect. He grunted with each swipe, putting all his effort into it. He hadn't known that slashing a human body repeatedly was so tiring. His lungs burned and his arms ached with each swipe. If it weren't for the black ooze flying through the air, splattering the floor and covering Kelly's face he'd have been questioning if he were actually cutting the man.

While Kelly sliced and diced, he noticed Bic rise to his feet and creep up behind The Maniac. Bic wrapped his arms around the man's tank-like frame and squeezed. The veins in his head and arms bulged as he struggled to control The Maniac. Kelly knew there was no way his friend would be able to keep hold of the giant for more than a few seconds.

"Kill this motherfucker!" Bic shouted.

"I'm working on it!"

With Bic struggling to maintain the bearhug grip, Kelly jabbed the shank into The Maniac, thrusting it forward and pulling it back again and again. It felt good to stick that fucker. Felt good to poke him for Reese.

"Don't stop!" Bic said.

And Kelly *didn't* stop, couldn't have stopped even if he'd wanted to. He was a man possessed, lost in the music of violence, dancing to a tune that only men who'd done violence recognized. There was no drum beat to follow, the rhythm of this tune was the wet squelching noises echoing through the dark room with each thrust of the shank as Kelly stabbed again and again. The putrid stench of the vile, black substance coursing through The Maniac's veins made Kelly gag, but still he continued the assault. Reese would be avenged at all costs. But as Kelly's arms grew tired, and each breath became increasingly difficult to take, his vicious attack slowed considerably. He looked every bit the lunatic he'd become when overtaken by the violent spell—arms, face, and chest, all covered in the black sludge.

"What the fuck are you?" Bic said, the tremor in his voice reinforcing Kelly's knowledge the assault had born no fruit.

The Maniac remained stoic, silent, the blank visage of his face etched forever among the scarred and charred flesh.

Kelly mustered all his strength and pulled the shank back once more. Bic screamed, "Die Fucker!" as Kelly rammed it forward, but The Maniac spun around at the last minute. The shank plunged into Bic's back, flesh parting like warm butter as the tip pierced his skin until it had sunk deep, puncturing his lung. Blood pooled around the handle and ran along Kelly's, coating it in his friend's warm, red essence.

The moment the shank pierced Bic's flesh, The Maniac sprang into action, no longer content to take everything Kelly dished out. He pumped his legs backward, pushing his two opponents into a stone pillar with enough force debris and chunks of stone to break loose, clattering around them. One such hunk of stone crashed on top of Kelly's skull, and, after a sharp pain, he felt nothing more.

He collapsed to the ground like a sack of potatoes. A large wound appeared in the place where the stone had collided with his head. Blood rushed from his broken skull and through the fragments of bone. His exposed brain seemed to pulsate as his body gave out.

Kelly's grip on the shank remained true even as his body collapsed. The force of his falling body pulled the shank down and out, tearing Bic's flesh as he fell to the ground next to Kelly.

The Maniac stomped Bic's skull like a child squashing bugs. His eyes popped from his skull as his head crumpled. Blood rivers ran from his ears. The Maniac continued stomping. Brain matter squirted from the ruined head like a Gushers fruit snack.

The Maniac grabbed the shank that had been used on him and shoved it into Kelly's face. He was already dead, but it didn't stop

Lee Harris from sticking Kelly's eyeball like a pig, piercing the orb. Gooey ocular fluid squirted from the wound. Lee Harris didn't care that both men were dead. He continued stabbing and slashing the dead man's body and face with the same reckless abandon Kelly had used on him earlier. Kelly's DNA painted the surrounding area. Blood spray coated the walls, ran down the stone pillars and pooled around his mauled frame.

One last time, he jabbed the metal into Kelly's chest, hitting the breastbone. The tip of the shank snapped off and at last The Maniac was finished. He tossed the broken weapon aside, shoved both of his hands into one of the larger punctures in Kelly's chest. He twisted and wriggled his hands until they were wrist deep in the cavity, a violent fisting of the wound.

With a grunt, The Maniac pulled Kelly's ribcage apart with a crack and ripped his heart from his chest. He dropped the dead organ to the ground and turned in the direction Lewis and Murphy had fled.

***

The sounds of violence echoed down the hallway behind Murphy and Lewis as they made their way down the dark tunnel, putting as much distance between Glenwood and Lee Harris as possible. Murphy had no clue what was transpiring, but he had no intention of finding out.

That some sort of undead ghoul really had been waiting in the bowels of Glenwood was a tough pill to swallow, although he had witnessed it with his own two eyes. It was amazing the lengths the human brain will go to in order to protect itself. But he couldn't let his brain tune this one out or deny it. Doing so would surely invite a horrific end.

Glenwood truly was hell. Human violence, atrocities, ghosts, corpses reanimated by some sort of evil presence. Murphy needed to be free and clear of this place. After that, maybe he could spread the word. People had to know about this. Glenwood needed to be leveled, nuked even. A ghoul like The Maniac shouldn't exist, it was an affront to humanity. A real-life killer straight out of a cheesy 80s slasher flick.

Murphy pressed on despite the heaviness in his chest. He blamed the cigarettes for that one, a habit he'd only picked up after getting locked up. He justified the foul addiction in his mind by telling himself it eased his stress, allowed him to pass time and relax in a place where relaxation was seemingly impossible.

Behind him, Lewis stopped running, clearly spent. He wasn't a smoker like Murphy was, but he was older and didn't make an effort to work out the way that Murphy had most of the time he'd been in prison. It was a fantasy of Murphy's to come home "prison jacked" and ravage his wife like they were on their honeymoon again. In his mind, he thought that she'd be excited for him to come home with a chiseled physique, but in truth, she preferred his dad bod, and he was only projecting a childish fantasy onto her.

Murphy went back to Lewis, who was bent over, hands on his thighs.

"I can't keep going man, I'm fucking done," Lewis said.

Murphy grabbed his friend's arm and draped it over his shoulder. "I'm not leaving you here with that fucking lunatic. Put your weight on me and let's fucking go. If it's too much, we can hide until you feel up to moving again."

They hobbled down the hallway, which had been getting steadily wider until it had doubled in size. The water running steadily at their feet told Murphy they were headed in the right direction. Thankfully, because of the width of the corridor, the water wasn't deep, only enough to get the bottom of their shoes wet. The last thing either of them needed was soaking wet feet. It could still be some time before they were able to take their shoes off and relax.

Murphy could feel Lewis still struggling with his injury. He said to Lewis, "Just down this corridor, man, keep going. We're almost there."

Heavy footfalls and splashing water echoed behind the escaping convicts.

"Shit, he's here," Lewis said.

"Just keep going. Look down the tunnel. I think it's getting lighter. That's gotta be the end!"

"Fuck man, we're so close. Don't let him catch up."

As the words escaped his lips, The Maniac's steel baton whipped through the air, the heavy handle whacking Lewis in the back of the head. He dropped to his knee, dazed from the impact.

Lee Harris appeared from the darkness behind them, closing the distance in a few long, quick steps. Logic dictated it should be impossible for a man that size to move as quickly as he had, yet he did. The existence of The Maniac defied logic. Why should anything else about him be dictated by previously held notions about what was or wasn't possible?

EXPIRATION OF SENTENCE

Lewis rose to his feet and turned, ready to defend himself, but he wasn't ready for how quickly Harris had reached them. The Maniac scooped up the baton and swung it in a downward, backhanded motion. It cracked Lewis in the face, shattering his cheekbone. Fragments of teeth rained down like candy from a piñata, scattering on the ground. The sharpened tip of the baton had slashed his face, parted flesh and left a window in his mouth made of sinewy strands of skin and meat. Blood poured from the gaping wound as Lewis lay face down on the ground. He coughed blood, and another tooth flew out of his mouth, clinking onto the floor beneath him.

The Maniac raised the baton again, ready to end Lewis. The attack had happened so quickly neither man had seen it coming, but now Murphy was ready to die for his friend. He sprinted as fast as his legs would take him, spearing Harris, but the man was built like a brick shithouse and the attack didn't budge the monster. Murphy had done more harm to himself than anything else. The impact sent a stab of pain through his shoulder, but there was no time to react. Their lives were on the line. Ignoring the pain, he wrapped his arms around Harris and pumped his legs like a piston, trying to take Harris to the ground.

There was a split second where Murphy thought he might take The Maniac to the ground, but the ghoul was too strong and Murphy's grip too weak from the stinger. Harris' feet moved maybe an inch before he planted them in the ground, stopping any momentum Murphy had. He interlocked his hands together, creating a club with his massive mitts, and hammered down between Murphy's shoulder blades. The pain was incredible. The air rushed out of Murphy's lungs. He might as well have been hit with a sledgehammer. He crashed to the ground flat on his face and Harrison raised his leg, quickly stomping down. Murphy's first instinct when hitting the ground was to roll away and create space, an instinct that prevented his brains from being pulped. The enormous boot hit the ground where Murphy had been an instant after he'd moved.

Scrambling to his feet, Murphy took a defensive stance, though he still had trouble lifting his arm from the stinger. The Maniac mauled face remained emotionless. To him, Murphy must be nothing more than a bug to be squashed. Another death to fuel the evil lurking within Glenwood.

Murphy surveyed the area, searching for something, anything, he could use as a weapon. He was smart enough to know he had no chance in hell to win a hand-to-hand fight with the creature who'd taken out Reese, Kelly, and Bic single handedly.

He saw large chunks of stone littering the surrounding ground, but nothing else. Having no other option, Murphy grabbed the largest one within reach and chucked it at Harris. A wave of triumph spread throughout Murphy; his aim was true. He knew it the moment the stone left his hand.

The rock sailed through the air and pelted Harris square on the cheekbone. A sickening crunch echoed through the cave-like depths of the basement. Harris' cheek exploded; the orbital bone destroyed. The monster's eye dangled from its socket. Black, chunky ooze flowed from the gaping wound it The Maniac's face. Maggots wriggled around in the sludgy pool of fluid spreading on the ground. Other than visually observing the physical damage done, there was no indication Murphy had done anything to Harris. The fucker hadn't even flinched.

What would it take to stop this abomination? Could Murphy kill him? Cripple him? He couldn't be sure of either of those things, but one thing Murphy *was* sure of was that if he didn't figure something out quickly, this crypt in the bowels of the prison would be his final resting place.

Out of the corner of his eye, Murphy saw Lewis rise to his feet. If Harris was aware of Lewis, he made no sign. He simply watched Murphy gather a few more large rocks. Maybe death by a thousand stones would do the trick, or at least slow the fucker down. One by one, he chucked everything in the surrounding area that looked as if it would hurt. Rocks, chunks of metal, anything he could find. Most of the projectiles found their mark, but none of it did the physical damage the first stone had, nor did they appear to slow Harris down in the slightest. The Maniac, unfazed, stalked ever closer even as Murphy backpedaled, continuing to throw everything but the kitchen sink. Had there been a ditch sink, Murphy'd have thrown that, too.

While Harris was distracted by—or indifferent to—Murphy's assault, Lewis crept up behind the behemoth. His gaze was trained low, and he moved in step with Harris. At first Murphy had no clue what the hell Lewis was doing, but as he moved closer, Lewis extended his arm toward something strapped to Harris' leg.

EXPIRATION OF SENTENCE

A large canister of Sabre Red pepper spray!

There was no way to know if the canister would still work. Who knew how old the thing was? And if it worked, would it be effective against the abomination? Either way, they were out of options. Maybe Lewis would buy them enough time to escape.

Lewis took one more step in tandem with Harris, who was now in striking distance of Murphy, and reached for the canister. For a moment, the velcro on the holster held true before finally releasing. Lewis snatched the canister, but that moment of resistance where the velcro held was all it took to blow Lewis' plan to shit.

Harris turned, and in a lightning quick motion, brought the baton down on Lewis' wrist. There was a sickening snap, like a tree splitting in a hurricane, and Lewis dropped the canister, falling to the ground, clutching his shattered wrist.

Harris picked up the canister and aimed it at Lewis' face. He held it there for a moment before unloading a blast of orange fog into Lewis' wide open, screaming mouth. The spray painted his entire face and chest orange. It entered the micro abrasions on his face and coated his eyeballs.

Murphy, still rolling around on the ground in pain, heard him choke from the intense burning and respiratory reaction the concoction of ten percent oleoresin capsicum caused his friend to experience. The residual spray in the air burned Murphy and caused him to cough. He could only imagine how his friend felt at that moment.

Lewis rolled around on the floor, screaming and clawing at his face. There would be no departmental policy mandated shower after this use of force. Lewis was getting the full effect.

Harris stood over Lewis and sprayed again, unloading the rest of the canister on Lewis as he continued to scream like a madman. Anyone who'd been hit by OC before knew it caused men to go insane. The itching and burning. The feeling that you couldn't breathe, even though you knew the fact you were talking and screaming, meant you *were* breathing.

Snot, vomit, tears, and blood were everywhere. Harris tossed the empty can aside and removed a set of handcuffs from the pouch on his belt. A quick swipe of the metal hoop with his finger popped the cuffs open with a ratcheting noise that echoed through the tunnel. He clutched the open cuff in his bear paw and swung downward, using the claw-like tip of the cuff to cleave through

Lewis' eye. The end hooked through his eyeball and Harris grunted, pushing harder until his untold strength forced the metal through thin bone behind the eyeball, giving Lewis the first ever transorbital lobotomy performed with a set of handcuffs. Lewis' legs jerked violently for a few moments before going stiff. His body slackened; his life essence evaporated.

Lewis was dead.

Murphy witnessed this and scrambled to his feet, the pain in his body miraculously gone with the additional dump of adrenaline that had hit his body. The fight-or-flight response working as biology intended. He said a silent prayer for his friend as his legs carried him away from The Maniac as fast as they were capable of moving him. Right now, there was no time to stop and mourn the loss of his friend. That would need to wait until he escaped from this hellhole, a feat which looked more unlikely with each passing moment.

He understood now what he hadn't before. The evil present in Glenwood had existed long before Glenwood existed. When the riots happened and the place was reduced to rubble, it hadn't dissipated; it had simply latched on to a bad man and lingered within him, transforming the man into a deathless killing machine. Murphy couldn't be sure, but he thought whatever the *evil* was, had dug in its hooks once more; new building be damned. O'Rourke wasn't Casper the Friendly Ghost. He hadn't shown Murphy a way out to help a man at the end of his rope. No, O'Rourke was an extension of the evil present here, a way to ensure the presence was given the fuel it needed—blood and misery.

If he escaped this hellscape, Murphy knew nobody would believe his story. He knew it sounded like horse shit, like the internal ramblings of a man whose brain had gone soft from too much time in segregation with no human interaction. Not long ago Murphy himself thought so. Evil, he had once thought, was tangible. Real. Rooted in humanity. But now he knew the truth: *evil* existed outside the boundaries of humanity as well. Lunacy, the idea that a *place* could be *evil*, but now that it had shown itself, he recognized it for what it was and realized that himself, Lewis, and the rest of the inmates of Glenwood Correctional Institute had been living in a place where *evil* was the norm.

It had been hibernating.

Biding its time.

Growing stronger.

Now it stalked him. Hunter and prey.

Closer to the exit now, the bright, inviting light of freedom cast aside the darkness, vanquishing its enemy as it has since the dawn of time. Murphy's heart raced. From adrenaline and fear, yes, but from hope, too. He'd been locked up for years, his freedom taken from him. Before his stint at Glenwood, he'd never quite understood the beauty of freedom. How could he have understood when, from the moment he'd been born, he had never had to fight for, or otherwise earn, his freedom?

But once that freedom had been ripped away, Murphy served his time, dreaming of an early release. Of the day he'd be free once more. Dreamed of a home cooked meal, of hugging his wife and son. Dreamed of the day when he could wipe his ass behind the privacy of a closed door or go to sleep and not have to hear the moans of another man masturbating on the bunk beneath him. Things you rarely consider until they are no longer a part of your life.

The parole board had ripped those dreams from him when they denied his early release, but here, in the bowels of Glenwood, it reappeared—an actual light at the end of a tunnel.

But just as the light will vanquish the dark, darkness reappears, embracing the world in its cold, empty embrace.

Murphy's hopes were snuffed out, just like the light was each evening. Extinguished with the realization that a massive, grate-like cover stood between him and the outside world, its chain links cruelly exposing an outside world they would not permit him entry to.

Behind him, heavy footfalls signaled The Maniac's final approach. Though walking, he moved with an uncanny speed. Of course he did. He was no man; he was evil personified.

Harris said nothing as he towered over Murphy, who sunk to the ground, defeated. He had given up hope of escaping either monster, Glenwood Corrections, and The Maniac of D Block, so what use was it to fight? If he were lucky, his resignation would bring a swift death, rather than the untold agony Harris' earlier victims had faced.

Murphy thought of his wife. His son. She had been right all along. He'd been selfish in taking a man's life. It didn't matter that the scumbag had gotten off with a light sentence. He'd served his time, piece of shit or not. Murphy was neither judge, jury, nor executioner, but for one ill-fated moment in time, he fancied himself all three, and it had ruined the lives of his entire family. They'd continue to pay for his mistakes. Maybe in death, their debt would cease.

Murphy looked into Harris' mangled, rotting face. "Do it, you son of a bitch."

Harris said nothing. His massive chest rose and fell. It seemed even in death the body remembers such autonomic functions. Beside him, O'Rourke materialized.

"You tricked me," Murphy said.

O'Rourke shook his head. "I did no such thing. I gave you a map, nothing more, nothing less. I made no promises to you. We all make our own choices. *You* never seem to make the right one. Always looking to take things into your own hands rather than let them play out naturally. But no matter, we all leave Glenwood one way or another." O'Rourke winked out of existence as suddenly as he had appeared.

Out of the corner of his eye, Murphy saw the baton crashing downward. He felt a moment of impact—an intense pain in the top of his skull. The sharpened metal defense weapon pierced through his skull and skewered his brain, exiting from his chin with a gout of blood, skull fragments and brain matter exploding from the top of his skull and the newly formed hole in the soft skin behind his chin.

Murphy served his time, in Glenwood, and on earth. He'd finally reached the holy grail of the incarcerated—expiration of sentence.

ACKNOWLEDGMENTS

JOHN DURGIN

Where to begin. A collaboration like this takes a lot of planning and communication. I'd like to start by thanking John Lynch and Jay Bower, for without them this book wouldn't exist. They reached out to me directly to ask if I'd be a part of it, and I accepted in a heartbeat. Which leads me to my next acknowledgement.

Scares that Care and Joe Ripple, along with Brian Keene, have not only been impactful to the families they help with the organization, but also the horror community in general. Without them, the event wouldn't happen. Without them, authors like me, Lynch, and Bower, would never have met and networked to the point where we felt doing a collaboration would work. So, thank you to both of them and the organization for everything they do.

I'd also like to thank my wife and kids as always, because they put up with my boxes of books and swag all over the house, as well as my early morning/late night writing sessions and the tired bags under my eyes that come from those sessions.

I cannot forget my beta readers, Danielle Yeager and Heather Ann Larson, who significantly improved the flow of my story with their feedback.

Matt Seff Barnes deserves another shoutout for once again providing an amazing cover.

I'd also like to thank Candace Nola for her amazing edits to our book. Not only is she an amazing writer, but her edits made our book so much better.

Thank you to all of the authors who provide a blurb to our book and took the time to read ARCs. Joshua Marsella, Steve Stred, Megan Stockton, Brennan LaFaro, thank you so much for your kind words and amazing blurbs.

And lastly, thanks to all of the ARC readers and anyone who takes the time and money to give our book a chance.

The Conservator thanks you as well. Until the next batch of stories he releases . . .

ABOUT THE AUTHOR

JOHN DURGIN

John Durgin is a proud active HWA member and lifelong horror fan who decided to chase his childhood dream of becoming a horror author. Growing up in New Hampshire, he discovered Stephen King much younger than most probably should have, reading *IT* before he reached high school—and knew from that moment on he wanted to write horror. He co-founded Livid Comics in late 2020, co-creating and writing his debut comic titled *Jol* (pronounced Yule), a Christmas horror series for all ages. After publishing that, the itch to expand his writing was one he had to scratch. Through Livid, he wrote his second comic which was released in the spring of 2022 titled *Dead Ball*. In 2021 he started submitting short stories in hopes of getting noticed in the horror community and launching a career. He had his first story accepted in the summer of 2021 in the Books of Horror anthology, and an alternate version of the story in the Beach Bodies anthology from DarkLit Press. His debut novel, *The Cursed Among Us* released June 3, 2022, to stellar reviews. Next up, his sophomore novel titled *Inside The Devil's Nest*, released through D&T Publishing in January of 2023, followed by his debut collection, Sleeping In The Fire in June of 2023. In 2024 he is set to have two more novels and a novella release through DarkLit Press and Crystal Lake Publishing.

www.johndurginauthor.com

twitter.com/jdurgin1084
instagram.com/durginpencildrawings
tiktok.com/@johndurgin_author

ALSO BY JOHN DURGIN

The Cursed Among Us
Inside The Devil's Nest
Sleeping in the Fire: A Collection of 9 Horrifying Tales

Coming soon from John:
Kosa—early 2024
Consumed By Evil (the sequel to The Cursed Among Us)—late 2024

ACKNOWLEDGMENTS

JAY BOWER

This project began after meeting both John Lynch and John Durgin at Authorcon 2 in Williamsburg, VA in 2023. Lynch had a table right outside my room and all weekend long we chatted about books and horror and everything else. I met Durgin but we didn't get a chance to talk much since he was in another section of the event, but I did make it a point to connect with him because I was so impressed with his talent.

After leaving, I stayed in contact with Lynch through texting and I was itching to do some type of collaborate project with him. I took a chance and asked if he'd like to work together. He was onboard right away. In our discussions, we decided we needed a third author to join our madness and both of us immediately suggested to the other that we'd love to work with John Durgin. We reached out and he joined without hesitation.

These past few months of working together has been a blast. Both Durgin and Lynch work diligently on their craft and being behind the scenes with them has taught me so much. I'm thankful for their insights and I'm honored to call them friends.

I have to thank Joe Ripple, Brian Keene, and all of the Scares That Care family for hosting Authorcon. Without the event, this book might never have existed.

I want to thank Joe and Crystal Lake Entertainment for taking our humble collection and turning it into other amazing editions.

I'd like to thank Candace Nola, a badass author in her own right, for editing this book and helping our stories shine.

I want to give a shout out to Matt Seff Barnes who crafted an amazing cover for our book.

I'd like to thank Daydream Studio for all the custom interior artwork.

My readers have been so amazing and I can't thank them

enough for their support, their love, and their friendship. Most of them reside within Bower's Basement of Humanity and to all the Cellar Dwellers out there, YOU are the best! None of this happens without you.

Finally, I'd like to thank my wife for supporting me in my crazy endeavors. She's been my everything and no amount of thanks will ever convey how deeply your love and support mean to me.

ABOUT THE AUTHOR

JAY BOWER

Jay Bower is a horror author living outside St. Louis, MO in the forest of Southern Illinois. He spends his time reading, writing, and convincing his wife the dark stories he writes do not involve her.

For links to all his books, visit his website. There you can also get a free story for signing up to his reader list.

jaybowerauthor.com

facebook.com/jaybowerauthor
twitter.com/JayBowerAuthor
instagram.com/jaybowerauthor
tiktok.com/@jaybowerauthor

ALSO BY JAY BOWER

Horror Novels:
The Dark Sacrifice
Soul Eyes
Useless Creatures
Dreamwraith
Slaughter Lake (Co-written with David Viergutz)
Master of Demons
Cadaverous
The Brownsville Nightmares (Collects The Dark Sacrifice, Soul Eyes, and Dreamwraith)
Every Time I Die

Dead Blood Series:
Dead Blood: Book One
Dead Blood: Book Two
Dead Blood: Book Three
Dead Blood: The Complete Series

Short Story Collections:
Hanging Corpses

ACKNOWLEDGMENTS

JOHN LYNCH

I always draw a blank when it comes to these. First and foremost, I'd like to thank my wife for taking care of the kids so I could attend Authorcon 2, a trip we were originally supposed to take together before we realized that it wouldn't be the smartest idea to take the little ones until they are older. Instead, she suggested I still go, but take my brother. At the time, I'd only planned on going as a fan, but then I released two books and availability for more vendor tables opened up so I jumped on the opportunity. If not for her undying support in allowing me to pursue writing, I wouldn't have gone and I find it highly unlikely Jay would have still asked me to collaborate with him. This book may still have come to fruition, but most likely in a much different form.

I want to thank Jay and John for their friendship and constant support. I'm happy to call you both friends.

Candace Nola and Matt Seff Barnes for their work on the editing, and cover of this book.

Joe Mynhardt at Crystal Lake Entertainment for giving us an opportunity to make this project even bigger, with artwork by Vincent Chong.

There are a lot of great local authors in Southern New England, and I must thank Aron Beauregard for being a local inspiration and a friend. Speaking of local authors, shout out to Gage Greenwood and Brennan LaFaro for their support and friendship. Southern New England is proving there are other horror hotbeds in the greater New England area than just Maine.

Thanks to Duncan Ralston for his continued support and guidance. Duncan does a lot to help other indie authors, myself included. Daniel Volpe is deserving of thanks as well for his kind words, support, and friendship.

A lot of readers have supported me this past year, far too many for me to remember. Kiera, Chaz, Rachel, Christina, Jonathan, Meghin, Dustin, Stephanie, Spike, Maritza, Mike, Margaret, Carli,

Sarah, and Nancy were all integral in spreading the word about this book on social media. From TikTok, to Facebook and Instagram, readers have helped more people get eyes on The Warrior Retreat than I had hoped. I know I'm forgetting people, and for that I apologize. My brain is Swiss cheese these days, please forgive me.

Thanks as always to my 2/3 brothers. Our unit may be gone, but your sacrifice will never be forgotten.

ABOUT THE AUTHOR

JOHN LYNCH

John Lynch is a Horror writer and Marine Corps veteran from Rhode Island.

johnlynchbooks.com

twitter.com/johnlynchbooks
instagram.com/johnlynchbooks
tiktok.com/@johnlynchhorror

ALSO BY JOHN LYNCH

The Warrior Retreat
Woe To Those Who Dwell on Earth

THE END?

Not if you want to dive into more of Crystal Lake Publishing's Tales from the Darkest Depths!

Check out our amazing website and online store
or download our latest catalog here.
https://geni.us/CLPCatalog

Looking for award-winning Dark Fiction?
Download our latest catalog.

Includes our anthologies, novels, novellas, collections,
poetry, non-fiction, and specialty projects.

WHERE STORIES COME ALIVE!

We always have great new projects and content on the website to
dive into, as well as a newsletter, behind the scenes options,
social media platforms, our own dark fiction shared-world series
and our very own webstore. Our webstore even has categories
specifically for KU books, non-fiction, anthologies, and of course
more novels and novellas.

Follow us on Amazon:

Readers . . .

Thank you for reading *The Conservator's Collection*. We hope you enjoyed this anthology. If you have a moment, please review *The Conservator's Collection* at the store where you bought it.

Help other readers by telling them why you enjoyed this book. No need to write an in-depth discussion. Even a single sentence will be greatly appreciated. Reviews go a long way to helping a book sell, and is great for an author's career. It'll also help us to continue publishing quality books. You can also share a photo of yourself holding this book with the hashtag #IGotMyCLPBook!

Thank you again for taking the time to journey with Crystal Lake Publishing.

Visit our Linktree page for a list of our social media platforms. https://linktr.ee/CrystalLakePublishing

Our Mission Statement:

Since its founding in August 2012, Crystal Lake Publishing has quickly become one of the world's leading publishers of Dark Fiction and Horror books. In 2023, Crystal Lake Publishing formed a part of Crystal Lake Entertainment, joining several other divisions, including Torrid Waters, Crystal Lake Comics, Crystal Lake Kids, and many more.

While we strive to present only the highest quality fiction and entertainment, we also endeavour to support authors along their writing journey. We offer our time and experience in non-fiction projects, as well as author mentoring and services, at competitive prices.

With several Bram Stoker Award wins and many other wins and nominations (including the HWA's Specialty Press Award), Crystal Lake Publishing puts integrity, honor, and respect at the forefront of our publishing operations.

We strive for each book and outreach program we spearhead to not only entertain and touch or comment on issues that affect our readers, but also to strengthen and support the Dark Fiction field and its authors.

Not only do we find and publish authors we believe are destined for greatness, but we strive to work with men and women who endeavour to be decent human beings who care more for others than themselves, while still being hard working, driven, and passionate artists and storytellers.

Crystal Lake Publishing is and will always be a beacon of what passion and dedication, combined with overwhelming teamwork and respect, can accomplish. We endeavour to know each and every one of our readers, while building personal relationships with our authors, reviewers, bloggers, podcasters, bookstores, and libraries.

We will be as trustworthy, forthright, and transparent as any business can be, while also keeping most of the headaches away from our authors, since it's our job to solve the problems so they can stay in a creative mind. Which of course also means paying our authors.

We do not just publish books, we present to you worlds within your world, doors within your mind, from talented authors who sacrifice so much for a moment of your time.

There are some amazing small presses out there, and through collaboration and open forums we will continue to support other presses in the goal of helping authors and showing the world what quality small presses are capable of accomplishing. No one wins when a small press goes down, so we will always be there to support hardworking, legitimate presses and their authors. We don't see Crystal Lake as the best press out there, but we will always strive to be the best, strive to be the most interactive and grateful, and even blessed press around. No matter what happens over time, we will also take our mission very seriously while appreciating where we are and enjoying the journey.

What do we offer our authors that they can't do for themselves through self-publishing?

We are big supporters of self-publishing (especially hybrid publishing), if done with care, patience, and planning. However, not every author has the time or inclination to do market research, advertise, and set up book launch strategies. Although a lot of authors are successful in doing it all, strong small presses will always be there for the authors who just want to do what they do best: write.

What we offer is experience, industry knowledge, contacts and trust built up over years. And due to our strong brand and trusting fanbase, every Crystal Lake Publishing book comes with weight of respect. In time our fans begin to trust our judgment and will try a new author purely based on our support of said author.

With each launch we strive to fine-tune our approach, learn from our mistakes, and increase our reach. We continue to assure our authors that we're here for them and that we'll carry the weight of the launch and dealing with third parties while they focus on their strengths—be it writing, interviews, blogs, signings, etc.

We also offer several mentoring packages to authors that include knowledge and skills they can use in both traditional and self-publishing endeavours.

We look forward to launching many new careers.

This is what we believe in. What we stand for. This will be our legacy.

Welcome to Crystal Lake Publishing—
Tales from the Darkest Depths.

Printed in the USA
CPSIA information can be obtained
at www.ICGtesting.com
LVHW012345271123
764922LV00001B/2

9 781957 133690